WHILE I HAVE YOU

A C Harlow

Copyright © 2021 A C Harlow
Cover photography by: Lilawa.com//Shutterstock

The moral right of the author has been asserted.

Apart from any fair dealing for the purposes of research or private study, or criticism or review, as permitted under the Copyright, Designs and Patents Act 1988, this publication may only be reproduced, stored or transmitted, in any form or by any means, with the prior permission in writing of the publishers, or in the case of reprographic reproduction in accordance with the terms of licences issued by the Copyright Licensing Agency. Enquiries concerning reproduction outside those terms should be sent to the publishers.

This is a work of fiction. Names, characters, businesses, places, events and incidents are either the products of the author's imagination or used in a fictitious manner. Any resemblance to actual persons, living or dead, or actual events is purely coincidental.

Matador
9 Priory Business Park,
Wistow Road, Kibworth Beauchamp,
Leicestershire. LE8 0RX
Tel: 0116 279 2299
Email: books@troubador.co.uk
Web: www.troubador.co.uk/matador
Twitter: @matadorbooks

ISBN 978 1800462 243

British Library Cataloguing in Publication Data.
A catalogue record for this book is available from the British Library.

Printed and bound in Great Britain by 4edge Limited
Typeset in 11pt Adobe Garamond Pro by Troubador Publishing Ltd, Leicester, UK

Matador is an imprint of Troubador Publishing Ltd

WHILE I HAVE YOU

A C Harlow grew up barefoot in Australia. When she was 6, she looked after wild rabbits and had a pet kangaroo. At 21, she moved to the other side of the world for love and other adventures. At 30, she helped establish a Cambodian children's charity and supported a brilliant young Cambodian woman through university. She now lives in London where she studied novel writing at Faber Academy. *While I Have You* is her first novel.

Instagram – a.c.harlow
Facebook – AC Harlow
acharlow.com

For my favourite people – you know who you are.

PART ONE

JUSTIN

She appeared. A mess of damp caramel waves, bare limbs and clinging clothes; satchel strap stretched diagonally across her chest.

Justin dropped the soil he had been wiping from the counter to the floor.

The girl browsed until she found the lavender. She gently stroked the plant, brought her fingers up to her nose and closed her eyes as she inhaled. *Are some senses heightened when others are closed off?* Justin wondered.

'Is there anything I can help you with?'

She turned and looked at him. 'No… I'm sorry. I've been looking for a part-time job… it was raining.'

'After school?' He couldn't tell her age.

She nodded. 'And weekends.'

He hadn't thought about hiring anyone. 'Know anything about plants?'

She shook her head.

'Ever had a job before?'

She shook her head again, looked a little embarrassed.

'Well, that doesn't matter, everyone has to start somewhere.' He could make allowances.

'What's your name?'

'Leah.'

'Lovely name. I'm Justin.'

She smiled and let something on the floor turn her attention from the compliment.

Justin glanced down to see what she was looking at; noticed her mosquito-bitten legs and her frayed cotton pumps.

'I love the tiles.'

She squatted down and traced one of the patterns.

'I'm surprised you can still see them. They were beautiful when I laid them – Moroccan. They're so old and filthy that I'd almost forgotten they were there…'

'They're still beautiful.' She dusted her finger off on her skirt.

'I'm happy you think so.'

She rose.

'I could use some extra help, why don't we give it a try?' He wanted eye contact.

She looked up. 'Really? Thank you.'

'Do you have some time now? I could show you around.'

The longer she stood there, the longer he wanted her to stay.

LEAH

Leah was all nerves. She imagined that Justin was amused by her discomfort and inexperience. Why else would he give her a chance? Perhaps he was just a generous person. She wasn't about to question. She'd left her name in several shops that morning but none of them had an opening.

She followed him through the shop. Candles and ornaments competed for shelf space; glass lanterns, planters and mobiles hung from the rafters; greenery climbed the walls, looking for a way to reach the sun.

Justin opened the door to the outdoor area. 'The rain has given up,' he announced.

As Leah's eyes adjusted to the glare, a green oasis came into focus – a bountiful maze of herbs, flowers, fruit trees and overflowing tubs. She wondered how many times she had walked past, completely unaware of the shop's existence.

Justin rattled off some names but she knew she would retain none of them.

'You will love this one: Chocolate Cosmos.'

Leah bent down to the delicate maroon petals. 'It does actually smell like chocolate!'

She listened as Justin talked about the way the sun and shade shifted around the garden during the day, about watering and overwatering, the temperature of the greenhouse and deadheading.

'I can go over the rest some other time; I don't want to bore you to death.'

'It's not boring. I just don't know how I will remember everything.'

'Oh don't worry about remembering all this. It will all become as clear as mud once you get going.'

Leah noticed a tall, wooden, shed-like structure, concealed almost entirely by enormous drooping purple flowers. 'What's in there?'

'My hideout.'

'Does anyone else work here?'

'Yes. Andy most days. And Ella runs the flower workshop Thursday to Sunday. Sometimes my brother, when he's not abroad.'

Up close Leah could see that Justin's eyes appeared to be painted from turquoise water; almost too pretty to belong to a man. She found it difficult not to stare.

★

On Monday, Leah managed to sneak up on Justin in the outdoor area.

'Hey there.'

'Hi.'

Her cotton dress had thin straps; a low V revealed a tanned chest. The sun silhouetted the lines of her body but hid the details of her face and eyes. Her hair ran wild, over her bare shoulders; the sun had burnt the natural colour so that the ends were almost blonde.

'How are you?' he asked.

'Okay.'

She said very little but soon, as her shyness subsided, there would be lots of adolescent blether. It really was only a matter of time before she would do or say something childlike and he would be reminded of her age.

'Where would you like me to start?'

'Maybe some pruning, but first I have something for you.'

Justin jogged off and returned with an apron which he gently, almost ceremoniously, hung around her neck. *The Potting Shed* now covered her chest. She crossed the straps behind her back and tied them in front. Looked at him expectantly.

'Perfect.'

Leah felt a warmth radiating from Justin as he stood next to her and showed her where and what to cut.

'Okay to have a go?'

Leah nodded and took hold of the clippers.

'Just shout if you need me.'

He walked away, taking the invisible heat source with him.

She cut through her first stem; it felt strange, like she'd severed someone's limb.

Justin stopped by several times to check up on her, probably to make sure she wasn't massacring all of his plants in one afternoon.

'Edward Scissorhands needs to step aside. You're a natural!'

'Very funny. I'm sorry for being so slow!'

'There's no rush when it comes to the clippers. People tend not to buy plants with blood all over them.'

She laughed and immediately felt less anxious.

Justin was encouraging without being patronising, and he kept asking her opinion on things in the shop.

'What do you think?' he asked. 'Window boxes are a very personal thing. Would you buy one that was already planted?'

'Depends on what you put in there.'

He smiled. 'Good point – no one wants a shit window box.'

At six, Justin went to find her. She'd swept up an enormous pile of debris and was bundling it into the green waste bin with her bare hands. He berated himself for not giving her gloves.

'Thank you, Leah – that's brilliant. I need to give you some gloves though. You must be exhausted. First day…'

'No, I'm okay. I liked it.' She smiled and brushed her hands down the front of her apron. 'I'll just go and wash my hands.'

'Wait.' Justin lifted his hand towards Leah's hair. She stayed remarkably still. For a moment he hesitated, then very carefully picked out the fragment of foliage.

'Thank you.'

'See you Friday?'

'Of course.'

Leah arrived home to an empty flat and picked at some food. Her mother Josie worked in central London in an art gallery, organising events and exhibitions. She worked odd hours, often in the evening, and for as long as Leah could remember had adopted a hands-off approach to parenting. Josie hated confrontation and never conformed to whatever other mothers had decided was the right way to parent. Leah was free to do as she pleased but had never bothered to engage in much that would anger her mother – there seemed little point. They were more like roommates than mother and daughter, which suited them both.

Leah couldn't think when she had last seen her father. She remembered the unceremonious way that he had packed and left – without warning, explanation or apology. It had confused and upset her deeply at the time. He'd quickly found another wife and fathered two more daughters who needed his undivided attention and the contents of his wallet. Her half-sisters were sweet enough, but they both had an air of privilege Leah found difficult to tolerate. They were privately educated, their clothes expensive and their rooms beautifully decorated. After their birth her father's appearances in her life had become increasingly rare. His excuses seemed reasonable at first, but after years of him having important business meetings that couldn't be moved, of being otherwise engaged with his younger daughters, and of simply forgetting, Leah and her mother had given up inviting him to school events and birthdays, until it became the norm for him to just not be there anymore.

It was an unusually warm night for September. Leah showered and lay in her bed with her hair still wet to keep her cool. As she tried to fall asleep, she couldn't help but think of Justin and the way he had been with her. Difficult to pinpoint what it was exactly, but Friday could not come quickly enough.

As Justin showered and stumbled around naked in the half-light, careful not to disturb the familiar form of his wife on the other side of the bed, he tried not to think about the shape of Leah's calves as she rose onto her tiptoes with the clippers. He also tried not to think too long and hard about the precise size and position of the small, chocolate beauty spot under her right eye that he felt so overwhelmingly compelled to touch.

★

Justin was out the front, unnecessarily rearranging a display, when Leah jumped off the bus on Friday. He had wanted to see her before he introduced her to Ella and Andy, to reassure himself that he wouldn't trip over his growing fascination with her in front of them.

'I didn't scare you off on Monday?'

'Not at all.'

'Ready to meet the gang?'

'Sure.'

He took her straight through to the flower table where Ella was arranging hydrangeas.

'Ella – Leah, Leah – Ella.'

Justin thought he detected a raised eyebrow at his choice of a new casual. 'She has green fingers and toes,' he justified.

Leah shook her head modestly. 'Working on it.'

'Good to meet you,' Ella said, peering over her thick-rimmed glasses like a headmistress.

'Let's find your apron and I'll introduce you to Andy.'

Andy practically ran over when he spotted Leah wearing the apron.

'How's it going?'

'Okay.'
'Schoolgirl, yes?'
'Yes.'
'What year?'
'This is my last.'

Her last year, what age did that make her? She was a teenager with teenaged boyfriends and gossiping girlfriends, homework, a family to look out for her, probably even a single bed covered in soft toys from childhood and a list of chores on the fridge. Not to mention all the things that were yet to happen – like university, travel and marriage – all the things that had already happened to him.

'We'll be in the greenhouse,' Justin said, turning away. 'It's baking in there and the sprinklers aren't working.'

The greenhouse smelt of lemons, basil and over-ripe tomatoes.

'Nothing attracts death like death so we have to get rid of any sign of it. Pull off all the split tomatoes and pop them in this container, trim anything that is brown – if the leaves are still green but wilted they should come back to life with water. But don't stay too long, you will pass out.'

As she made her way down the rows of drooping vines, Leah listened to the muffled voices outside, trying to make out what was being said. She watched for Justin moving past in his faded red T-shirt and blue shorts. When she was done, she took a broom and swept the floor.

Justin returned with a glass of water and made sure she drank it.

'Beautiful job – and so clean in here.' He inspected her tub of split pickings. 'Dinner tonight!'

'I could stay in here forever. It's so warm, and the smell is delicious.'

'But you must come out – can't have you fainting on day two.'

They moved to the cool of the shop and Justin asked her if she could dust and tidy the ceramics and glassware. It was busy and loud – customers shuffled around with their carts and baskets while staff shouted out locations of plants and delivery dates.

Leah struggled to steady her hands, terrified she would break something. She propped up a fallen sign describing the fair trade origins of the products and imagined Justin bartering for it all in the crowded markets of northern Africa, India and Nepal.

Justin stopped beside her to shift around some oversized pots. She felt the warmth returning to the space between their bodies; it made her look, she could have sworn there was a flame gently licking its way around the curve of her arm. His presence made her self-conscious, though; everything she touched began to wobble.

Justin noticed and she felt embarrassed.

'You make me nervous.'

He smiled. 'I'm not that scary am I?'

'No, not scary.'

'Then why so nervous?'

'I don't know…'

Ella's voice broke through their quiet conversation. 'Don't forget to take this bouquet home for Marcella – she wanted it for a friend's birthday. I'm off.'

Marcella?

Marcella.

Of course there was a woman at home. Leah hadn't even thought to look for a ring, but a quick glance confirmed that Marcella was a wife. Foreign, exotic, permanent.

'Thanks, Ella. Will do.'

Justin walked away. As the air turned cool in his absence, Leah kept her eyes on the crackle-effect vase she was holding and dusted it for too long. She felt a little stupid for the pang of disappointment she felt, not fully understanding where it came from.

'You hired a casual? You didn't tell me you were looking for someone. Can you even afford it?'

Justin had met Marcella in Argentina during his gap year. From there they had travelled together; shagging, drinking and arguing their way around the US, Asia and Europe. Their rows – sometimes about his inability to admire other women without her noticing and frequently about her inability to see the world through anyone's eyes but her own – were always followed by great sex and laughter.

They both returned home to their studies, but ended up back together each summer and for term breaks for the three years that followed. Justin had slept with a number of girls at university during this time; but Marcella, with her cute dark bob, firm arse and wild temper, somehow always had him over a barrel. She was his foreigner: separate, different, challenging. Seeing her at the end of each term became the thing he looked forward to during the monotonous months of study, when his string of pointless flings had rendered him bored and unforgivingly dismissive. He craved Marcella because for most of the year he couldn't have her; his memories of her and their sex morphed into something he wanted them to be. His need to have his fix of her, to be with her and bury himself deep inside her, he decided, was what it meant to be in love.

Marcella grounded Justin and refocused him when he drifted. He forced her to drift when she became so focused that she was unrecognisable as the free-spirited girl that he had met when he began his travels. She was in a hurry for everything – to work and make money most of all. He wanted to take his time to find out what it was he wanted to do with his life.

Justin loved Richmond Park and when Marcella came to London they would cycle through it together. She'd always ride at the speed she wanted her life to progress – faster than him, faster than she needed to, missing everything he noticed along their way. At some point he would make her stop and lie down under a tree and look up through the branches and just listen – to be still and quiet and empty of essays, undergrad job applications and debts. For a few minutes, at least, their connection would be more than just physical, more than something they had grown into, or would become, as they planned their lives together; it was about the moment they were in.

After university, they moved in together and took whatever work they could find. Three months later they sat together, cross-legged on their mattress on the floor, the only item of furniture in their studio bedsit in Twickenham, and stared blankly at the small piles of books, clothes and CDs stacked up around the skirting boards.

'We can't even fit a cot in this room.'

It was a strange thing for Marcella to say, he thought, and would have been the last item on his list of concerns about bringing another person into the world. But who spoke sense in the face of such adversity? A baby was not part of her plan and could not easily be slotted into the life she had mapped out for them both.

It was the first time he had seen Marcella cry, and the first time he had taken her into his arms and lied that it would be okay. The newly discovered vulnerability in her, which was half his fault, made him feel beholden to her. His marriage proposal was blatantly reactive, but she made no remark on it; possibly happy in the knowledge that he would have asked her eventually, regardless. She sniffed a 'yes' and buried her face against the petrified gait of his heart.

The equal measures of loss and relief that came with the late miscarriage seemed to cancel each other out. It both tarnished and cemented them, took something away and presented something else in its place.

Some fifteen years after losing their first child, the subject of trying for a baby kept finding its way across their dinner table and into their bedroom. The timing was appropriate – they could afford it and there was room for a cot in their three-bed townhouse. He could find no reason to refuse her.

Justin had pre-empted Marcella's practical accountant's response to having to pay another wage out of the income from The Potting Shed.

'I'm only offering a few hours, so it won't cost much. It just takes the load off; the place is a pigsty. I'll see how it goes.'

'Male or female?'

'Huh?'

'The casual!'

'Oh, a girl – she's very quiet, just gets on with it.'

'A girl. How strange.'

'Why's that?'

'Just assumed it would be a boy, with all the physical labour.'

'Not much of a feminist, are you darling?'

'I guess not… By the way, did you remember the bouquet?'

'Shit!'

★

Saturday was an endurance test for Leah. The customers filled all of the available space in the shop; they were relentless in their queries, dithery in their selection, yet impatient to pay once they'd made up their minds. Leah learnt the till and stayed there, smiling, wrapping ceramics, looking for appropriate bags and boxes for purchases and arranging home deliveries.

When Justin made her take a break for lunch, she found a spot behind the greenhouse where customers were not admitted. Justin joined her.

'There you are – you know you can always take your break in my office. There's a sofa. You wouldn't have to sit on a bag of compost.'

'Thank you. I will when we no longer have sun.'

Leah smoothed her skirt down to cover herself a little.

'How are you getting on? It's pretty manic on the weekends.'

'I think I have the hang of the till… better to be busy than quiet.'

'True. Well, you are doing a great job. You are lovely with the customers.'

She smiled, thankful for the praise. 'They're very forgiving of my lack of knowledge.'

Andy interrupted: 'Justin, can I get your help on something?'

'See you in a bit.'

Their time alone together was so brief.

Justin had never felt so irritated to be interrupted. He was aware that Leah was learning about him through his interactions with other people, but she remained aloof and enigmatic whether she intended to or not. There were times at work when he wanted nothing more than to be allowed to fade into the background and to go about his day without having to speak to anyone or make any decisions. His favourite time was always before the shop opened and after it closed; he loved being alone amongst the plants, loved the solitude and silence. He wanted to be interrupted by Leah though. There were less and less people that Justin met that he felt he wanted to really get to know, but for some strange reason Leah had intrigued him. He wanted to gently prise open the tight lid she had on herself and get her talking. He had never found someone so young even remotely interesting. Teenage girls were loud and their conversations senseless – they shouted over each other and laughed at the most ridiculous things. They were also oblivious to their flesh bulging out of their too-tight clothing, generally vain and selectively stupid. If anything, he had found teenagers a little grotesque. Why, in the few days that he had known Leah, did she seem so completely, wonderfully, surprisingly different? He was wary of paying Leah too much attention in front of the others. It irritated him that he had to be so mindful at all; couldn't two people discover a connection, whatever the age difference? He and Marcella had never possessed each other, they'd allowed each other complete independence and had never questioned each other's motives when they'd met new people, but with Leah it would be different. It just would. *Monday*, he thought to himself. *Monday they would have to themselves.*

'So how's the new girl getting on? What's her name again?'

Justin was taken aback that Marcella had thought to ask about Leah at all, let alone the minute he walked in the door. Or perhaps he just had a guilty conscience; he hadn't considered taking anyone on before Leah appeared that day. She was also conspicuously pretty; there was no getting away from that.

'Leah. She did really well; a natural with the customers, smiled under pressure.'

'Leah, nice name. How did you find her again?'

'She came in looking for work.'

'Oh...'

Oh – the shortest, most loaded word in the English language.

'Enough about work – how was your day?'

'Boring old housework, shopping. Dinner's almost ready. Thought we could have an early night...'

An early night always intimated the same thing.

'Can't wait.' He kissed Marcella on the head and slapped her bum.

Justin was fully aware that it wasn't so much the sex that

Marcella wanted as the baby it might produce. It wasn't that he no longer wanted to make love to Marcella – he was still deeply attracted to her. But their lovemaking had become more functional than fun; the animal breeding instinct had taken over and once implantation took place their sex life would never be the same again. He couldn't help but think about that, too. He'd been warned, even though he had laughed at the notion at the time. Marcella's body would become a vessel for their baby. It would progress to nourishing the baby and by the end of that stage it would be just plain exhausted. And just as it was returning to a fit state, it would probably be reserved for another baby.

He thought about the women he had been with before he'd married Marcella. He thought about their bodies, their scents, how they tasted, their ways of giving and receiving pleasure, the different sounds they made when they came – none of which he would ever experience again in his lifetime.

Marcella took him in her mouth but stopped him going down on her: 'Just fuck me.' She turned her back and lifted her oversized T-shirt. He found his way inside her with his fingers, but she didn't want to waste time; she pulled his cock in and arched her back so that they were locked together. She was forceful and insistent, and from behind, a faceless mess of hair – an anonymous vagina that wanted to be filled. He clamped Marcella's hips down hard and moved faster, until she made her wild pleasure-pain moans that made him come.

Leah was too tired to meet up with anyone after work. She spent most of the evening in the bath constructing a mental image of Marcella, and then several images of Marcella and

Justin. There they were, husband and wife, greeting in the hallway after a long day at work; snuggled up on the sofa; sitting down at a dinner table set for two; in bed with their two pillows and their two bodies lined up next to each other. Assuming of course they didn't have a child. Justin hadn't mentioned one, but maybe he wouldn't have even if they did.

Leah turned her thoughts away from Justin. *There was Ollie.* Ollie was cute and uncomplicated. Perhaps she would say yes to going out with him, or not – she really needed to throw all of her spare time into her final year at school. She also needed to save up so that she could go away somewhere in the summer and have some savings for when she started uni.

*

Sunday was as intense as Saturday. Leah manned the till again – she was yet to match the names of plants with the plants themselves, so it made sense for her to stay put.

Leah gracefully accepted the constructive criticism Ella ladled on her when Justin was out of sight. And when Justin was in the room, Ella seemed to constantly bring up Marcella's name.

'What's Marcella up to?'

'Not sure.'

'Isn't she popping in?'

'Doubt it.'

'Shame. How is she anyway? Still fit as fuck? Boot camp every day?'

'Yep.'

'Puts the rest of us to shame.'

'Leah, why don't you take your break?' Justin suggested. It was barely past midday.

'I don't mind working through; it's pretty busy.'

'No, I insist. You need to eat.'

Leah took her sandwich to the same concealed area as the day before. She sat down on the topsoil bags this time; they were firmer than the compost. 'Fit as fuck' ran through her head. Marcella was now not only foreign and exotic; she also had a perfectly toned body. She ate quickly and lay down on the bags. She let the sun touch her skin and transport her elsewhere.

Justin found Leah in her lunch spot again, stretched out on her back, arms shielding her eyes from the glare of the sun, belly button revealed where her top had ridden up. Leah didn't notice him so he remained perfectly still while he fixed the previously unseen parts of her body into his memory. He wanted to ever so gently run the tip of his finger along the waistband of her skirt.

As he turned to quietly leave, to just get that image out of his head, he brushed against a windchime, alerting her to his intrusion. Leah removed her arms from her face and there was a pause, a moment where she remained partly exposed and he couldn't turn away. He watched as she righted her top and rose to leave.

'You don't have to come back in yet.' *Just stay right there. Talk to me. Don't move. Forget the bloody shop.*

'I do. My break is over.'

Justin was occupying the small passageway that ran behind the greenhouse. He didn't plan to not move; he just wanted her to stay, wanted some time with her.

He watched as Leah sucked in her stomach and made her body concave as she slid past. He felt only the fine hairs on her forearms and the almost touch of her chest as she drew her breath in deeper.

And then she was gone. Back to smiling at customers and back to not being right up close to him.

Justin didn't return to the shop immediately. He disappeared into his office and locked the door behind him.

He needed to be alone. Alone, with the picture of her flesh still on display and the memory of her body so close to his in the passageway. Tomorrow he would be in her company again. He would continue to examine her movements as though she were an undiscovered wonder of the natural world. He would unstitch the seams of her clothes with his thoughts and touch whatever skin he could with his invisible hands. She wouldn't mind that, because she wouldn't even know he was doing it.

★

On Monday Justin rushed around trying to get all the jobs done so that there would be nothing for either of them to do when Leah arrived at four, quite defeating the purpose of employing her. Then he thought it might appear too obvious, so he pulled out some trays and seeds. That would keep them quietly busy and in one place.

Leah seemed quiet for the first half hour. Had he frightened her off when he had refused to move out of the way? She hadn't seemed uncomfortable at the time; it was he who had been unnerved, mainly by the intensity of his attraction to her. She had blushed and smiled a little –

the look on her face at that moment was burned into his memory.

'How was school?' Could he not have thought of a more mundane question that separated them instantly?

'School is school. Did you like school?'

Leah had a knack of turning Justin's questions back on him to avoid having to talk about herself.

'Um, let me think.'

'I bet you were naughty and didn't like being told what to do,' she mocked.

He laughed at her accuracy. 'Pretty much. I wasn't good with rules or authority. Even now I can't imagine having a boss. I can't picture you misbehaving, though. You seem very together.'

'Not sure about being together but I don't think anyone can afford to mess around these days. Competition for university is so high, graduates struggle to get jobs, blah-blah. I feel like I've been lectured on that for the last four years.'

These days. As opposed to back in the day when he was her age, many, many years ago, when there were more jobs and she was wasn't even conceived of.

'What do you want to do?'

'I'm not sure, and I really ought to know by now.'

'What subjects are you taking?'

'English, History and Religious Studies.'

'Interesting. What would you say your greatest strengths are? Research? Creativity? Analysis? Writing?'

Leah looked like she had thought about this question before and found no definite answer. Bemused by his interest in her future, she shook her head, smiled, then expertly shifted to a more comfortable topic.

'Did you always want to own your own business?'

'Actually, I think I wanted to be a journalist at some point. Honestly, though, I completed an entire English degree without a clue of what I wanted to do with my life. You have time. You have the world at your feet.'

She shook her head again, embarrassed.

It was part of her charm, that she didn't know she could take what she wanted from life. There was something about Leah that everyone would eventually want a piece of when they discovered her. Justin wondered how long she would find even him interesting. Her mind was expanding every day, her world growing bigger and bigger as opportunities and choices presented themselves. One day she would be at the centre of something extraordinary; that was obvious, just not to her yet. His world was doing the opposite, narrowing and becoming more repetitive, more predictable and less exciting with every year.

They carried the full seed trays to the greenhouse and gently watered them.

'You'll see how rewarding it is to grow something from seed. A bit like giving birth to silent young. You take these tiny specs you can barely hold in your hand they're so small, and pop them somewhere warm and cosy. They soon sprout into delicate, needy little creatures. You feed them, protect them from the elements, gently encourage and nurture them – sometimes I even talk to them – then you take a step back and marvel at how quickly they grow and blossom.'

'Then sell them to random strangers and hope that they won't kill them?' Leah finished.

Justin laughed out loud. 'Brutal! But you're so right! I

take it for granted that my babies live when they leave here, but it's probably a fifty-fifty survival rate at best. That's it, I'm shutting up shop and keeping all the plants for myself. It's the only way I can be sure they'll live!'

'Will my services no longer be required?'

'Your careful hands I trust.'

Justin looked at her small hands – he wanted to hold them in his and feel how soft they were. Instead he walked away, uncertain about his ability to contain himself.

Justin put through a few orders while Leah cleared up their mess; unfortunately the clock hadn't failed to work and was still moving time on.

When Leah hoisted her bag over her shoulder, Justin had no way of keeping her there. There were so many trapped words stuck somewhere inside him that would not, and should not, come out. Leah looked at him, as if waiting for him to say something. He could think of nothing to say that was appropriate.

'So, I will see you Friday, then,' she finally said.

That hurt, actually, the enormous negative that suffocated the positive. He would see her Friday but there were three empty days in between.

'Okay, well, bye,' she chirped.

'Bye,' he managed.

The minute the door closed between their worlds, he immediately began to replay the two hours that had just been.

★

On Wednesday Ollie asked if he could watch the English

Literature film with Leah. She agreed. It would be a good distraction, she thought. It would normalise things and help her to move on from the ridiculousness of her burgeoning feelings for Justin.

She found, though, that Ollie was not the distraction; Justin was. He was all that she could think about. She went over and over their conversation, trying to figure out what had made him think that she had the world at her feet. Did he mean it or was it just flattery? Encouragement? A fatherly pep talk?

Halfway through the film she felt Ollie watching her.

'You do realise the television is that way, don't you?'

'Lee-lee, why can't you just say yes?'

'I don't want to go out with anyone. It's not personal.'

'You know you want to really…'

She laughed as Ollie rested his head on her shoulder like a loyal dog.

'Just one snog and I'll leave you alone for the rest of the film. Promise.'

There was something so daft about his request. A kiss should just happen; the pull between two people should be magnetic. Did he actually think that one snog would bring them closer together? She would prove to him that this was not how it worked.

'The whole, entire, rest of the film?' she asked.

He nodded.

She paused the film, straddled him, took his face in her hands and kissed him. He tasted of Pepsi, smelled of boy sweat, and his face was covered in a fine layer of blonde hair punctuated by a few angry spots.

After a minute or two she removed herself from his lap

and curled up on her side of the sofa, flicking the remote so that she could re-engage with the film.

'No way!' he whined.

'Shhh,' she whispered, 'you promised'.

Ollie slapped his head in despair and readjusted his cock. 'Such a fucking tease, Leah.'

Marcella announced that she would come to the shop on Friday to work on the books: 'I have lots of time in lieu; I can just leave work early'.

'No need. I can bring them home.'

'Be nice to come in; it's been a while.'

He didn't want Marcella to meet Leah. She would no doubt accuse him of hiring her simply because she was pretty. And would she really be that far off? Moreover, she might ask Leah awkward questions. He surprised himself at how protective he felt.

'Honestly, it's just so hectic at the moment; I wouldn't be able to sit down with you. Pick a quiet day.'

'Next Monday?'

'Mondays are an arse – the place is a pigsty and I have to do the orders. Tuesday? Tuesday is quiet and I can help you out.'

'Okay, Tuesday it is.'

Justin was completely unaccustomed to lying to Marcella. He wasn't able to define what he was guilty of but he knew that he was guilty. He had never given a shit about which day Marcella came in to do the books; but he was beginning to map out his time in terms of Leah days – torturous as they were with their interrupted conversations, stolen glances and awkward interactions, like the one that had occurred in the small space where she took her lunch break. It was like a circular barn dance where they never ended up as partners, never linked arms, never embraced. The days between the Leah days were just there to get through.

He hadn't thought about whether he was happy or even content with his life until he met Leah. It hadn't mattered, it was his lot, it had evolved that way and he had actively participated in that evolution. Out of nowhere a state of restlessness had arisen; an unease that ate at him and fed him in equal measures. Leah arrived and he felt alive. She was mesmerising, sweet, humble and entirely undemanding, yet had his full attention. Then she left and took the heat with her. Yes, that was strange, he had never felt the cold before; but when she left the room he felt a physical chill, like the energy had been drained from his body. It was exhausting, switching from everything to nothing all the time, pulling himself through the time between.

Justin began to analyse what he and Marcella had become over the years; the traps they had fallen into simply by existing and letting the days repeat themselves. They argued more and joked less and then sometimes didn't argue at all, and that in itself was a sign that neither of them cared enough. He and Marcella had been together so long that neither of them had even noticed that they'd grown into some sort of middle-class cliché. Even their ambitions were predictable and in line with everyone else's. Career, period townhouse, imaginary baby, imaginary child's graduation day, and so on. Their life was decided, from such a young age, from that miscarriage.

Marcella mothered him and this was the thing that

bothered him most of all. He had allowed it because it meant that there were fewer arguments, but he'd also relinquished a huge part of his independence. Perhaps all women eventually assumed the roles men's mothers once enjoyed in preparation for becoming mothers themselves. Marcella told him what to do with his dirty shoes and his soiled hands when he walked in the door, just as his mother had done. She told him when dinner would be ready and constantly made comments about what she saw as his time-wasting activities, just as his mother had. Even the tone of her voice when she beckoned him from the other end of the house had begun to take him back to his youth.

★

Mondays. Mondays. There should be more Mondays in the week, Justin decided.

'I have nothing for you to do.'

'How come? I saw the state this place was in yesterday. There has to be something left for me to do.'

'You work too hard. You are at school all day, homework every night, I'm guessing, and four days here. Aren't you tired?'

'I like to be busy.'

Justin paced around with a cup of tea while Leah awaited instruction.

'Do I look tired?' she asked.

He moved in closer, inspected the area under Leah's eyes and found only the perfect little freckle.

'No, most definitely not. I, on the other hand, am knackered and look like an old Basset Hound.'

'Now that is hilarious! You always glow. Probably because you work outdoors so much. Besides, I have you down as more of a Beagle than a Basset: playful, forgiving, full of energy. Don't you have any days off?'

'Every now and then.' He smiled. *A Beagle?*

'Then put your feet up.'

She took a pillow from the shelf, plonked it onto a high-backed bench and patted the seat.

He obeyed. Amused.

Leah left him sitting there and returned with a scrubbing brush, a bucket and a rag.

'Leah, what are you doing?'

'Just my job.'

She lifted her skirt above her knees, knelt down, dipped her brush in the bucket and began to scrub at the Moroccan tiles. Justin watched, momentarily dumbstruck, as she steadied herself with one hand and made quick, small circles with the other.

'No, Leah, you really don't have to…' he said, unable to bear it any longer.

'Let me, please. Look at the difference.'

'I can't let you.'

'You can't stop me.'

She rinsed the brush then began to dry the area she had scrubbed with the rag. He tried not to look at her bottom and the kitten-like arch in her back; he almost had to cover his eyes. Leah days were full of possibility and the length of time that 'possibility', as a thing in itself, could be fed off and enjoyed was immeasurable.

'Wait.'

He returned with some kneepads.

'If you insist, I must insist. Stand up.'

Leah stood still, afraid her legs might collapse while Justin squatted in front of her and attached the kneepads. She felt wet inside, imagining his hand sliding up the inside of her leg.

'Thank you.'

'Let me find another brush, I'll be right back.'

They scrubbed in silence, past their usual finishing time of six. Leah's legs were cramping and the palms of her hands in spasm by the time she finally stood with Justin to admire the transformed tiles.

'It's stunning, really beautiful. And there I was thinking we could have the afternoon off. Slave driver!' Justin mocked.

'Worth it, though.'

'Definitely worth it, and I quite like you being the boss for a change.'

'You couldn't handle the workload,' she teased.

'True. I'm shattered. Can I buy you a drink at the café around the corner to thank you?'

The idea sent Leah spinning. *Alone, in a café…? Yes, let's, and let's forget that you are married while we are at it…*

'You don't have to do that. I'm just doing my job. I should get home anyway: homework.'

Perhaps it wasn't unusual for Justin to meet up with women in cafés, to have perfectly platonic interactions with them over a drink, but Leah knew that anything she wanted to say yes to so desperately left her open and exposed – it would mess with her head and have her dreaming up scenarios that could never come true.

'Okay, if you're sure I can't convince you. But I'm driving

you home. And I'm not giving you a choice on that one. St Margaret's, right?'

Justin's old jeep was a mess; not built for comfort, just moving plants around. Leah felt like an intruder sitting in the passenger seat. She wondered if there might be traces of Marcella in the glove box – an old shopping list in her handwriting, sunglasses, a hair tie or some lip balm. She tried not to think about it. The music was loud. Something Indie she couldn't recognise. Her hands were pressed together, in between her knees, ankles crossed over. She wanted to appear relaxed but realised she had no idea how to.

'Will your mum be worried about you coming home late?'

'I doubt she will be home.'

'What does she do again?'

'Events. At a gallery.'

'Are you close?'

'In some ways. She's out a lot so our paths don't cross every day. We are not like those mothers and daughters that talk about anything and everything. I think she prefers not to know too much. She has enough going on in her own life. She's not good at choosing men. Or maybe she's not good at being in a relationship.'

'Do you wish she was around more, in the evenings? It must get kind of lonely at times…'

Leah shrugged and looked out the window. 'She's always worked, so I think I'm used to my own company. And I'm always doing homework, which is kind of solitary anyway.'

'Do you see your dad much?'

'Not really. He's the busiest man in the world. And he's

kind of awkward, a bit closed off. He has another family too.'

'It's a shame that you feel like he's closed. Blokes are a bit useless.'

Leah smiled, feeling she should react in some way. She had chosen not to think too much about her father, sometimes she even said out loud to herself: 'I don't have a father, and I don't need one'. She let the window down a little – she wanted to change the subject, ask him something about himself, but was momentarily lost for words. She was relieved that Justin was perceptive enough not to push too hard.

'Not all blokes are useless,' she finally said.

Justin wasn't useless, and he wasn't closed or cold or uninterested. He was the opposite of her father. He had paid her more attention in the short time they had known each other than her father had in all the time since he left.

It stank outside and the fumes quickly infiltrated the car. It was noisy too. Leah wound the window up again. She wanted it to just be the two of them and the beautiful track that was playing. It felt so different to being at work – in the car there was no one to hear them, look on or interfere.

'Who is this?' she asked.

'The music? Ben Howard – *Every Kingdom*.'

'I like it… next left.'

'Oh, are we almost there?'

'It's that one there. Thank you for the lift.'

'Any time.'

Leah's mother wasn't in. She ran upstairs, downloaded *Every Kingdom* and played it loud enough in her room so she could still hear it as she found herself something to eat. She pulled out a cucumber, washed and peeled it and took it to her bedroom. She gently inserted the cucumber. It was wet, not too big. She moved it in and out, softly at first and then deeper. But it wasn't the touch of another person, it wasn't Justin. She used her fingers to make herself come.

Justin sat for a moment and pretended to be checking the messages on his phone in case she should look out of the window – he wasn't ready to leave. He looked up at the typical Edwardian terraced house that had been sliced into flats and wondered which one was her bedroom window, if it was at the front, if on occasion she forgot to fully draw the curtain before she changed at night. He could still feel her in the car beside him, still see her thigh bent at a right angle over the edge of the worn leather seat, her hands pressed tightly between her legs. She sometimes seemed to not know what to do with her hands; she often covered her mouth when she spoke, or tucked her hair back behind her ear.

But she wasn't there anymore. Their time, as ever, had been brief. She had grabbed her satchel and bade her farewell and however much he wished that in a carefree moment she'd flung her arms around him and kissed him on the cheek as she said her goodbye, she had not. Because she was not someone who did things without considering the consequences.

Justin wondered if this was perhaps how men who preyed on young girls behaved; if they sat outside their houses waiting for them to walk past a window. He turned the key and drove away, away from all the madness of wanting more of Leah than he should. She was just too fucking young.

Even if Marcella didn't exist, he would be slandered and abandoned by even his closest, most forgiving friends.

★

Ollie pursued Leah at school. He put his arms around her waist when she was getting her books out of her locker and tickled her – she tugged free and laughed him off. Had she not met Justin she might have given into him by now – they'd be fumbling around in each other's bedrooms when their parents were out, thinking they were in love.

'You going Sat'day night?'

'Huh?'

'Joseph's'

'Probably not; I have to work and, after that, homework.'

'Lee-lee, now look. You're only young once. You're being boring and soon you'll be wearing maroon velvet slippers and watching *Coronation Street*. You *are* coming, even if Ness and I have to drag you kicking and screaming out of that garden shop you live in now.'

'Okay, okay! I'll come.'

He threw her a you-can't-resist-me-forever look and galloped down the hall like a triumphant stallion.

★

The Potting Shed was full of people trying to squeeze the last few weeks out of their gardens before autumn turned into winter. Leah had memorised the location of most of the plants and was now able to recommend hardy perennials for shady beds, specialised composts for flowers and vegetables and knew which kitchen herbs didn't grow well together. Their regular customers remarked on the tiled floor they had never even noticed before. Leah's favourite place was the greenhouse; it was warm and quiet in there and she made it her domain.

Autumn had browned petals and crisped leaves at an alarming rate. Leah had seen everything come out, only for some of it to die a number of weeks later. It was a shame that some things had not been purchased and enjoyed and now had to be discarded.

Leah began to take her lunch break in Justin's wooden office. She sat cross-legged on the sofa and looked around; taking in the boards of inspiration on the walls, the mess of papers on his desk, the coffee cups he'd abandoned and the clothes he had slung over the armrest. She was in amongst his things. She could smell him and see him there with her, even when he wasn't actually in the room. She imagined the conversations they would have, remembered those they'd already had, and thought of all the things she wished she had the courage to ask him. She was aware of the bed that was in the loft space, aware that he slept in it when he was too tired to go home and that his brother used it when he came back from working abroad. One day, perhaps, she would sneak up there and fall into a deep sleep on Justin's bed. Maybe he would even find her there.

An hour before closing, Ollie showed up. He stood awkwardly under the ornate wooden archway that Justin had shipped over from India and never priced because he couldn't part with it.

'Ollie, what are you doing here?'

Leah walked over to him, flushed with embarrassment

– someone from her normal, dull world had penetrated her fantasy, full-of-possibility world.

Justin watched from a distance as Leah was approached by a teenaged boy. She seemed surprised and quickly linked arms with him in an attempt to shift him towards the exit.

Who was this boy that she felt able to openly clutch on to? It immediately exacerbated the frustration he felt at never being able to touch her; not even in a friendly, casual, meaningless way. Andy had taken a liking to Leah. Of course he had. Who wouldn't? He hung around her like a dog; succeeded in making her laugh, flattered her, touched her constantly. Justin couldn't touch her like that, so playfully and naturally, not without anyone remarking on it, or finding it inappropriate. He couldn't touch her at all. His touch would be loaded and incriminating. Leah was polite to Andy, without being overtly flirtatious in return. It wasn't Justin's place to be jealous, and any sign of it would arouse suspicion. So he held back. All that he could do was give them unconnected tasks in separate corners of the garden centre and encourage the little prick to go on more dates.

Justin watched the two of them together – the spotty, skinny kid and his beautiful, elegant Leah. He wasn't in her league, not even close. There was no way he was properly aware of Leah's uniqueness, nor could he fully appreciate her sweet, gentle nature. He didn't have a clue, not at his age, an age Justin remembered being only too well. All boys at that age are stupid and self-serving. She was just a pretty girl to him: a potential shag or a girlfriend he could boast about to his friends. The kid probably seemed innocent enough to Leah, but no boy of that age is ever really innocent. They are driven by a single, relentless goal. Surely he wasn't bright enough to win Leah's affection anyway. He wanted to take the little shit to one side, just to be sure. He had no right to, of course, but the thought was there, grating at him despite its lunacy.

Inane jealousy; it really was ridiculous, and a surprise. The boy was probably only a friend, perhaps he was even gay. Justin made a decision then to introduce himself.

'Justin.' He held out his hand.

'Hi. I'm Ollie. So sorry to disturb Leah at work. I'm not staying.'

'Good to meet you, Ollie. No apology needed – it's nice to meet one of Leah's friends.'

'He was just leaving,' Leah interjected, turning Ollie on his heel.

'You really don't have to rush off.'

'No, no, I do. I know she's busy. See you at eight?' Ollie asked Leah.

She rolled her eyes, nodded and walked him out. She returned almost immediately.

'I'm so sorry,' Leah said.

'He's cute,' Ella called out.

'He's just a friend.'

'Oh really,' Ella teased, 'a see-you-at-eight kind of friend?'

Justin didn't join in the banter, he just feigned amusement.

'Andy, you missed it. Leah's boyfriend was just in,' Ella persisted.

'No way! Where is he? I need to eliminate him!' Andy half shouted. 'You didn't tell me you had a boyfriend. We have plans, you and I!'

'He's just a friend! I don't have the time for a boyfriend.'

Justin felt irritated, then pissed with himself for feeling irritated, but images of Ollie and Leah together kept forming. He'd feel her up and stick his tongue down her throat like the inexperienced imbecile that he was. Maybe they would even fuck. This is what she was supposed to be doing, though. Who was he to deny her the freedom, joy and experimentation of youth? It disgusted him just the same.

After knocking off early, Justin drove like an arsehole through the traffic and found Marcella at home in the bath. He pulled his clothes off and joined her. The water lapped over the edge as he entered her, his hand clutching hard to the back of her neck as he moved their bodies through the water.

'Hate to be a killjoy, but the water is going everywhere,' she said.

They moved to the bed where Justin proceeded to lick every inch of the flesh that was his, that belonged to him, that no one else had the right to touch. He pulled Marcella's legs apart so he could lick inside of her and for once she didn't dictate, didn't resist and came within seconds. And then he was inside her; the perfect rhythm of them, uninhibited, right, accepted.

Leah wove through the stumbling bodies; her friends were either dancing or getting off with each other in every corner of Joseph's living room. She'd made herself a drink with some of her mother's vodka before she'd left for the party and felt relaxed but not overly drunk.

Ollie was leaning on a windowsill, lapping up attention

from a girl they both knew well. He excused himself when he saw Leah and made a beeline for her. Ollie was tall; when he hugged her she nestled into his chest. It felt familiar and safe.

'Now that has made my night.'

'I can't.'

'I know, I know. I'll take what's on offer, however small.'

Leah looked up as he took her face in his hands and kissed her before she could pull away.

'Come back to mine?'

She nodded.

Leah shimmied herself out of her skinny jeans.

Ollie inexpertly removed her underwear and then his own.

His hard on stuck out like a diving board.

She was astonished at how quickly she had ended up completely naked on his bed, his parents unaware and snoring in tune with each other in their room down the hall.

Ollie moved quickly and nervously, rummaging for a condom. She wasn't sure what he was more afraid of: waking his parents, messing it up, or the possibility that she might change her mind at any second. The thought *was* there but she talked herself around it; it had to be now, it had to be Ollie.

He tore the packet open and snapped the thin rubber over the diving board.

She helped him inside.

A sharp, shunting pain in a space that was too small and not wet enough.

Not entirely unpleasant but not as advertised in films.

★

Sunday was uncomfortable. Aside from the splitting headache and the tenderness and stinging between her legs, Leah felt inexplicably as though she had cheated on her own fantasy. She felt coolness from Justin all morning, or imagined it. She wondered whether she was wearing a sticker on her back announcing her abandoned virginity.

Justin detested himself. He'd had sex with his own wife to forget about the girl/woman that had tortured him, without trying, since the day they met. He was aware that he was acting like a cock around Leah and she was probably wondering what the hell she had done to deserve his juvenile silent treatment, but there was no shaking his mood or his wrath for the injustice that came with meeting the right person in the wrong decade.

He did the only mature thing possible. He hid in his office for most of the day. He even napped on the bed in the loft, despite the shop being full of customers. When it was near closing he came downstairs but stayed in the office; he sat at his desk and stared out of the window. Every now and again he caught a glimpse of Leah: smiling, glowing, working hard and behaving like a normal human being. He buried his head in his arms and waited for what there was left of the day to pass.

He must have fallen into a light sleep. Someone entered the room; without looking he knew that it was Leah. He slowly lifted his head out of his arms and turned to face her.

'Are you okay?' she whispered.

'Of course.'

'Missed you today.'

'I'm sorry. I just had so much paperwork.'

Her smile was so warm it made him want to weep.

'I thought you might be hiding for some reason.'

'No, not from you. Did you have fun at the party?'

'It was okay, if you like being around drunk teenagers.'

'Did you get drunk?'

'Not really.'

'Did you kiss that boy?'

Of course it was an intrusive question, but he'd asked it anyway.

'Ha! Very funny. No.'

He imagined that she was lying.

'Poor sod.'

'He's just a friend. It would be weird. How was your evening?'

Such an expert at shifting the subject.

'Oh, very boring.'

'See you tomorrow.'

'Yes. Bye.'

★

On Monday Justin made sure the tiles were immaculate, the shop tidy, orders placed and the shelves full. When Leah arrived, he turned the *OPEN* sign to *CLOSED* and locked the door.

'No one comes after four anyway,' he said, matter-of-factly.

He led her to one of his favourite corners where he'd

positioned a small table and two chairs. As soon as he saw it through her eyes – the table and chairs, the fresh mint tea, the pitta bread and hummus – he realised at once that it looked like a date. She was coy enough not to mention it.

'Think of it as a delayed induction. I like to get to know my staff several weeks after I've hired them!'

In fact, he wanted to discover all of her, layer by layer, until he knew everything.

'And what would you like to know?'

She sat down, made herself comfortable, limbs all neatly folded.

Just everything would suffice. What you read, what you eat, what you look like when you are sleeping, what your dreams are – you know, that kind of stuff. 'Tell me something I don't know about you.'

'No, that's way too broad. Let's start with you, it will ease me in.'

Her favourite trick, turning the tables.

'How long have you been married?'

Anything but that... 'We met very young, at the beginning of both of our gap years. We travelled all over the place, any chance we could, on as little money as we could. After uni we moved in together, fell pregnant, lost the baby, married anyway.'

'I'm sorry – about the baby.'

'We were too young to look after a baby.'

'Your wife, Marcella, what's she like?'

'She's an accountant. She's feisty, organised, focused. She's definitely too good for me. I'm a chaotic, ineffective nuisance who hates to make plans.'

Justin did not want to talk about his wife and he wasn't

sure how much Leah really wanted to know. He imagined she asked out of politeness, or in an attempt to seem mature, which she clearly was – he couldn't imagine learning about one of her boyfriends and remaining calm and collected.

'You must have planned this place and you can't be that ineffective – you're running a business!'

He loved that she had such a high opinion of him and wouldn't allow him to degrade himself. He had somehow made The Potting Shed happen, that was true, but it was not through a process of well-considered order and design.

'Okay, new topic. Name a country you still want to see,' she said.

'Hmmm, I haven't thought about that for a while. I'd love to do more of Asia and South America, but the world is large and changes all the time – the places I saw when I was eighteen would all be unrecognisable now. I used to live for my next trip.'

'You wouldn't travel now? You can't trust anyone with the shop?'

He wasn't sure if it was a question or simply fact. Perhaps it was a suggestion. They could disappear together, to a parallel universe, make love on the peak of a mountain under unprejudiced stars.

Justin poured the tea into the little coloured glasses he'd so carefully carried back from Marrakech in his hand luggage.

'Maybe. I don't know. Perhaps I've become like everyone else: settled, sensible, attached to the daily routine. Although working for myself beats working for some other twat.'

He was half mocking himself and half embarrassed that perhaps most of what he was saying was entirely true. Not to mention the fact that Marcella was an enormous part of his daily routine.

'I think what you have is incredible. Look where you spend your days.'

'You are right, of course, this is my own private utopia. Although I could do with more sun, and a beach… then it would be almost perfect.'

Almost. What would be more perfect was if Leah was in his utopia more, and if their days didn't have to be broken up by other people.

'And you created it yourself. Nobody handed it to you and you didn't do it for anyone but yourself. What could be more rewarding?'

'I have no doubt that you will make far more amazing things happen in your life.'

'I'm not so sure. But thank you for thinking so.'

'I'm very sure. Now, over to you. Where would you like to travel?'

'I don't know. Just everywhere. I wouldn't even know where to begin. I've only really been to Europe.'

'I don't think you need to know. I think what matters is wanting to. I can't understand people who don't want to travel, who don't want to know how the rest of the world looks and feels and tastes. Everywhere is the perfect place to begin your journey.'

Everywhere would be wonderful with Justin, Leah thought. She imagined the luxury of just having more time with him. Every conversation they had seemed to bring them closer and yet there were so many gaps, so many topics they avoided, not to mention the force field around her body that kept Justin away. Leah wanted Justin to touch her but knew he would not. He was always careful not to overstep. She remembered the day he'd stood in the passageway and made her squeeze past him to get through. She'd felt the warmth of him drawing her in towards his chest, the burning sensation that always seemed to ignite between them, but he hadn't actually touched her and she wasn't sure he ever would. He was too sensible, too aware of the consequences.

*

On Friday a sharp draft of cool air made Leah turn to the door to see where it had come from. She wasn't sure why, but she knew immediately it must be Marcella. She saw her profile and then her back as she gave Ella a hug. The discomfort, which should have made her retreat to the safety of the greenhouse, instead, fixed her feet to the floor. Marcella then turned so that she was facing forwards. She had striking features; thick, dark hair, olive skin and an immaculate figure.

Leah watched as Marcella put her grocery bag down and began looking around, picking up items from the display – things she obviously recognised, things she didn't – and rearranging them.

'This place is looking rather good, actually.'

'So, what has kept you from visiting us for so long?' Ella asked.

'Just working like a dog in the week, trying to relax on the weekend. Alone, of course! You know, I sometimes think that I should get a job here if I want to see Justin.'

No, Leah thought, *that would be a terrible idea. Do not do that.*

'Probably the only way,' Ella agreed.

'Where is he?'

'In his office, I think.'

Marcella clocked Leah in her Potting Shed apron and made her way towards her. This was it; she was going to know just by looking at her that she thought of her husband, a lot, and in a way that could not be mistaken for anything other than what it was. Marcella would force a confession out of Leah, rip fistfuls of her hair from her scalp and kick her down the street.

'I don't believe we've met. I'm Marcella.'

They shook hands, like gentlemen on opposing sides of an imminent war.

'Hi, I'm Leah.'

Leah saw Justin stride over. He briskly embraced his wife and kissed her on the cheek. She patted his lower back.

'So, how are you finding it? No doubt Justin has you slaving away.'

'He keeps me busy. It's nice to finally meet you. I'd better go and help that customer over there.'

'Got a minute?' she heard Marcella ask Justin as she followed him into the office.

She wondered at their conversation, whether they ever rowed, whether affection found its way into their time alone in the office. They stayed inside for the longest time – long enough for Leah to picture them having sex on the mattress in the loft. The idea of seeing the two of them walk out with flushed cheeks and tousled hair ground a stabbing sensation into the centre of her stomach. She asked Andy to grab her bag for her when she saw him heading for the office.

Leah had missed calls from Ollie and a text message.

Would she pop over after work – his parents were away for the night? She replied that she would. Why not? Justin would go home with his wife after work. They might see a film or go out for a meal, make love and fall asleep in their shared bed. It made perfect sense for her to see Ollie.

Another message appeared on her phone.

Sorry not to have said goodbye. Thanks for today. J.

A reassurance of some kind?

No problem. See you tomorrow. L.

Justin had watched Marcella appear in the shop and, for a moment, it was as if he was having an out-of-body experience. It was happening, he was watching, but he couldn't prevent it. The look on Leah's face, his own blood rushing up through his cheeks and into the top of his head, the innocent actions of his wife, whom he immediately, unfairly detested for stopping by. What was surprisingly clear was that his main concern was for Leah. It was not that Marcella might suspect something, or feel insecure when confronted with the pretty young girl he had hired, which, of course she commented on, just as he had predicted, but for what her presence might do to Leah.

He wasn't sure how or when his own wife had become the imposter but, at that moment, she really was.

Ollie attempted to make Leah dinner.

'You do know this is not a date, Ols?'

'Well, I'm hungry and you look emaciated. You clearly don't have time to eat any more. I know I'm not the best cook but pasta pesto is pretty hard to cock up.'

After dinner, he asked if she would like to go upstairs.

She agreed. As long as he knew it was just a bit of fun there could be no harm in it.

The music was loud – it helped to dull the feeling that she wasn't sure she wanted to be there. She laughed through his half striptease but declined to attempt one in return. He lay her down on the bed that stank of boy and gently pulled up her top. He was trying to be in less of a hurry and she found it endearing. She wanted to allow herself to be wet so that it would hurt less. Ollie stuck his tongue in her mouth, touched her on the outside of her clothing until he could wait no longer. Leah looked up at the ceiling as he removed her underwear, all too aware of how closely he was examining the lower half of her body.

He was a little rough; she told him to lick his finger so he would be softer. He improved. He took a moment to get the condom on, then pushed his way in. The pain was slightly less but it still felt unnatural. She tried wrapping her legs around his body. He lifted her backside up with one arm to lock her in closer. There was still a feint line between what hurt and what felt good. A few minutes in and Ollie sped up, rammed it in once more and was done, tortured by his orgasm and its speedy arrival.

I am now a person who has sex, Leah thought quietly to herself as she lay on Ollie's bed half naked, her top lifted and breasts exposed. *Choosing the moment to lose your virginity is one thing, but going back for more, that's something else altogether.*

★

The following Monday, after an excruciating weekend of half conversations in between serving customers and of Leah again feeling strangely guilty for having slept with Ollie, Justin said something unexpected.

'I know it's a bit off the wall, but do you think you could take a day off school tomorrow and spend it with me?'

Leah was completely thrown. Adrenalin shot through her veins, pulsed up into her forehead. How could she yearn for something and fear it in equal measures?

'I'm sorry – it was just a thought. I was thinking you might like a change of scene… probably highly inappropriate of me to ask.'

Perhaps it was inappropriate, but she wanted to accept.

'Have I made you uncomfortable? I'm so sorry, don't…'

'No, I just wasn't expecting you to… Where would we go?'

'I need to visit some suppliers in Eastbourne… but it needn't take long. We could take some lunch and eat it on the Downs. Just be nice to get away for the day.'

'I could take a day off, I guess. I have a lot of spare lessons on a Tuesday.'

'Is that a yes? Only if you're sure?'

'I'm sure.'

PART TWO

It wasn't until he had Leah in the car next to him that Justin realised the potential enormity of what they were doing. How would he justify this if they were discovered together? He imagined a few quick, believable responses in his head. An essay she was doing on Fair Trade, perhaps? A keen interest in the business? He thought about sharing his thoughts with Leah, to be sure she was on board and willing to lie at a moment's notice but, in truth, he didn't know her well enough to be sure she wouldn't use the scenario against him if she felt uncomfortable at any point. It felt like the most unlikely thing in the world – Leah didn't have a malicious bone in her body. She also seemed wholly unaware of the power she had over him. She wasn't trying to seduce him; he was simply seduced by her, just as she was, all gangly limbed, shy and uncomfortable in her teenaged skin. If anything, he could only imagine that Leah would defend him passionately. But he still couldn't be sure.

Ultimately, if they were seen and questioned, it wouldn't matter how much either of them protested that nothing had actually happened and that nothing was going to happen, he would be branded a pervert. There was something between them that was gently evolving: something pure, something unique, and something Justin was treasuring every minute of. It sickened him to think of it in any other way, but he knew what society did: it decided for itself, found names for people and took great pleasure in stringing them up.

At that moment a car pulled out in front of them, forcing Justin to slam his foot on the brake. He imagined the worst possible outcome then – a car accident – they would be found together, no questions asked, no rebuttals made.

He looked over at Leah – as they left the city and hit the motorway her entire body seemed to finally relax. She had slipped off her shoes and was sitting cross-legged, hands resting loosely in her lap. To remark upon the obvious need for discretion would be loaded and maybe even damaging to whatever it was they had. She would assume he didn't trust her; or thought of her as an unreliable, blabber-mouthed child. So far she had belied her youth in every other regard; she had done nothing *but* keep her cool. And if she wasn't thinking in that way at all, she might take it as an announcement of his intentions – he didn't want to alarm her. He wasn't sure why, but by coming here today she must trust him, despite the musings he was having in his head about her body, her face, her skin, her mouth...

Leah had so far only drip-fed information about herself to him. He wasn't sure if it was subconscious or if she somehow quickly vetted everything she was going to say before she said it so that she never revealed too much. There was so much more to her, so many more layers, and Justin wanted to discover them all.

'Okay, favourite film?' he began.

'Ah, twenty questions. My favourite game.'

'Yes. And there's no backing out, shying away or running off home. We have several hours.'

'*The Piano*,' she decided.

'I've seen it. Loved it. Interesting choice. Why?'

'It just really moves me. A woman who through some sort of trauma can no longer speak, so she speaks through her music. But more than that, there's something about the way the love affair begins. It's not just that it is illicit – he brings her to life, doesn't he, and gradually releases her from herself and her husband, her captor…'

Justin nodded, not sure how far to probe.

'And then there's the bad guy, who turns out to be the good guy…' he added.

'Yes. I love that. And, of course, the dramatic scene where the husband chops off her finger – which kind of makes the film. She sort of falls to the ground at an angle, as if the loss of her finger has distorted her equilibrium.'

'Perhaps the loss of her finger is symbolic of her lover too – that to lose him is like losing a body part,' he added.

'Yes, I think you're right. Or maybe the stolen moments she had with him were worth losing a finger for.'

'True love, hey. I'd like to see it again one day.'

'I have it on DVD.'

'Excellent, I'll pop over and watch it at yours then, shall I?'

'Sure. My mother won't find that weird. She'll make us both popcorn and bring us soft drinks.'

Justin looked over and caught her smiling.

'And yours?' she asked.

'My mother would bring us strong tea and Bakewell tarts.'

Leah laughed. 'Your film!'

'Hmmm. Has to be *Paris, Texas*.'

'I've not seen it. Tell me about it.'

'I guess it's about atonement. The beginning is perhaps the most poignant part of the film. A very thin man walks out of the desert with an empty bottle of water. He appears to have been walking for days. Nothing is explained for a long time but it's clear that he has been through something traumatic... We eventually learn about his possessive, passionate relationship with a much younger woman – Natassja Kinski – that ended under the most disturbing circumstances. There is some brilliant storytelling, and nothing comes quickly, you have to wait and learn.'

'Sounds intense. I'd like to see it.'

'Then I won't tell you any more. And that's another date, then,' Justin joked.

Leah smiled again.

'Right, next question. Favourite book?'

'It has to be *The Collector* by John Fowles,' she answered immediately.

'How old are you!'

'I found it in the villa last year when I had run out of things to read. Someone must have left it there. I read it in two days, couldn't put it down.'

'Tell me about it, I haven't read it,' Justin lied. He wanted to hear her describe it.

'Man steals girl, locks her up, adores her, she dies.'

'Well, now I know the start, middle and end there's no need to read it. Pretty light read, then?'

'Sorry! I didn't mean to spoil it! Although, there's far more to it, so you could still read it. Their relationship is fascinating; how it shifts and evolves, and the bleak thoughts she has, especially towards the end of the book. I cried, I mean really cried, when she died.'

'I might read it anyway. If it affected you that much, I would like to understand why.'

'I think it affected me because she was so young; she had so much to look forward to… she was just becoming a woman, then it was all taken from her; all of the pleasures and emotions she wanted to experience, like being in love… taken by this man's sick need to keep her locked up. Did I mention the butterflies? He collects butterflies and pins them into little glass boxes. He collects beautiful, delicate things so that he can keep them to himself and look at them when he wants to. That's what it's about. Psychotic greed. It's devastating, actually.'

Justin nodded. He wanted her to go on – he'd never heard her speak so much or seen her so animated and affected – and yet he wanted her to stop, too. He had begun to feel like the Collector himself. He'd taken Leah from her perfectly sweet teenaged life so that he could have her to himself.

'And yours?'

'Probably *The Unbearable Lightness of Being*. But I won't tell you what happens because I think you would like it and you should read it. It has everything – passion, love, complex relationships, tragedy – that's all you need to know.'

As Justin drove they talked more about films, music, books and the people – past and present – who had woven themselves into their lives and left a mark there. She told him she had decided to apply for a degree in English; she wasn't sure what she wanted to become but she knew she would enjoy the literature and could think more about her career options later. He found that the further away they were from London the more she was willing to open up; or perhaps she just felt more comfortable the more time she spent in his company.

They talked about travel and restlessness, or rather a constant need Leah seemed to have – that he certainly recognised in himself – to find out what might be on the other side of the mountain. They talked about other cultures that were built on different principles to the ones she had grown up with. She wanted to know everything Justin had seen and done and the impact it had on him. Justin found himself jumping all over the place, from one country to another, the chronology didn't matter, just the memories. He remembered the desert he had crossed, the jungle that had almost swallowed him, the dives he'd made, the borders he'd talked his way across and the sellers he'd bartered with in stinking hot bazaars.

He found it strange that now, after all the countries he had visited and after all of the extraordinary people he had come across, there was Leah – the most intriguing of them all – in her beautiful simplicity. And she had appeared without him having to seek her out. Instantly she had brought vivid colour to the fading edges of his every day; challenging him, making him laugh, reminding him of the things in life that made him feel truly happy.

Leah had it all in front of her; a lifetime of choices, risks, experiences and adventures. And he was one of them. This, now, being alone together for the day, was one of them and he wanted to live up to her expectations.

Leah stayed in the car while Justin went in to talk to his

suppliers. She received a message from Vanessa but didn't reply. She'd thought about telling her about her connection with Justin, but she knew she would be met with confusion, unwanted questions and, ultimately, disapproval. It would come out wrong, no matter which details she chose to include or exclude. Vanessa would simply think it was wrong. She would warn her that it would end in tears, that he was married and too old. She might even call Justin a pervert, which he was not. He'd done nothing to make her feel uncomfortable; he'd simply made her want more of him than he could ever give her. She wasn't even sure herself what she actually wanted from him, she just knew that the time they had together was never long enough. She wasn't prepared for judgement, not from anyone, or for what she and Justin had to be tarnished by friends who weren't able to understand. Besides, technically nothing had happened – it was merely an attraction.

She took her seatbelt off and ran her hand over the steering wheel and the worn leather of the gearstick that Justin had just been gripping in his hand. She watched strangers walking past the car going about their day, and relaxed into the seat – they had no idea who she was or that she wasn't supposed to be there. Justin could take her and keep her somewhere; she wouldn't try to leave. They could talk forever then; one hour would just roll into the next. She wouldn't need the outside world. No one would particularly notice she was even gone. She would be a missing person for a time, then mourned, and afterwards she would be remembered as someone more interesting than she really was by the simple fact of her disappearance.

When Justin reappeared she sat herself upright; pulling

her wandering mind back to the present as he shoved some boxes into the boot.

'That was quick!'

'Of course. We have far more important things to be doing than this.'

Leah followed Justin along the edge of the cliff as the wind dotted them with a light, salty spray. They chose a spot to sit and eat; the sea spread out in front of them with all its secrets and history and constancy. How many millions of people, for how many millions of years, had sat on a shoreline and spoken to the drama of the waves? Leah's jumper, which seemed warm enough in London, was stupidly thin out here. Her entire body shivered.

'Hey, you're freezing. Take my jumper. I should have warned you about the wind up here.'

'No, no, then you will freeze. I'm okay, honest.'

Leah put down her sandwich, hugged her knees and shuffled closer to Justin's body; using him as a shield against the elements. How warm it felt there, only a few centimetres closer – the flames that always rose up when they were in such proximity engulfing her. She wondered if he might put his arm around her; she was willing him to but he did not. Not even in this wind and at this temperature, with a storm forming on the horizon.

'What made you ask me here?'

The question, which had started out as only a thought in her head, had come out as a perfectly audible sentence. How he answered would affect her so profoundly that she was not sure she wanted to hear it. What was it about her that had held his interest up to this point? Was it really just an unusual friendship he wanted? Did he mean to act as a sort of mentor and offer her advice and encouragement out of some kind of pity? The latter was the last thing she wanted from him. She wanted, instead, for him to push her back into the grass, to kiss her mouth and feel her warm skin under her clothing, to find her stomach, her back, her breasts.

'Why do you think I asked you to come with me today?'

'Well you haven't hit me over the head with anything yet, so I don't think it's anything sinister. I'm guessing you were just worried about falling asleep at the wheel on the drive back and needed someone to keep you awake.'

'That's it! You got me.'

The space between their bodies was so warm; she was almost tempted to remark on it and ask if he felt it too.

'This is my favourite day,' she added.

'Tuesdays?'

'Of all the days I have known you.'

'And mine.'

'No interruptions.'

'No one else.'

Leah unfolded her legs and lay back in the grass. The sky had been washed over with charcoal, creating vast expanses of deep, watery grey. It was beautiful, dangerous, magnificent.

Justin lay down next to her. He turned to face her but she stayed that way, staring up at the sky.

'How long can you stay here?' he asked.

'How much food and water do we have?'

He looked up at what she was seeing, and at that moment the clouds undid themselves and the rain fell out. It landed on them as they looked up, forcing them to shut their eyes.

It burst on their cheeks, seeped into their clothing. Neither moved. It was strangely exhilarating.

As the storm gained momentum they couldn't help but relent and laugh, turning to each other. It was then that Justin reached out and touched the freckle under Leah's eye, just for a second. He withdrew, turned back to looking up at the crying sky.

'You haven't answered my question. Why me?' Leah asked.

He looked around; searching in his mind for the correct way to define need and lust, and his obvious selfishness, without any of it sounding reprehensible or sordid. He thought of so many things about her that made it impossible for it not to be her, and yet couldn't tell her any of the reasons.

'You appeared. A day like this,' he finally said.

'So it could have been anyone who had come in that day, at that time? I'm pretty sure a granny came in just after me.'

He laughed. 'No, it could never have been anyone else.'

After a time, a long time of nothing more being said, Leah sprung up onto her feet.

'You needn't worry, I won't tell anyone we were here.'

Her statement seemed to come from nowhere and pulled him out of the moment.

'I know. But thank you for saying so.'

He stood up with her. They were now both completely soaked, shivering on the Downs without a single person in sight.

'You're married. I have no intention of hurting you or your wife.'

He brought his hand up as if to steady her need to

reassure him. He wanted to kiss her forehead, her nose, her lips. He wanted to taste inside her mouth and not talk about the world they would be returning to after this day. He would have liked for her to reassure him of something quite different – that one day, when it was right, when they would somehow be allowed to, they would kiss, even if just the once.

But she did not say that they would kiss one day.

Instead she bit her lip and turned away from him.

Justin watched her walk away, back towards the car. She wasn't herself. He followed a few steps behind. Had he somehow upset her?

If Justin wasn't going to kiss her, Leah wasn't going to stand there and wait to be kissed. As she marched off she immediately wondered if she *had* waited that long as she willed him to take her face in his hands. It was also entirely possible that she had misread the situation altogether. But there was something in the way that he had looked at her… She thought she had reassured him of her discretion but, actually, she had probably just confused him and said something that didn't need to be said; stopped him in his tracks. She was confused herself. Had she actually wanted him to kiss her? The thought of them kissing made her anxious. Did she want the fantasy or to just enjoy it from a distance? What would it be like? To kiss a man? A much older, married man? And what would happen after? Would he immediately recoil at the realisation that she was inexperienced and young? Would he regret it and pull away from her, or she him, out of shyness or fear, completely obliterating their connection? Leah wasn't ready for that possibility.

Leah curled back into her seat, her body turned towards Justin, her frustration and confusion slowly dissipating with the warmth of the heating. She stared at Justin as he drove and studied his profile. Wet hair, eyelashes, skin, lips, stubble, slightly rounded, ski-jump end to his nose, small hole in his sleeve, scar on his arm, prominent veins on his left hand. She felt that they were both in control and yet no one was. They were on the edge of something: words unsaid and actions not taken. Even to have spent a few hours alone together was a victory.

Leah appeared to soften, but there was quiet between them now. Justin felt her eyes move over the left side of his body as he drove. It was usually *he* that did the examining. It was *he* who knew every stitch of *her* clothing from memory. The colours and patterns of her favourite skirts, the pulled thread on her cardigan sleeve, the grey cotton vest with the lace around the neckline. It was *he* that looked for signs of the flesh that her clothing concealed. He would love to be in the passenger seat right now; watching her drive without her being able to turn away or cover her face with her hair. All he could do was steal the occasional glance.

After a time, Justin saw that Leah had closed her eyes. When he thought she might be asleep he gently tucked her fallen strands of hair behind her ear.

No, he told himself, *just no*.

★

The following Friday Andy asked Leah out. He'd spent the afternoon flirting with her, as he always did, and had become increasingly physical. The minute she rejected him, Leah knew it would make things awkward. But he wasn't Justin. He was just Andy: harmless, fun, uncomplicated. She told him it wasn't him; she just didn't have the time to see anyone with school, homework and work (and spending all of her available headspace on Justin).

'Yes, and that is very admirable, but you still need to have fun! That kid who came in is actually your boyfriend, isn't he?'

If only she had thought of that as an excuse, but she wouldn't have actually wanted Justin to think she was seeing Ollie.

'Ollie is definitely not my boyfriend!'

Justin arrived at this point. They had all stayed back to help with a stock check and general clean up.

'Justin, tell this beautiful girl to go out with me.'

'Leah, are you interested in going out with this filthy man-child? He has dirty nails, he's South African, he eats from Subway, sings terribly and lives in a flat with two other similarly unkempt Neanderthals.'

'Unfair! I am actually a remarkable singer.'

'No, you're not!' Ella piped up.

Leah laughed, thankful for the interruption.

'I'll finish the greenhouse.'

'She was about to say yes!' Leah heard Andy joke as she walked away.

She willed Justin to find an excuse to join her. She had only half an hour left.

After a few minutes Justin came in and stood opposite her, picked at some dry leaves.

'How was the rest of your week?'

'Okay,' she answered.

'I would like to have that day all over again,' he said.

Leah smiled, but only for a minute, then looked down at the plant she was deadheading.

'If I could read your mind,' Justin began.

'I'm glad you can't.'

'Sounds ominous.'

'It's just that… '

'You can tell me.'

'I can't.'

'I can't tell you either.'

'Tell me what.'

'That I think about you too much.'

The idea of this left Leah raw rather than pleased. It made it harder that he had now actually admitted it out loud. At least she could have tricked herself into thinking his feelings were not returned, not fully. At least that might have helped her to eventually stop thinking about him.

'I know that feeling.'

'Of wanting the thing you are not supposed to want?'

She nodded. 'You have a wife.'

'And I'm old.'

'You're not that old.'

'Okay, then you are young. It's all relative. There are twenty years between us.'

'Do I seem young?'

'No.'

'And you don't seem old. But you do seem to be married.'

She was aware that the way she had said it had made it sound like a mistake he had made in the past and couldn't undo.

'I know I am. I wasn't expecting this.'

'I could leave.'

Even though she had said it, she wasn't sure what she really meant – did she mean now or forever? Both options brought on a sharp, piercing stabbing in her abdomen.

'That's a terrible idea.'

Andy swung the door open. It made her jump.

'Sorry, didn't mean to give you a fright. Ciao, guys. I'm off. Oh, and Ella said bye.'

'See you tomorrow. Thanks for staying back.'

'Bye, Andy,' Leah said, still feeling embarrassed about rejecting him.

The door swung back and made a clicking sound as it closed tight.

Leah looked at it and imagined being locked in there all night, in the warmth, with Justin.

'I should go too,' she said.

'Do you have to?'

She didn't answer but she didn't move either.

Justin walked over to Leah and brought her body in close, so that it was tight against his. It was the first time he had really, properly touched her. He felt her soften even as his heart thrashed in his chest. He could smell her so clearly; her soap, her beautiful uniqueness. After a few minutes she gently pulled away. Her cheek was pink from where it had been pressed against him and she seemed a little faint.

'We need some air.'

He took her into the office and sat her on the sofa with a glass of water.

'Drink. Rest. Wait.'

Justin quickly checked that everyone was gone, locked the door and sat down next to Leah on the sofa. Without saying anything Leah immediately lay down and rested her head in his lap. She curled her legs up to her chest and placed her hand on the top of his thigh. It felt like the most natural thing in the world and yet his heart was thumping around loosely in his chest, completely out of rhythm. He stroked her hair to calm himself but the beating only quickened. As he ran his fingers gently down the side of her face and over her eyelids, Leah's eyes closed. He wanted to savour every second of their closeness, but he too fell asleep.

When Leah finally woke she looked panicked. She stood up quickly and struggled to find her footing in the darkness.

'What time is it? I have to go.'

'Let me drive you.'

'No, I'm okay.'

He watched as she stumbled around in a hurry, gathering her things.

'Leah.'

But she was already gone. Bolted, in fact. Out of his office and straight through the shop. He followed but he was too slow – he heard the front door close and she was gone.

It occurred to him that it was actually pitch black outside and very late. Justin made his way into the night – he could just about make out her form in the dark and hear her pumps hitting the path leading to the bus stop. He didn't want her getting the bus.

The bus was nowhere to be seen so Leah ran to the next stop, just to make some distance, struggling to breathe in the cool air. Was it fear that made her run? Was it excitement? Was it that they had come too close? She wasn't ready for it to be over, or for it to begin.

Her mother was in when she arrived home. She was never in on a Friday night.

'You could have texted to tell me where you were.'

'Sorry, I had to work late.'

'But this is really late. Do you think maybe you are doing too many hours?'

'No, it's fine. I still get my homework done. This was a one-off, anyway.'

In truth, when exams came up in the New Year, she would have to reduce her hours. Less time with Justin, more time in between.

'There's some take-out if you want it.'

'Why are you in?'

'Shocking migraine.'

'Oh. Doesn't sound good. Have you taken something for it?'

'Yes. It should kick in soon.'

'Okay. Night.'

'Night.'

Leah thought about texting Justin that she couldn't come in on the weekend because she was ill, but decided that it would be too much of a statement. And she had to see him – there were already too many days that she didn't see him and all of those days were long and dull and their only purpose was to lead up to the days when she would see him. Justin would have interpreted her running away as fear – he would assume that the situation had made her uncomfortable. And if she didn't go to work he would pull away again, go back to not touching her at all. She didn't want that. She would tell him it wasn't him: *he* hadn't *done* anything, *he* was the perfect gentleman. It was she that had put her head in his lap and slept there, quite of her own volition, and then run away, like a child.

On Saturday Justin attempted to catch Leah's eye as soon as she arrived but she avoided him. He tried to talk to her a number of times during the day, but she cut him off, said she was in the middle of helping a customer. Justin needed to know Leah was okay and yet she refused point blank to make it possible for him to ask.

At five, when Leah was due to leave, Justin asked her to come into the office, in front of everyone, to discuss some banking error to do with pay. She couldn't wriggle out of a perfectly legitimate request from her boss.

'Please close the door.'

Leah did so, then stood in front of the closed door and fixed her gaze on the sofa. Justin looked at the sofa too, at the soft dent they had made when they had sat on it the night before.

Justin spoke first.

'I feel I may have…'

'Of course not. I was half asleep. I don't know why I reacted the way I did. I'm sorry. I think I was just a little disoriented.'

'I'm not asking for an apo…'

'But I'm giving one. I shouldn't have done that.'

'I'm not that scary am I?'

'No, but I shouldn't have put my head in your lap. I didn't run because of you. I ran because of me. I'm so sorry.'

Justin could see how hard Leah was trying to hold tears back. Suddenly everything felt incredibly heavy. They had moved from one place to another and then retreated, and it had all happened too fast, without him having control of it one way or another. He wasn't sure what to say next, how to reassure her.

'Leah, I loved you resting your head in my lap, it felt perfectly natural and innocent to me.'

'I don't feel innocent.'

'Leah, it's okay…'

'You have to stop being you, Justin. Can't you just be a bastard or something? I can't be alone with you. You are not mine to be alone with.'

Justin realised then that he had never thought of himself as being owned by Marcella, but that was exactly what marriage was – a branding, a certificate in sole proprietorship.

'Do people really belong to other people? I don't think they do. Are there really rules about who can be alone with whom? Who wrote these rules? And a bastard? To you, fuck no, *that* I will never knowingly be. I want to be your friend, your confidant, your encouragement, your sounding board; even your pillow if you need a nap. There isn't anything wrong with that, Leah. Unless it messes with your head. Then, of course, there is something wrong with it. God, that's the last thing I want to do.'

'I don't think Marcella would agree that it is okay for us to be close like this.'

'Why? Because you are a beautiful young girl? Not all friendships are conventional. Why can we only be friends with people our own age, people we wouldn't be attracted to, people that society deems are okay for us to be friends with?'

'So that we don't upset our loved ones, I guess. In any case, I don't know that I see you as a friend.'

He could profess innocence until he was blue in the face but he could not argue with the truth.

'Thanks a lot. And there I was thinking you did see me as a friend!'

'Justin, you know what I mean! You are more than a friend.'

'Does it mess with your head? Us spending time together? Or just me, in general…?'

'Yes, both, but not in a bad way. I think maybe I like having my head messed with.'

'You might retract that statement somewhere down the line. And then I'm going to feel like a real prick.'

'You can't take responsibility for everything.'

'Yes, I can. And anyone looking in from outside would see it that way too. They would say that I have power over you and can influence and manipulate you simply because I am older and more experienced. They would say that I lured you into my office and my car and fed you bullshit stories about how big and exciting the world is. Oh, my God, I am such a cliché guru.'

'Yes, but you are my first guru. I will always remember you fondly for that. Though I have to admit that I am still waiting for the words of wisdom…'

Justin laughed, relieved that she could find some humour in the situation.

'First guru! You should only ever really have one guru; otherwise it all becomes very confusing. Now let me think…

Okay, here goes. First words of wisdom: Never trust a guru.'

'Do you trust yourself?'

'Actually yes, I trust myself, but I can't stop wanting to know more about you and I can't stop wanting to spend more time with you. And I do have a tendency to look at you too much.'

'Well, there's no harm in the first two if you trust yourself. And the third is important, looking; you have to check on my work, and you need to make sure I don't steal money out of the till or have food in my teeth before approaching a customer… bosses should be looking.'

'Yes, that is very important. But I don't like looking at Andy, he's too ugly.'

Leah laughed. 'You can trust me too, boss.'

He smiled at her calling him boss, but was lost somewhere between looking too much and wondering if he was being honest with himself.

*

Sunday was less awkward. Justin hoped they had somehow managed to lighten the weight of what was happening between them. Andy had been out on a date the night before, having been rejected by Leah.

'How did it go? Think you might go out again?' Justin asked.

'I think I will see her again – I need to fill the time until Leah changes her mind.'

'If you can't be with the one you love, Andy,' Justin quipped, hoping quietly that it would be the end of his pursuit of Leah.

'What did you and Marcella get up to last night?' Ella asked.

Justin wasn't sure when he had begun to feel guilty about talking about his life. He kept his answer brief: 'Dinner with friends. Too much booze'.

The real response would have been slightly different: *I had dinner with Marcella's friends, at Marcella's insistence. He's a twat and she is loud and obnoxious; and there was my wife sitting across the table laughing, perfectly happy and chatty. My wife who I do love, actually, but I thought about Leah the whole time anyway. Later, my wife and I had drunken sex on the livingroom floor, because we can, because I am used to doing that after a night out. Well, actually, I was drunk. She only had one glass. She spread her legs wide for me so I could make myself come. But I felt very little pleasure in it. Not because my wife is bad at sex, but because my head is a fucking mess and I am not in control of who appears there. The truth is, it is beginning to feel like I am being unfaithful to Leah; even though she is not mine, and I am not hers, and I don't believe in ownership anyway.*

★

Justin was sure that Leah would decline his invitation for another trip to Eastbourne. Their last conversation had at least broached the subject of how they might be allowed to hang out together under the guise of an unconventional friendship. However, despite denying himself his reservations, he was aware of hers, and needed to be sure he wasn't pushing her too far. He had to ask, though, he longed for more time alone with her; it was all he wanted all of the time and, without it, he found it difficult to focus. He didn't care what they did with that time; he just wanted to know that they would have some.

Leah didn't decline as he had assumed she would. 'Sure, why not,' she replied casually.

★

In all of the other hours of the week when she was not with Justin, Leah went through the motions: she turned up to class, she did her homework, she finally completed her statement and uni application, she ate, slept, talked to her mum, texted her friends (although she had recently neglected them all shamelessly). In the few hours she was with Justin she was not a daughter or a teenager, she was just Leah, and in that time everything else had little meaning unless it was in the context of their conversation. It made it harder to leave work, harder to accept that her time with him was not really her reality – just stolen minutes. She couldn't have felt more disconnected, more removed or less interested in her actual life. Justin had done that somehow; eradicated the stuff that didn't mean anything and made it almost impossible to carry on with a normal teenaged existence. All that really mattered now were the conversations and experiences she had, or might have, with him. And for whatever reason, Justin longed for her company too. She felt it all the time. He devoured any knowledge of her and his interest made her feel more intelligent, more mature and more desirable than she knew she was. She loved the person that she was when she was with him, the person he was gently cajoling out of her, and she looked forward to becoming the person he thought she was capable of growing into. She would strive for that extra layer to herself – that ability to see and feel and experience with an open mind.

Leah wasn't sure why she said yes to the trip, but she didn't seem to be able to say 'no' when it came to spending time with Justin. Somewhere in between declaring that she could not be alone with him, and craving his attention the minute she didn't have it, she had lost her will to deny herself him. She decided what mattered was what they did when they were together; not that they were spending time together. Men and women all over the world maintained platonic friendships; surely she could manage to not lay her head on his lap again? They could just talk and laugh and eat sandwiches on the edge of a cliff – and that would be okay. He wouldn't force anything else, as was his way, and she would control herself, simple as that.

The wind was violent out; it seemed to turn the minute they entered Eastbourne. They stopped in a pub and ordered chips to warm up.

'Tell me another thing I don't know about you?'

Leah had grown used to his questioning; although she wasn't sure how she managed to retain his interest with her juvenile answers.

'I love to swim,' she announced.

'We have something in common.'

'Outdoors, though. Not in those public pools full of pubes and verrucas.'

Justin laughed out loud. 'Lakes? Rivers? Beaches…?'

'Yes, absolutely. It's liberating, isn't it? I see a body of water and I just want to dive into it. I'm always diving in my dreams.

Most people dream they're running when they are restless; I dream of diving and swimming for miles. In my dreams I never get tired, my limbs move in perfect unison, I don't lose my breath, I cross entire oceans and pass many countries on my journeys…' Leah paused to look outside the window at some people getting out of their car. 'I think I feel safer in the water than I do on land. I'm terrified of heights; but I went paragliding once and because I could see the water below me, I felt nothing but calm. And I love to swim at night. It always feels like a stolen, naughty thing to do.'

'Mmmm. Night swimming, for sure. And naked swimming,' Justin added.

She knew he hadn't said it to be provocative, but her mind was immediately full of images.

'I haven't yet, but I can see the appeal… I guess I'm always naked under my clothes.'

Justin cleared his throat and looked out the window. She'd made him blush.

Justin continued: 'I've swum in some beautiful places. You're bringing it all back. That magical feeling of weightlessness'.

'That's it, weightlessness, and when I'm in the sea I feel so small and insignificant. I like that feeling – that I matter less – that in the grand scheme of life I am just a dot in a vast, deep body of water somewhere in the universe.'

'What is your favourite place to swim?' he asked.

'Anywhere in the Med… Mind you, I haven't been to many places. What about you?'

'Probably the thermal spring along the Dalyan River in Turkey. Without any tourists around, of course. Simple, rustic, beautifully warm. Not that I mind a cold swim.'

'Thermal? Sounds healing.'

'Better than any expensive spa retreat – just you, the fish, the occasional turtle and everything going back to zero. No stress; no thoughts about time or what needs to be done that day.'

Leah drifted off to a place like the one Justin was describing, with him and no one else, both of them naked.

'I have so much to see and do in my life. I need to find a career that will allow me to travel,' she said, sighing, almost exhausted at the prospect of exploring the world, knowing she wouldn't want to leave anything out.

'I'd love to be in your position and have all the adventures to look forward to.'

'You could have more, do them all again... You're all grown up – what's stopping you?' she mocked. *Do them again – with me.*

Justin wasn't done travelling yet; there was so much more of the world he wanted to explore, especially now that he was older, now that time had changed the world. But Marcella wanted a child and that would put an end to adventures for a long time. She was not the kind of woman to sling a baby onto the side of a camel and ride through a desert with it. Marcella would plan every month of the child's existence down to the last detail. Was Justin really ready to have a child with Marcella? His head was all over the place, full of Leah. He lived for their exchanges. How could he carry on that way if he became a father? Perhaps he could put Marcella off for a while; rethink the whole baby thing somewhere down the track.

They both looked out the window as the trees fought against a spitting gale.

'Nice day for a swim?' Justin suggested.

'Perfect. Not a cloud in sight,' Leah answered.

'There's a beach about fifteen minutes from here. I'm game if you are.'

'I'm always game. I got in the car with you, didn't I?'

'Fair point.' He couldn't argue with that – she certainly trusted him more than she should. Justin paid up and they almost ran to the jeep, covering their heads from the rain.

They arrived at the empty car park.

'Let's not think about this too much or we will chicken out. We need to leave some clothes in here to change into when we come back. How many layers are you wearing?'

'Only a jumper and jeans.'

He rummaged around the back seat.

'You can wear this old T-shirt to swim in if you like, then your clothes will stay dry.'

'Okay. Perfect. Thank you.'

'It probably stinks.'

'Of you?'

'Yes, sorry.'

'I think I can handle a bit of your stink.'

He turned away from her and tried to focus on something outside his window so that she could change. The temptation to turn around too soon was unbearable.

'I'm done.'

Leah was irresistible in his T-shirt; she had brought her knees up to her chest, hugged them in close and used it to cover her legs.

Justin whipped everything off awkwardly within the confines of the jeep. He was shivering by the time he finished

– the feeling of being almost entirely exposed making him unsure of himself.

'So, shall we do this?'

'We are doing this.'

And with that he opened the door and was out of the car, standing in the mist in his pants, freezing his nuts off and hoping to God that no one would pull up in the car park. He doubted it – no one else would venture out in this weather.

Leah followed, running along in her bare feet, holding the sides of the T-shirt down.

They paused at the top of the hill.

Justin gently tugged on Leah's wrist. 'Come on. We're in this together now – no backing out.'

'I'm with you.'

Leah squealed as the gravel pierced the soles of her feet.

'Perhaps we should have worn our shoes!'

'Maybe. Oh well, let's just run!'

They bolted down the path that led to the beach. When they drew closer to the shoreline they gathered even more speed, but stopped dead the minute they made contact with the bitterly cold water.

'We have to do this quickly, there's no other way,' Leah panted, staring at the sea, psyching herself up. And then, as Justin watched, she ran at the water. Her dive was fish-like; graceful and violent at the same time. She surfaced again as Justin looked on gobsmacked. Where was the shy girl who had appeared in his shop that day?

'What's up? Forget your wetsuit?' she mocked.

That was it: Justin ran towards the exhilarating, chilling feeling of being alone with Leah, half naked in the rain with only the vast sea as their witness. This was that parallel world he thought of so often – the one where he was ageless, wifeless and burden-less. He was in it now.

He watched Leah dive and glide through the waves, then plunged after her; the cold pulsing through his skull and freezing his brain.

They stayed in the water for less than twenty minutes, but it was more than enough.

'I think we've conquered the sea, wouldn't you say?'

Justin had an urge now to wrap Leah up and get her warm again before she caught pneumonia. He watched her emerge. All of the curves of her body were now visible under the heavy, wet skin of his T-shirt. A turquoise bra sliced over her shoulder. Goosebumps. Long, very long, dripping hair. Blue lips.

She walked out of the water leaving her mermaid tail behind; but she was still all mermaid, even without the tail, he could see that now. Justin had always thought of her as otherworldly, but until now he hadn't been sure which world it was. It was clear to him in that moment that the sea was where she came from, where she came alive, where she would always find solace. She was born to swim, to be naked, to grow her hair out long and wild and to tantalise men from the safety of their boats. Men would dive in, stupidly, and swim down to the ocean floor with her; hoping for some time alone, hoping for a kiss. They'd stay down with her for so long that they'd forget they needed to surface for air or simply choose not to. Despite being able to swim they would drown rather than leave her. She could drown them all if she wanted to – all the men that came across her.

'Got to keep warm. Race you to the car.'

Before she climbed inside the jeep he saw Leah quickly pull off his T-shirt. Justin was already in the car, pumping up the heating; she couldn't see that he'd stolen more than a few glances through the passenger window. The shape of her small pert breasts inside her bra, her ribs under her skin, her flat stomach and belly button, her spine when she turned around.

Leah rung the T-shirt out and held it up against her to cover what she could as she scrambled in and pulled the door to.

'Here, let me.'

Justin took the T-shirt from her and stuffed it into a plastic bag. They struggled to get their dry clothes over their salty, sticky, frozen skin and wet underwear. When they were finally covered Leah held her hands up to the heater vents. Her lips were still blue.

'Worth it?' Justin asked.

She nodded and smiled, but was shivering all over.

'Hot potatoes?'

'Sorry?' she asked.

'Turn around. I'll show you what hot potatoes are.'

Justin gently moved her wet hair to one side so that he could have access to her back. He then cupped his hands and blew hot hair through the opening he'd made.

'More!' she begged when he paused to catch his breath.

Every place Justin blew on felt instantly warm, right through to her core. He blew at the embers again and again, until flames rose up her back and surrounded them both. The closeness, the inexplicable pull and the energy it created; it was not enough and yet much too much.

Leah settled back into her seat and stared out of the

window. She wasn't sure which she loved and needed more – just Justin, and by that she meant all of him, everything about him – his arms, his chest, his eyes, his way with the world, the soft, gravelly tone of his voice. Or was it the attention he paid her, and his determination to draw more and more out of her. They were quite separate things. She could have adored him quietly, from a distance, even if he hadn't paid her any attention. But the fact that her interest in him was reciprocated, that was the catalyst, that was the thing that would sustain her and make her want more. Had anyone, ever, been this patient and persistent with her? Had anyone risked everything for just an hour or two alone with her? She needed both – her love for him and his for her. The idea that she might not always have the latter, that it could be a short-lived fascination, completely terrified her.

'I guess we'd better head back.'

'Guess so,' she whispered, feeling instantly punctured and deflated at the thought of the day needing to end at some point.

Justin rummaged through his CDs, found something called The National and popped it in. He didn't start the engine and pull out of the car park, though, he just sat there and stared into the space in front of him as the music filled the car. He had beautiful hands: their lines, the darker pigment from working outdoors, the fine little hairs on the backs of his fingers. Leah reached over and covered Justin's left hand with her own, traced her fingers over his, then around his wrist and up his forearm. She watched as he closed his eyes, as though by not seeing her he could somehow maintain some self-control. Touching him like this was a way for her to be intimate with him in a way that was almost acceptable; it was just a hand, just a touch. He turned his hand around, where the skin was paler, so that she could trace the inside of his palm. *We could do this forever*, she thought. *Make love with only our hands.*

Leah curled up on her side as she had done before.

'Promise you'll be nice?' she asked, or rather told him – she wasn't sure which.

Justin looked her in the eye then. 'How could I be anything else to you?'

She smiled at his answer, then, as Justin turned the key, she closed her eyes so she could begin to relive the last few hours before even a second of their time together slipped from her memory.

'Where have you been?' Leah's mother had never really asked this kind of question before she had started working at The Potting Shed – it made her uncomfortable. 'Your hair looks a mess.'

'I went for a swim at the leisure centre.' Leah kept her distance – she clearly smelled of saltwater not chlorine. 'Just feeling really stressed about school lately. It helped.'

'Do you want some dinner?'

'No. I'm so tired – think I'll have an early night.'

Leah crawled into bed fully dressed. She wanted to undo nothing of the day; she wanted to still have the scent of Justin and the sea all over her. She could have no expectations – he couldn't be her lover and even their friendship would have to remain a secret – but he had promised to be nice.

★

The following Friday, after work, Justin asked Leah to stay back after everyone left. She sat on his desk and flicked through a catalogue; swinging her legs in the space underneath where the chair was supposed to be – Madeleine Peroux on LP.

He sat on the sofa and watched her; a thing he would do for hours if he could. It occurred to him that Leah had become like an addiction. Seeing her was all that mattered, all the time, and actually being alone with her in a room was something he now lived for and tried constantly to engineer.

He imagined how Leah might have come to be; how all of the elements came together to create her – water, earth, fire and air – all of them at their peak and vying with each other. And then, when they receded, this extraordinary being appeared: an Aphrodite-mermaid-girl-woman with long, long hair and the life-affirming energy of all the elements combined. The world belonged to her; she could take what she wanted from life. She would come to understand that one day. She would begin to recognise her value, her strengths, her beauty and her gifts. Justin could help her to realise them all. In fact, he could quite happily make that his mission in life and derive more satisfaction from that than achieving any more ambitions of his own; even if it had to be quietly, from the sidelines. After a time, when she finally understood just how special she was, he would most likely desperately regret the encouragement he'd given her and wish he had been more selfish, and looked instead for a way to keep her for himself, like the Collector. Before he knew it the last thing he would see of her would be the flick of her caramel mane and her incandescent, turquoise tail disappearing into the water as she swam off to more exciting shores. And that would be that, she would be gone forever. It was inevitable.

When Leah clocked him looking at her she closed the catalogue and put it down. There was so much they never talked about. She wore the look she often had in his presence, like she wanted to say something but didn't have the courage to test the water.

'I feel like there's something you want to say,' he said.

'There are lots of things I would like to say, but never will,' she announced.

'Why?'

'You know why.'

'Should we talk about Eastbourne?' he asked.

She looked confused.

'I'm not sure what I trusted myself not to do, but I think…'

'Out of the kindness of your heart you warmed me up because I was shivering,' she said, quite bluntly. 'Do you think we need to draw imaginary markers that separate our bodies from touching? Do we need to say that friendship is the only thing that will ever be between us?'

Justin thought about Leah's question for less than half a second.

'I think it would be a terrible idea. If someone said to you, for whatever reason, you would never visit a Greek island in your lifetime, you might be really disappointed with how the life you haven't even lived yet was going to turn out. You might even resent the person who told you. However, if you lived your life knowing you could visit a Greek island if you wanted to but, in reality, spent time in Spain, Italy, Turkey and the South of France, and just never got around to it, you would still die a relatively happy woman.'

She looked slightly perplexed, then thoughtful.

He carried on: 'There's no need to say nothing will ever happen. In fact, there is a very distinct need *not* to say it; because when you say it, this is what causes the damage, not the unknowing. It would end something before it has even happened. Or rather, kill the magic of possibility. Possibility is wonderful and its purpose underestimated. Take away possibility and life is dull and repetitious, and then it just ends.'

It was an extravagant analogy, but he was sure it made perfect sense.

'So…' she joined in, 'until someone says nothing will ever happen, there will always be possibility.'

'Yes.'

'That I will go to a Greek island?'

'Yes.'

Leah was relieved they would never have this conversation again, but glad they'd had it too, because it meant that the possibility remained. She wondered how long they could orbit each other without colliding. Two halves of a planet separated by light years, both uninhabitable: one without gravity, the other without oxygen. All around them now were an infinite number of possibilities, like spinning matter in space. She wanted to grab at them, snatch them, pull them in close.

'I love you,' she confessed.

'Not half as much as I love you,' he told her, then walked over, picked up the palm of her hand and kissed it.

★

Marcella came by the shop again the following week, causing Justin to go through the same psychosomatic convulsions as before. She waved and smiled at everyone but didn't stop to talk, and they left together almost immediately, at her insistence.

In the café around the corner Justin and Marcella sat opposite each other; she huddled over and he stretched out. He wasn't sure what she could possibly want to talk about that they couldn't discuss at the shop. On the short walk over a myriad of potentially thorny topics of conversation had come to mind. Leah, for one. Had someone spotted them together in Eastbourne? He felt sick to the stomach as the waiter walked away with their order.

'I'm pregnant.'

'What? Are you serious? Oh my God!'

'I know. It's hard to take it in, and it's early days, but I really am pregnant!'

'I'm in shock. Did you just take a home test?'

'Yes. I took three… We are going to have a baby, whether we are ready or not!'

Justin hugged his wife. Marcella's excitement had changed her in an instant; softened her and made her look younger, more vibrant. He was surprised by his own overwhelming joy at the prospect of becoming a father. He buried his face in her hair. It smelt familiar; comforted him in his weakened, pathetic, irredeemable state.

'Let's not tell anyone yet, until the twelve-week scan.'

'Absolutely.'

Wow!

Shit.

Leah.

This would destroy them.

It just would.

Justin had some time before Leah would have to find out. It seemed ironic that they had just talked about not drawing a line and not eliminating possibility; a fantastical conversation they both dived into with their eyes closed. He had to prepare himself, and the words he would choose. Each time he played out the conversation in his head the result was the same. Leah would see this as the end of possibility. She might feign happiness for him, but she would be hurt. She would draw lines between them very quickly; big fat ones in order to protect herself. And every time he looked at her for too long she would remind him that he was married with a child on the way.

He could feel it instantly – the loss of her.

How long could they wait to share the news? Longer than the twelve-week scan? Maybe. Just to be on the safe side?

In order to receive one beautiful gift into his life, Justin would have to give up another.

PART THREE

Justin was in the habit of rushing around and getting everything done on Mondays, but when Leah arrived the shop was still in a terrible state. She took to the floors while he did the orders. When they had only half an hour left, he locked up the empty shop and told her to come and sit with him outside. She tried to refuse, insisting there was more to clean, but he wouldn't take no for an answer. He appeared with a blanket, put it around her and walked her over to a bench.

'This bench is leaving tomorrow and you haven't sat on it yet.'

Leah sat down, brought her legs up and crossed them, as she always did. It was as though she didn't like her feet to be touching the ground.

'It is okay for us to be friends, isn't it? I mean there's no actual harm in it, is there?' she asked, peering up at him from her perch.

'Absolutely, completely okay.'

'So what do friends talk about?'

'I don't know. Let me think. Are you seeing that boy?'

'Ollie? No…'

'Poor kid.'

'What do you mean?'

'You're stringing him along by his balls.'

'I'm not! He knows exactly where he stands!'

'Right. Well, he's standing pretty close in line. I'm just saying. Him and Andy.'

'Very funny. Andy isn't standing in any line; he moved on pretty quickly.'

'I wouldn't be so sure about that.' Justin realised then that he was finding it difficult to conceal his jealousy.

They were quiet for a time after that. Justin wasn't sure what to talk about – the pregnancy was on his mind. Leah was in front of him, but she wouldn't be for long, and he was so far from ready to lose the essence of what they were.

Leah broke the silence: 'I loved our swim, I thought about it for a long time after'.

'Me too. I loved seeing you in your natural habitat – little fish.'

She giggled. 'I was also thinking, you give good hugs; for a friend.'

'Any time. Nothing quite beats actual physical contact when you feel like shit.'

'And you smell good.'

He liked that for whatever reason, that thought had come to her then.

'I'm not even going to go into what it feels like to hug you or what you smell like – as a friend – but I have more hugs to give, if you should ever need one.'

Someone rapped on the door. Justin got up to answer it.

When he returned Leah was up and about, pretending to look busy.

'Paranoid?' he mocked.

'Maybe a little! Must have a guilty conscience. It is that time of the evening, though. I really should go home and do some homework.'

'Such a shame.'

'I kind of need a hug, though,' she said coyly.

Justin reached out and pulled her in close. They held on to each other, finding more in their physical contact than they had been able to in their stilted conversation. Justin slid his hand softly across her upper back, over her clothing and the bump of her bra strap. He rested his chin on the top of her head where he imagined he might plant a kiss. Her hands found her way under his T-shirt, on to his lower back. Her touch was cautious, her hands small and cool. She gave him a little squeeze and sighed, pulled away slowly, looked through him.

'I feel so much better, thank you.'

Justin's cock had expanded several inches and was now an aching, bowing branch trapped behind his underwear and jeans.

'Oh, and don't forget, you won't see me for three weeks.'

Shoot a man while he is struggling with his erection. Of course she was having time off, she had told him about two major pieces of schoolwork she had to complete and a family Christmas engagement. He had simply chosen to not remember that she would be away.

★

After the initial disappointment, loss and frustration, Justin actually felt that Leah's temporary absence really was for the best. Everything became about the pregnancy. He and Marcella had gone from talking less and less to talking incessantly about the baby, the things they would need to buy, the birth and the child that would appear at the end of it all.

Marcella read pregnancy books in bed at night – remarking upon her discoveries and inserting post-it notes beside the important passages she would need to refer back to later – and spent hours browsing the internet for all the best baby products. Justin joined in where he could and read at least half of what she asked him to. Marcella also began to eat everything that was not nailed down – she said it helped with the sick feeling that was not even remotely limited to mornings.

They attended an early scan after a small amount of unexplained bleeding that turned out to be nothing. The memory of the miscarriage, all those years earlier, resurfaced and tainted some of their joy at being pregnant now. They saw it, though, the tiny wriggling prawn, and listened to its galloping heartbeat; again Justin was surprised at how much he wanted this, and at how that sound alone could actually cause him to cry.

The Christmas trees arrived and Justin brought one home. He was ideologically opposed to cutting down trees for a festival, but this one could be kept and allowed to continue to grow. Marcella loved the tree and was excited by the idea that the following year there would be gifts underneath for their baby.

Life was good, life was exciting: a child was growing.

And still Leah remained in his head; less when he was at home, where everything was about the pregnancy, but always, always when he was at work. He thought about the times when it had been just the two of them in his office; Leah coy and slightly uncomfortable, unknowingly flirtatious. He had never forced her to stay and yet anyone looking in from the outside would see it differently; they'd say he was controlling her.

Towards the end of the three weeks Justin noticed the days were growing longer, cooler, darker, more tedious. Leah was absent from them and that took the joy out of everything. Leah would bring the sun back; she would make the days feel lighter again. He imagined the pain that would come if she left for longer, if she left altogether. Of course she would, one day, leave altogether, to head off to university, to travel. The thought of his life without her somewhere in it was unimaginable.

★

Leah forced herself to commit to her schoolwork until she was crying with tiredness. She had allowed herself to fall behind and was now panicking. University offers were coming in; she needed A's, all A's. In all her years of school she'd achieved nothing less, but she wasn't so sure now. She realised then how heavily she had flung herself into her fantasy world with Justin. Who was she now when she was not with him? She was disinterested in her friends and had given Ollie the cold shoulder. Sweet adoring Ollie, who deserved so much better. She dragged herself around the house and barely spoke to her mother. She saw her father, stepmother and half-sisters for Christmas but they all felt like strangers; like a perfect, harmonious family from the

1950's that she was looking in on. She wasn't sure where she fitted into that picture, since she was just a burden from her father's previous life. All that she could think about was Justin. She'd never felt more connected to another person in her life and simultaneously so hollow at the same time.

She worried that in her absence Justin might realise that their connection had already gone too far and that he must pull back. He would realise that he could return to his wife with his morals still relatively intact. She wanted to text him and remind him that she was still there, still Leah, still needing his attention and affection. Of course she didn't contact him, not even on Christmas day, she couldn't be sure that Marcella wouldn't be with him or that someone else wouldn't pick up his phone. Just a phone call perhaps, on a Monday, when he really should be alone? She recognised her own desperation and resisted.

By the time the three weeks had passed, Justin was another three weeks closer to having to tell everyone they were expecting. Leah reappeared at the shop accompanied by the sound of leaves fighting their way in, and the slam of the door as it was pulled to by the wind. She looked amazing, lifting him instantly. Nothing was gone, nothing lost.

'Hey stranger! How was your Christmas?'

'It was okay, how was yours?'

'Quiet. Get your essays and revision done?'

'I did, thank you for the time off. Did you miss me? My ability to clean, I mean?'

'We have all failed to keep the floors shining in your absence. And yes, you were missed. Very much so.'

'Shall I get the broom, then?' And off she skipped.

He let her go; not because he wanted her to sweep the floor, that was the last thing he wanted her to do, but because he could think of nothing to say. Because balancing uncomfortably on the tip of his tongue was this enormous, wonderful, miracle-bombshell that would change everything. Everything. And nothing. Because they had not actually done anything and had not promised themselves, or each other, that they ever would. He would not be able to forget about Leah even with a child on the way, he was certain of that now, now that he had missed her and seen her again. He would simply continue to feel tormented by his feelings for her while becoming even less able to express them.

After cleaning, Leah found Justin in his office and he poured them both tea. He had lit the fire. Their time apart had done something to them, but Leah wasn't sure what. He was quiet, still attentive, but distracted. Perhaps she was slowly losing him as he felt the need to return to his adult life and his adult wife. She wouldn't fight it when it happened. One day he would stop asking her to sit down with him; he would stop fussing over her and asking her questions about how she was, and who she was, and she would just have to get over it.

Leah sat down on the rug in front of the small wood stove. It was the first time she had seen it lit. The wood made a gentle cracking sound as it burned – the only thing that could be heard in the calm and quiet of Justin's space. She wondered how long she could stay. Maybe she could become one of the things he had collected on his travels and kept here instead of in his house, due to Marcella's dislike for it. Justin sat down on the sofa behind her. He stretched out and put his hands on her shoulders.

'Shuffle back.'

Leah did so, until her back was resting against the base of the sofa and she was tucked into the space between his legs. He wrapped his arms around her in a bear hug and whispered in her ear.

'Now, I want you to close your eyes and relax or this won't work. I'm just going to help you with your exam stress.'

'Okay, they're closed.' She was far from relaxed, though.

Justin gently slid his hands under the collar of the loose top she was wearing. As he began to massage her shoulders, neck and upper back, her head slowly fell forward. It was his turn to observe her at close range: her skin, her spine, strands of hair, silver earrings, the pale pink satin of her bra strap, a small birthmark on her right shoulder, tiny goose bumps. So many perfect details to take in all at once.

'Is this okay?'

'No, it's wonderful.'

'I mean, do you mind that I am… are you comfortable?'

'Of course.'

'You're not going to run off?'

'Very funny.'

Leah's body began to slacken as the knots were pressed out. After a time Justin could feel her almost collapsing and he put his arms around her again, holding her tight to keep her upright. He breathed her in, remained still, waited for his heart to slow a little.

'Thank you,' she managed, her voice weak. 'Where did you learn to do that?'

'Actually, I don't know. I expect from being massaged myself.'

He moved off the sofa and on to the floor beside her.

'You're not a bad friend to have – but I feel I owe you something in return.'

'You don't owe me anything. Just stay a little longer.'

'Too easy.'

He rose to add wood to the fire.

'My half-brother is coming back soon.'

'I've forgotten what he does.'

'Tristan. He's a teacher with restless feet. Doesn't like to stay in the same place for too long so teaches English abroad, sometimes in slum areas and remote villages, sometimes at International British Schools; although that tends to be when he runs out of money.'

'Sounds like an interesting way to live your life.'

'I think it probably is. He'll be staying here, sleeping upstairs.'

'Are you close?'

'He's a lot younger so there's a bit of a generation gap, but, yeah, we are good mates.'

'We won't be able to hang out like this when he is here…' Leah concluded.

Justin looked down at the ground, shook his head a little. 'I always look forward to seeing him, but the thought of us not being able to… there are so few places our friendship can exist.'

They sat quietly for a long time.

'Since we are here, sitting by the fire, I thought I might tell you a little story,' he said.

'Let's hear it,' she answered immediately, sounding excited.

'Around ten years ago, and approximately ten years into

your future, you and I are both travelling alone and meet for the first time at a base camp at the foot of the Himalayas, prior to a trek. You are struggling with your tent, I mean really struggling, and when we try to erect it together we find that it is fucked, a crucial pole is missing. It is getting dark and the temperature is dropping fast; you have no choice but to share with me. It is colder than you expected and despite cocooning yourself in several layers of clothing, your woollen beany and gloves and your thousand tog sleeping bag, you cannot fall asleep. Without saying anything we unzip our sleeping bags and reclose them together so that there is just one big sleeping bag and two strangers' bodies squished in together, keeping each other warm. And that is how we actually meet, or have already met. We just can't remember it.'

'I like that story.'

There was a moment of silence as Justin's story played out; as their other selves slept peacefully in their tent.

'What are you doing tomorrow, early afternoon?' he asked. 'I was thinking we could catch a film.'

They could arrive at the cinema separately and meet somewhere in the middle, in the dark. It was another way for them to be in each other's company, as strangers and friends, as two people alone and two people together at the same time. When she was in his car Justin had her where he wanted her, but without being able to engage with her properly. In a cinema she would be near enough that he would be able to touch her arm and whisper something in her ear to make her smile. Time together was all he wanted, but it wouldn't materialise of its own accord, he had to make it happen.

★

Leah received a text from Justin that he would arrive just after her. The small cinema foyer was quiet. It was the middle of the day; only a few mothers and children, no one she recognised. Leah took a seat in the middle of the empty theatre and nibbled at her popcorn; it looked like they would have the space all to themselves. She thought about whether there really was anything wrong with seeing a film with Justin. She had decided that if they were seen together, she would say that they had met by chance and it would have been strange not to sit with each other. She was satisfied with her lie despite its ridiculousness – why would either of them just so happen to be in the cinema in the middle of the day? She slipped her pumps off and perched her toes on the seat in front.

Just as the previews finished up, the double doors squeaked open. Leah turned, expecting to see Justin looking for her in the darkness. In his place a group of teenage boys with hoodies and low-slung jeans appeared, laughing and shoving each other along the aisle. Leah took her feet down and sank into her seat. She felt oddly vulnerable, alone in the dark.

The boys took seats behind her. From what she could hear it was a few rows back. Leah wondered if she should stay. *Where was Justin?* If she stood up the boys would see her and might harass her – there was something about the pack mentality of teenage boys that always made her uncomfortable. She could just stay, unnoticed, hidden as she was, until the film was over, and wait for them to leave. Justin would arrive soon anyway.

Then she heard the flick-back of their seats; they were moving. She hoped it meant they were leaving.

'Oh, look man, this poor girl's here all alone.'

Fuck.

'Hey, do you want some company, sweetheart?'

Fuck.

'Oh, come on, fellas, let's join this lovely lady.'

They approached from both aisles – four of them – and took seats next to her. Leah was trapped in the middle. She got up.

'Alright, darlin'? Can we share some popcorn?'

'Actually, I was just leaving.'

'Na, I don't fink so, sweetheart. Don't mind us.'

One of them took her popcorn and stuffed fistfuls into his mouth.

There was so much laughter but nothing they'd said was funny.

'Fuck, you're really hot – here, let me sit wiv 'er.'

They began to push each other.

'Nah, I saw her first, man.'

Leah tried to climb over the back of her seat but one of the boys pulled her back by her waist.

She wanted to tell them to let her go, to fuck off, but the words were wedged somewhere between her diaphragm and her throat.

One of the boys pulled her hard against him, locking his wiry arms around her waist and chest. He stank of cheap aftershave. Leah began to kick and writhe, trapped in the small space in between the seats.

'Hey, settle down, sweetheart. No need to freak out.'

'No!' she finally managed, her breath finally coming back to her.

'Help me out man. This bitch is going nuts.'

'Shut 'er up and get 'er down.'

Two of them forced her to the ground while the others looked on; laughing at her attempts to escape them. Leah fought like an animal; kicking violently as one of them lifted her skirt and tried to remove her tights. She felt dizzy and sick, unable to breathe, as she flailed and twisted in the airless darkness.

'Grab her arms and mouth.'

The boy by her head pinned her arms down with his knees, covered her mouth with one hand and cupped her breasts with the other. With the full weight of the boy on her arms the pain was excruciating. She tried to bite him.

'Don't you fucking bite me, bitch.' He slapped her hard across her face; her head instantly filled with a ringing sound.

Leah could feel her strength failing her.

The other boy knelt on her legs and crushed her beneath him. Now her legs were breaking too and his hands were pulling at her waistband.

Marcella had bled again.

'No! More than last time, Justin! For fuck sake!' Marcella screamed down the hallway.

They spent all morning queuing at the hospital and demanding to be seen. Only when they saw the tiny little wriggling being with its enormous heartbeat, were they reassured that everything was fine.

'For the moment...' Marcella repeated the doctor's words in the car.

'Well, they can't guarantee the baby will be born perfectly healthy from a scan. They're just covering their backs. It's fine today, that's what matters. You just need to rest up.'

'No. You're basically telling me that a miscarriage is inevitable. No amount of resting up will stop that from happening. You don't give a shit!'

Marcella had clearly discarded all reason.

'Let's not be completely negative – you heard what the doctor said, a lot of women bleed for inexplicable reasons and don't go on to miscarry. But if we do miscarry, it's because it wasn't meant to be.'

'What the hell, Justin? Not meant to be? Our baby is not meant to be?'

'I mean that if there is something seriously wrong, you could miscarry. Not because we are not meant to be parents, not because we don't deserve to be, and not because you think it doesn't matter to me, but because we would have no control over it.'

'And you think I am being negative? All you're doing is preparing for the worst. How practical of you. You're supposed to be reassuring me, not making me feel worse.'

Justin drove in silence. Marcella turned her back on him in the car and sobbed quietly to herself. Once home, she went straight upstairs to lie down. Justin followed her up and sat on the bed next to her with his head in his hands. It was still early days, they had months to get through; he wasn't sure how they would manage.

'There's no point just sitting there in silence, Justin. That's not going to save our baby. Just go and get on with your day and leave me the fuck alone.'

Justin felt like a conniving prick as he pulled out of the driveway. He had a wife at home, a baby on the way, and now he was on his way to spend the afternoon with his bit on the side. It was sordid, almost pathetic, and yet he could not stop himself from going to her.

Given their unplanned trip to the hospital, Justin was more than twenty minutes late for the film. He cooked up some lies to justify his absence, hating the fact that one day Leah would have to learn about the pregnancy.

The spotty kid at the counter had a problem with the till – something about the computer not letting him select a ticket for a film that had already started. Justin tried to remain calm and asked for any ticket to any film. The boy insisted he would have to see the film he paid for and muttered a rehearsed line about health and safety. There was no point arguing with the little dick. Justin nodded, growing increasingly agitated.

'Absolutely. Of course. I will watch this children's epic and I will enjoy it thoroughly, from beginning to end. In fact, I will even write you a review.'

The dick smirked as Justin paid for the ticket then raced down the corridor to find the cinema Leah was in.

It was dark, but something was happening down in the middle row. And Leah was nowhere to be seen.

Then he heard her.

Heard her muffled, petrified scream.

Adrenalin swamped him. 'Get off! Get the fuck off! What the fuck are you doing?' he shouted like a madman, leaping down the aisle, terrified of what he might find.

He threw himself towards the gang – there were two on the floor and two in the seats behind, egging the others on. One of them reached inside his pocket and produced a knife. Justin would have thrown himself at him even if he had been wielding a machete, but his first concern was for Leah and her close proximity to the weapon.

Justin put his hands up, as if to say he was backing off. Then he turned and ran back out.

'Call the police! Quickly! Someone help!' His voice was shrill, desperate.

Leah heard Justin's voice above the laughter and the sound of the film. She saw the knife and turned her face to the side, sure that the boy was going to cut her with it. Instead they pulled away abruptly, kicking her as they made their escape. It didn't hurt. The only thing she could still feel were the boy's hands on her breasts.

Leah curled into a small ball, making sure her clothes covered any exposed skin. She shielded her head and face with her arms as the lights came up and the film was turned off. Everything was very quiet then. The lights were so bright she couldn't bear to open her eyes.

'They took off through the fire exit by the front of the screen,' she heard someone say.

Justin was the first in a line of people who had come to pull her out from in between the seats. She could not release her hands from her face; could not look at him or have him look at her.

'Come on, love,' she heard someone else say gently, so gently it hurt to hear it. She felt someone touch her shoulder and recoiled further, made her ball tighter. The ball she kept herself in was safe. Pretending not to be able to hear, to be unconscious and incapable of movement, that was safe.

Other people tried to speak too, but she closed them all off, refusing to respond. She heard them ask Justin if he knew her. She didn't hear how he answered but she was certain he said no. It incensed her and yet she expected nothing different. His late arrival had allowed this to happen and yet none of it was his fault. It was hers: her fault for going, her fault for expecting, her fault for agreeing to sit in the cinema with another woman's husband. It was karma.

She heard someone say the police were on their way. And that was when she needed air. She had to get out. She had been willing herself to suffocate but her body came up looking to draw breath again. She uncurled herself, using the seat to pull herself up, ignoring the blurred mess of concerned faces as she stumbled towards the exit and swiped popcorn from her hair and clothes. She wouldn't sit and be comforted by strangers while they wondered what the boys had done to her. She would not be interviewed by the police. They would not learn her name and feel sorry for her and ask if they could call her mother. Justin would not be a witness and have to explain what he was doing with her in the cinema in the middle of the day. She was not in this scene; she was above it all, looking down from a corner of the ceiling. She pushed her way out of the theatre, into the foyer and through the heavy glass doors that led on to the street. The good people behind her urged her to wait for the police but she did not even acknowledge that they had spoken.

She realised then that she wasn't wearing any shoes.

But still she began to run. It was all that she could do now.

Leah ran down the street, faster than she knew she was able. She was free; with air all around her and air inside her body, she was escaping, she was getting away. If the boys were behind her now they would not be able to catch her. She was just too fast.

She ran for several blocks, past confused pedestrians and hooting drivers, not knowing if Justin was behind her but guessing that he probably was. She felt everything underfoot through her tights – the cold, the debris and all the filth of London. She spotted someone getting out of a taxi on the other side of the road and threw herself into the moving traffic to get to it.

She opened the door of the taxi.

'Leah! Stop!' Justin's voice was cut off as she pulled the door shut.

'Is that man bovering you, love?'

She could see the driver's concerned face in the rear-view mirror. She wondered what she looked like, all smashed up and hysterical, running down the street with no shoes and a man chasing her. She nodded.

'Aw-right, darling. Let's go.'

He turned the car into the rhythm of the traffic and they were away, away from the cinema, away from Justin.

PART FOUR

Justin's legs gave way as he watched the taxi turn off the main road; the back of Leah's head silhouetted in the frame of the rear window.

He had been late.

Leah had been on her own.

And she had been violated.

When Justin had arrived he was only able to offer himself as a concerned stranger.

The last few moments of the attack flashed through his head. The screams, the youths, the knife, and then Leah; shaking involuntarily, curled up in a foetal position, not responding. He wanted to vomit. He wanted to find the kids and actually physically harm them, one after the other.

She had run.

And he couldn't catch her. Again. She was always running away from him when he wanted so much for her to run towards him, into the comfort of his arms and stay there where he could hold her and keep her safe. She seemed to be running away from him as much as she was running from the scene of the attack. Justin was twenty years older than Leah. To the taxi driver, whose disgusted face he'd caught sight of as the vehicle had moved away, he was the threat. He was why she was crying and barefoot and battered. And the taxi driver, a stranger, was the one who saved her.

In the cinema and in the street his two worlds had crossed over and he hadn't known what to do. All that he could think in hindsight was what he should have done: He should have picked her up. He should have told everyone that he knew her and asked them to back away. He should have carried her home in his arms. But most of all he should not have been late.

Justin felt desperate then. Overcome by wave after wave of love and fear and remorse, he began to cry like a lost child in the street.

For her. For Leah.

His girl. His parallel girl.

Leah had never been more relieved to be alone in the house. She quickly removed all of her clothes, put them in a plastic bag, tied it up, and stuffed it in the bin under the rubbish that was already in there. She spotted a beaten, bruised, pallid figure in the mirror she passed on the way to the shower. In the bathroom she inspected her naked body all over, touched the raw and peeled back skin and the swollen hearts of all of the bruises.

They had not been able to remove her tights. They had been interrupted by Justin. She could still feel the boy's hands on her breasts – like a pair of heavy, dirty gloves – but they had not taken off her tights. There was at least one part of her body that had remained unsullied.

She would be able to cover almost all of the bruises and the carpet burns with clothes, anything else would be explained by a story about a tumble she had taken from a bicycle she had borrowed. She had her lie figured out, quickly and expertly.

She turned on the shower. When the water was warm she curled up and lay inside the tray and let it run over her body as she cried.

Justin couldn't go home. He could not go home and have Marcella shout at him. He drove to Richmond Park and sat in his car. He cried some more, punched the steering wheel and howled in the closed confines of the car. Then he called himself 'a fucking bastard, a stupid, selfish cunting bastard'.

He composed several text messages to Leah; none of them adequate or appropriate. They were all about *him* needing to feel better, *him* needing to know she was okay, *him* wanting reassurance and forgiveness. Piss poor apologies and declarations of vengeance; and how he would do anything, anything humanly possible, to undo the damage. He threw the phone on the dashboard, slumped over the wheel and closed his eyes. He wanted sleep to come and take him away. And he wanted to find that when he woke the incident in the cinema had all been part of a dream. He wanted Leah to be unhurt again, more than anything he would ever want in his life. He begged to a God he didn't even believe in to have the day over again so that he could do it all differently.

The phone wasn't broken. He had to send her something. He typed in another text and sent it: *Even if it takes the rest of my life, I will make this right again.*

He waited several minutes.

But there was no reply.

He waited an hour.

Nothing.

He wanted to drive to her flat and force his way in to see her and try to console her, but he knew he could not and would just have to give her time. He had done enough harm already by forcing his way into her life.

★

On Wednesday, Justin finally heard from Leah.

Would it be okay if I didn't come in this week? I have lots of homework.

Of course, take your time. Are you okay? Please can I see you?

No.

Can I call you?

No. Sorry, can't talk.

Torture. He deserved it. He spent the week pacing the floor of the shop and being blunt with everyone who tried to communicate with him. He drove by Leah's flat on his way to and from work in the hope that he might catch her coming or going, or maybe see her in her bedroom window, looking okay, looking like she would recover.

But he didn't see her.

★

There was no way of removing the feel of the dirty gloves from her breasts. They were simply there, the whole time, even after Leah washed and scrubbed her skin until she was raw. She imagined having her breasts surgically removed. In their place would be a flat, masculine, clean slate. And the vulgar feeling of being touched by a filthy, repugnant stranger would be gone.

She thought about going to the police and how all of the people in the theatre had told her to stay and wait for them. It made her paranoid that they might be looking for her now and the whole thing would end up on *Crimewatch*. There she would be, in black and white, the whole thing taken from the cinema's CCTV for the world to see. And maybe then they would all spot Justin running in and they would both be found out. But the youths wouldn't be identifiable, in the dark, with their hoodies and cheap aftershave. It was hard enough to convict a rapist, but a bunch of kids just forcing her to the ground and pinning her down? She'd go through all of the telling, all of the humiliation and judgement, and explaining why and how she came to be there, for nothing. And the boys would just be laughing at the other end of the courtroom. Laughing at her, laughing at getting away with it.

Her mother wanted details of the bicycle accident but eventually gave up when Leah burst into tears and told her to leave her alone. She spent a number of days in bed. She thought endlessly about how Justin would treat her differently now that she was a victim. He wouldn't dare touch her now, or even flirt with her. In fact he would probably recoil at the thought, now that she was damaged. This idea upset her more than the actual attack. It was as though something of her, her essence, had been ripped from her body while she was still alive and in its place was this revolting stain.

Leah was asked a number of questions at school; each time she told the story she came up with a new detail about the accident – the condition of the road, the way the tire had come off the jagged edge on the side of the bitumen and how she had skidded in gravel and toppled over the handlebars face first. Oh, and how embarrassing the whole thing had been – some bloke had pulled over to ask if she was okay and she had cried like a baby. She thought her story tremendous, flawless.

Vanessa winced at the sight of her face. 'Shit, Lee, must have been a bad prang.'

Ollie made the mistake of holding her arm, as he often did when he talked to her. She recoiled in agony; they had knelt on her arms and legs. They had knelt on her and pressed their mark into her skin. And now she could not be touched at all, ever again.

'Oh no! Sorry.'

'It's okay,' she lied.

'Let me come around and take care of you after school.'

She shook her head. His kindness was almost a cruelty. She didn't deserve any of it. 'You are sweet, but I can't. Too much homework.'

'You should be resting,' Ollie protested. 'You shouldn't even be here.'

'Can't get any further behind.'

'Are you okay? You just seem really shaken up.' Vanessa was so sincere Leah thought that she might lose it.

'Just hurts. I'm fine, though.'

★

The anxiety of returning to work and seeing Justin was almost more than she could take. She felt her heart racing as the morning arrived. She didn't know what to wear, she couldn't eat, she ran out of time, forgot her bus card. She was determined not to crumble when she saw him, adamant that she would not fall apart. She would not be different and she would not allow him to feel responsible or guilty. She was resilient and, moreover, she was still the girl he had been so taken with before that day. She was. She would prove she was, and everything would somehow be okay between them and return to what it had been before. She couldn't lose Justin and she knew that if he saw that the essence of her was not there anymore he would change, he would withdraw, they wouldn't laugh anymore, or talk about possibilities, he wouldn't touch the freckle under her eye, or tuck her hair behind her ear or examine her every feature the way he did. She couldn't lose him. Justin was all that was beautiful and remarkable in her life. Without him she was not sure how she would ever get out of bed again.

Justin made sure he was at work early on Saturday. For some reason he thought it might make the time pass more quickly. He cleaned the shop, tidied all the displays and opened the doors. His chores complete, he paced the Moroccan tiles until everyone else arrived; everyone that is except the very person he wanted to see – Leah.

And then she was there, with Ella and Andy, just a few metres away. Justin listened as she relayed a story about a bicycle accident.

He caught up with her as she made her way towards the office, leaving the other staff shaking their heads behind her. Up close her face shocked him. A yellowing bruise sprawled from her jawline to just beneath her right eye.

'Leah...' He had tears in his eyes.

'I'm okay, Justin,' she whispered. 'They didn't get what they wanted. They're just bruises.'

She entered the office and he followed.

The relief of knowing they hadn't raped her was almost overwhelming. There could be nothing worse.

Justin daren't imagine what was underneath her clothing, what they had done to the rest of her soft skin. He didn't know what to say, whether to touch her. He hadn't known how she would be after the attack; although he had hoped for anger, even if it was directed at him, anger and tears, lots of them. At least then he could comfort her.

'Can you stay late? Not to work, just to talk.'

'I can't. I have homework.'

'Of course, I'm sorry. I'm just so sorry.' And then he really was crying. He sat down on the stairs that led up to the loft space and covered his face with his hands, felt his body shuddering with each useless sob.

Leah walked over and ran her fingers through his hair. Then she bent down and whispered in his ear. 'It's not your fault.' She kissed his forehead. 'And you did save me.'

And then she left – before anyone spotted them through the window.

Justin was deeply ashamed of himself. He didn't deserve to be let off the hook, at all, let alone be comforted by Leah. It should have been the other way around.

After a time, he washed his face and went back outside. Leah was there manning the till, smiling and making polite conversation with the customers. At one point she stretched up to a high shelf to reach a pot. He saw carpet burns and bruises on her lower back. He cringed and looked away, speechless. She refused to stop for lunch and left promptly at four. He followed her down the street, making some excuse to Andy about her leaving her purse behind. He caught her at the bus stop. They were alone, side by side. She kept her eyes down on the ground and wouldn't look at him. At least she didn't run.

'I'm sorry for crying like that. Please tell me what I can do?' he pleaded.

She sat in silence, slightly shook her head as if to say no.

'Have you made a statement?'

'To the police? No, I don't want to.'

'I could come with you.'

'No, thank you.'

He shouldn't have pressured her about going to the police – she wasn't ready, or able, and was clearly struggling with her decision not to – he just wanted to help in some way, any way.

'Can I drive you home?'

'Here's my bus. See you tomorrow.'

'Okay, see you tomorrow.'

She didn't need him, didn't want his help, at least that was what she wanted him to think.

Justin left work early. At home he curled up on the sofa and stayed there without moving. His stomach churned, his head spun and everything ached. He hoped Marcella would stay out with her friend until late so that he could just be in his own headspace. He had no energy for anything or anyone.

Marcella crept in at some point and sat on the seat in front of him, waited for him to open his eyes.

'I've been a bitch lately, haven't I?'

'Cel, don't worry about it. You're pregnant, your hormones are all over the place and you're worried about the baby. It's normal.'

'Well, I'm sorry.'

'Me too. I should be more supportive, more patient, and try to understand what it is like for you. You are the one carrying our child, after all.'

'Have you told everyone at work yet?'

'I kind of don't want to jinx anything.'

'I know what you mean.'

'I'm going to wait a few weeks more.'

'Don't leave it too long. People get really offended when they're the last to know.'

★

Justin received a text from Leah. It said she would like to give it another week before coming back to work properly. Of course, he told her; though he wished she would come in so that he could find a way to talk to her.

On Sunday he did something he had rarely done in all the years he owned the shop – he called in sick. He closed the shop on Monday altogether. He wasn't sure if it was flu but he just wasn't able to get out of bed. The only day that meant anything was the following Saturday, when he would see Leah again.

★

'Hey, you're looking brighter,' he heard Andy say to Leah as she arrived.

'Yes, everything has pretty much healed.'

'Something is different too.'

'It's the jumper.'

'Love it.'

'A birthday present from my mother.'

'What, when was your birthday?'

'Tuesday.'

'How old?'

'Seventeen.'

'Happy birthday! Sweet seventeen – I keep forgetting how young you are. Hey, shouldn't you be eighteen?'

'I was put forward a year in primary school.'

'Oh, one of those gifted kids. That makes sense.'

'Not gifted, just keen; I was such a nerd in primary school.'

'And now?'

'I just can't wait for school to be over with so I can get on with my life.'

Her birthday? Shit! Justin hadn't known. His crimes against Leah were multiplying by the day. He'd promised to be nice and yet couldn't even remember her birthday.

'Doing anything special?'

'Not this year. Seventeen isn't really a big deal.'

'Every birthday is special. We should all be celebrating the day you were born.'

'Andy, you are such a sleaze, leave the poor girl alone,' Ella called out.

Leah laughed, amused by Andy's persistence and by Ella being her defender for once. What she liked about being around Andy was that he didn't know what had really happened to her. There was no pain in his eyes, no remorse, no guilt, he was just himself.

She knew Justin was in the corner, listening in. She hadn't gone out of her way not to tell him about her birthday, but it would have seemed odd to remind him, particularly now. And for what purpose; the expectation of a gift, a bunch of flowers, or an evening alone together? He couldn't give her any of those things. Besides, there was nothing that would lift her mood; nothing that would make her want to celebrate the day she was born. If anything she wanted to protest the stupid decision to bring her into this ugly world full of pain and longing.

After work, Vanessa popped over with a present and asked if, at the very least, she would come and see a film with her. The very thought of going to the cinema made Leah's entire body convulse. Vomit spun its way up like a tornado; through her gut and into her gullet, throat and then her mouth. She ran out of the room and emptied the contents of her violent memory into the toilet. Vanessa came after her and looked on horrified, held her hair back in a ponytail, asked if she was pregnant. Thankfully there was no chance of that. Must be gastro, Leah suggested, heaving again at an imagined waft of the boys' aftershave that she could still taste in the back of her throat.

She told her mother she was ill and spent the evening in bed trying to read the copy of *The Unbearable Lightness of Being* she'd ordered. It seemed an apt choice given her present unbearable, heavy state of being. She couldn't focus, though, kept returning to the same paragraph and reading it from the beginning, having not retained any of the words. She slept. Sleep was all that she wanted, all of the time. It was exhausting to be awake, to talk to people and smile and lie.

★

Justin asked Andy to come in on Monday morning to look after the shop for a few hours. He had to buy a gift for Leah. Before he even began, he knew it was going to be an impossible task. She would probably think of it as a pathetic token of apology, or simply an afterthought, which it was. Later, when she found out about the baby and told him she never wanted to see him again, she would probably throw it back in his face.

Ultimately, he just wanted to give her something beautiful; but it also had to be something she could keep without being asked too many questions. Despite the fact that he had chosen not to look for something locally, every time he entered a shop and started looking he felt like he was being watched. And everything he examined seemed feeble and not nearly enough for Leah. A journal to write about her travels one day? He couldn't find one pretty enough. Jewellery, it had to be. Something discreet. He'd never really noticed her wearing any. Occasionally some studs, but that was it.

Several hours later a bird pendant jumped out at him from its hiding place at the back of a glass cabinet. He thought of Leah, her delicate frame and grace, her ability to take flight when she needed to.

Back at The Potting Shed Justin attempted to wrap the little box in some of the brown paper from the flower shop, but removed it immediately. It was too bulky, too plain, too brown, too obviously from the flower shop. He tied some ribbon around it instead, which looked equally naff, but it would have to do.

He felt awkward around Leah all afternoon, with his gift hiding in his office – it was late, small, not enough. Leah was making every effort to be 'normal' and undamaged around him. He could see that. It upset him that she felt she had to pretend everything was okay. He wanted her to cry. Crying would be normal and make sense and he could put his arms around her. Or, better still, shout abuse at him, blame him. It would be so much easier to handle than the okayness she was intent on displaying for his apparent benefit. She worked tirelessly and silently, finding all manner of things to do to fill her time – cleaning and dusting and stacking and making everything perfect. Had she lost weight in the last week or so? She was so slight, anyway. Perhaps it was fragility he could sense. Even though she was in the shop with him, she just felt so distant.

At the end of the day Justin closed up the shop and went to find her. She was sitting in the office on her own, on the sofa, staring out through the window – surrounded by silence and heaviness. She looked tiny, almost childlike, with her legs bent up and a cushion clutched to her chest.

Leah sat on the sofa in Justin's office, unable to move any part of her body. She wasn't sure what had made her sit there or what was stopping her from getting up and leaving. Though she was looking out of the window, she could see only the events of that day replaying over and over. It was as though it was happening all over again – the pain, the fear. She was trapped, once again, unable to breathe in the space in between the seats.

Justin found her there and sat down next to her on the sofa.

And then she fell apart.

Shook.

Cried.

Shook.

She let him very gently fold her into his body as her tears rushed out. Each time she tried to stop herself it would all start up again. She wrapped her arms around his body and soaked his clothing as he stroked her hair and smoothed the water from her cheeks.

After a time the desperate feeling dulled a little. But she ached all over. The crying had released the net of resistance that had been holding her together, and now her body felt loose and unsupported. It was different than feeling numb. She could at least feel something now.

'I'm so sorry about your T-shirt,' she said, slowly pulling herself away. 'I must look a mess. I should go home. You have to get going.'

'Actually, I have lots to be getting on with here. Why not stay? I can light a fire. You can just cosy up, read, do your homework. I could grab some takeout.'

'No, I shouldn't…'

'Please. Let me look after you, just for a few hours. I don't want you going home like this. I can drop you back later, after the rush hour.'

He rose to make the fire. Leah thought about it. She didn't have the energy to get up anyway, the crying had drained her.

'Sit tight. Please.'

Leah looked up at him. There was an intensity in his eyes, as though he knew what was going on in her head as well as she did.

'Okay. Just a little longer. But don't let me stop you doing what you need to do.'

'What I need to do is make sure you are okay.'

As Justin arranged the kindling in the wood stove, Leah took out her revision notes; but her eyes were so swollen that she could barely see. She had supressed all of her emotions, trying to be strong in front of Justin. She'd been wandering around like a pot of boiling water and he'd lifted the lid and let the water spill out over the edge. She felt lighter now, for having allowed herself to cry in front of him; it had not been the humiliating experience she had imagined it to be.

The office started to slowly warm up. Justin grabbed his keys and left, but returned almost immediately.

'I almost forgot – I have a birthday present for you. It's not enough… I don't know how I managed to forget the date.'

He handed Leah the box. She untied the ribbon and opened it; and there she was, crying again.

'It's beautiful. Thank you,' she whispered as she immediately put it on.

The metal bird sat comfortably on her chest bone, nestled in against her skin.

'It looks beautiful on you.' Justin smiled, bent down, kissed her forehead and left for the food.

Leah couldn't focus on her revision so she lay down on the sofa and held the pendant in her hand. She hadn't slept well since the day at the cinema.

She woke up when she heard Justin come back in.

'I'm so sorry, were you asleep?'

'I must have just dozed off. I'm always falling asleep when I'm with you.'

'I can be pretty boring.'

She smiled.

Justin put the food down so that he could tend to the fire then disappeared upstairs and returned with a blanket, which he laid over her legs. They sat on the sofa together, huddled in the warmth, and ate. Leah refused to be changed forever by her experience in the cinema, she decided. This was something she would hold steadfast to. Crying had helped – Justin's acceptance of her crying had helped. He knew something about her that no one else did, and because of that, she felt closer to him.

'I guess I should head home.'

'Do you have to?'

'If I don't I will fall asleep on the sofa again.'

'That would be okay. Or there's a bed upstairs. You're welcome to it.'

'I'd be scared if you left me here over night!'

'No, I would stay here on the sofa. I wouldn't leave you alone.'

The proposition was extremely tempting; to be near Justin all night, to wake up together in the morning. Justin was the only person who knew what Leah had been through; there was no one she wanted to be with more. She wanted to not lie and not pretend and not make up stories about bicycle accidents.

'I couldn't. It would be too risky. I mean, how would you explain it to Marcella?'

'I've stayed many times. It's why I have the bed upstairs. All it would require is a text to let her know.'

'But if she found out, if she came in and saw that I was here.'

'She has no reason to come here tonight, or tomorrow morning, and there is just no way that she would. I really wouldn't suggest it if I thought there was a chance of that.'

'I don't want to make your life complicated.'

'It's much too late for that. But that isn't your fault, only mine. Would your mother question you?'

'No. I would text my friend to cover for me.'

'Good, then it's done. You text your mum and friend and I will get everything ready for you upstairs.'

Leah texted Vanessa, who begged to know where she was; then her mother, who said she was going to be out late anyway.

'Please don't go to any trouble,' she called from the bottom of the stairs.

She gathered her books and belongings, wondering if she was doing the right thing but knowing it was already too late to change her mind.

'Come on up.'

The loft was like a gypsy caravan. An elaborate embroidered quilt covered the mattress on the floor, no doubt a relic from Justin's travels, along with some richly coloured cushions. A soft, circular, Aztec-style rug filled the floor space. A light-well above the bed looked straight out into the night sky. Justin had also lit a fat candle that rested on a wooden crate by the bed.

'Wow, it's gorgeous up here! I think I would live up here if I were you.'

'Thank you. I love it too. Probably more than my house if I am honest. You can stay anytime you like. Do you have something to sleep in?'

'I do, thank you.'

'You're so welcome. Sleep well and just call down if you need anything at all.'

Leah changed into some leggings and a T-shirt she found stuffed in the bottom of her schoolbag. She wandered around the room looking at everything that was Justin's, everything that had meant enough to him to keep it. She lay down on the bed, splayed her limbs out as though she was making an angel in the snow. The bedding smelt of Justin and she rolled over to inhale the scent of him. She imagined him downstairs, lying on the sofa on his own and keeping the fire alive. She wanted to see him when he fell asleep. He had watched her do the same so many times. She could creep down later perhaps.

Leah pulled the quilt over her and lay on her side so that she could watch the flickering candle. She closed her eyes but she was unable to sleep. After all of his kindness, Justin was downstairs and not with her. It felt wrong that they weren't side by side, stealing time, just enjoying how close they could be with no one else around.

She received another message from Vanessa and immediately felt anxious about lying to her. Leah's assumption that she would not understand, would not be able to give her the support she needed, had made her withdraw from her. None of her friends knew anything of her life now, and she had shown little or no interest in theirs for months. Her relationship with her mother was no better; she had so many secrets that it seemed sensible to simply say as little as possible, to avoid slipping up on the lies.

The dirty gloves were beginning to feel a little lighter on her chest, their grip on her was lessening slowly, but their voices still echoed in her head when she was alone. The tears came again. She didn't think that there would be more; she had let so many go earlier. Her hair and the pillow were wet; she couldn't wipe them away fast enough, and she couldn't stop.

She wasn't sure how Justin heard her; she'd tried to be quiet, but she could hear the stairs creaking as he made his way up.

'Are you okay?' he whispered. 'Don't worry, I won't come all the way up. I just want to know if you are okay.'

'I will be. Thank you. I'm sorry if I'm keeping you awake.'

'Please, Leah, don't apologise. I will stay up all night if you want me to.'

'Do you think it would be okay if you stayed in here with me? It's okay if you think it's not a good idea.'

He tiptoed in.

'I would love to.'

Even in the low light Justin could see that Leah's face and hair were wet with tears. He carefully crawled in beside her, moved in close and placed his arm over her. She cried for only a few minutes more then drifted off. Justin stayed awake until Leah was in a deep sleep; their silhouette flickered against the wall in the light from the diminishing candle.

This is okay, he told himself. *This is okay.*

It wasn't, of course, but there was nowhere in the world he needed to be more.

★

Leah had risen before Justin. She must have showered because she was now sitting on the edge of the mattress with her clothes on, hair stringy with water. She looked beautiful, her cheeks pink and her skin glowing. But he could feel her imminent departure, and it was torture. She was still there and yet already gone.

'Thank you for letting me stay, and for putting up with me crying like an idiot. And thank you for keeping me warm last night. You're like a human radiator. I do feel better. I really do.'

He sat up in bed, rested his back against the wall. It was stiff. He had stayed on his side all night without moving so that he wouldn't miss a moment of being with her.

'I am so glad to hear it. Any time. You know that.'

'But it makes it harder.'

'Makes it harder?'

'Being with you more makes everything harder, better and more painful all at the same time,' she said.

'I know the feeling. But I would rather feel empty every time you left the room than not have you in the room at all. I think I like hard, and pain; because the alternative, not spending time with you, terrifies me.'

Leah's hand was resting on the bed in front of him. He instinctively picked it up and held it in his. He wanted to close the shop, keep her in all day, make her fires, breakfast, lunch and dinner, then lie down in the bed next to her again and watch her sleep. It could be his atonement, just looking after her day after day, making sure she had everything she needed to feel safe and loved and happy again.

But, of course, he could not. She would get up and walk out into the world outside again: where leaves and rain and snow fell, where traffic jammed and pollution fucked up the air, where schoolwork had to be turned in and exams studied for, where gangs of youths preyed on pretty girls in the middle of the day in a fucking cinema.

Leah unclasped her small hand from his as she stood up and immediately the room, and his entire body, felt desperately, unbelievably cold. It made him shudder. He was not the radiator, she was; heat left the room with her. But the sweet scent of her before her shower, of her sleeping and crying and breathing in his bed, would be on that pillow and on the sheets as long as he didn't wash them. He would still have that after she had gone.

She was always just out of reach, but never more than at that moment. Disappearing down the loft stairs she left him with a collection of final images: the back of her un-brushed hair, the knitted grey jumper that hung off her shoulders, her hand on the railing as it slid down. It occurred to him that he had missed waking up with her; missed watching her eyes open and adjust to the sunlight that fell through the light well. He rolled over onto her pillow and just breathed.

PART FIVE

February had come. It was a late Friday afternoon, everyone was in and the last of the customers had just left. Marcella had pitched up unannounced. More than sixteen weeks had passed, and numerous scans and procedures confirmed that the baby was indeed okay. Justin had run out of reasons not to tell everyone at work. The days of citing fears of saying anything too soon were behind them; to the point where Marcella was starting to question whether he wanted the child.

A heated conversation in the office lasted only a few minutes. They came out together. At Marcella's insistence they were going to break the news, without hesitation, before Justin could tell Leah separately. He had seen Leah several times that day; he could have told her when he'd had her on his own. Had he known that Marcella would appear and insist that today was the day, he would have told her. He felt incensed at himself for handling it all so badly. The least Leah deserved was to hear the news from him, and him alone, in private.

'So, gang, gather round. I have some news.'

'Sounds ominous,' Ella called out.

'Not at all. Marcella and I are having a baby.'

There were screams and celebratory hugs. Leah looked like she had been stabbed; the last person in the world he would ever have wanted to cause pain. He hadn't just hurt her – hurting her would have been breaking the news gently – the way he had executed the blow was unforgiveable. He should have told her before today; possibly even the minute he knew. She would have cut him off, of course, but he would have deserved it. But then he never should have allowed them to become so close in the first place, and it was too late for that too.

Leah found it difficult to draw breath. She sank to the back of the well-wishers knowing her turn would have to come. She couldn't run before expressing her joy for the happy couple because everyone would instantly suspect there was something between her and Justin. Hatred rose up inside her; something she immediately detested herself for feeling. Didn't this man and this woman deserve to have a child? Marcella was beaming with happiness. They were married, they wanted to start a family; there was nothing more normal in the world. And they had lost a child all those years ago – even if they weren't really ready for a child then; no doubt it was upsetting for them both. So why was she holding back tears? Had she been holding out for news of a separation? Had she hoped to bear Justin's child one day when she was no longer so stupidly, embarrassingly young?

A natural passageway eventually formed, creating a space for Leah. She hugged Justin awkwardly, averting her eyes from his, and smiled warmly at Marcella, who was thankfully still locked in a hug with Ella. She pushed the word out; the one she was forced to conjure up from the pit of her gut.

'Congratulations.' *I think you've just killed me.*

'How many weeks?' Ella asked.

'Just over sixteen. We had a few scares, so we wanted to be sure before telling anyone.'

'Wow, soon you will be halfway there!'

'Yes, put like that, it doesn't feel that far away at all.'

Leah's eyes were drawn to Marcella's lower abdomen which Marcella was patting. She could hear and see no more. She wasn't interested in the ins and outs of Marcella's morning sickness and baby scans and musings over whether it might be a girl or a boy. Sixteen weeks was almost four months. That's how long Justin had known and hadn't thought to tell her: as he arranged to meet her at the cinema, as he comforted her when she cried, as he lay next to her in his bed in the loft, as he continued to allow her to fall in love with him and abandon everything else in her life.

'It's really wonderful, exciting news. I'm so happy for you both. I have to rush off, though. Lots of homework, as ever. See you tomorrow.'

There was not a hint of resentment in her voice. She had sounded normal, like a slightly uninterested teenager. She wanted to feel calm, accepting, mature, composed. But deep down Leah cursed the day it had rained and she had taken refuge in the shop; then she cursed the days she had sat in Justin's car and been driven to Eastbourne and sat down on the grass on the cliff top, their swim in the ocean, the times she had curled up on his sofa in the office by the fire and, in particular, the night she had spent in the loft with him in the bed next to her. She regretted all the personal things she had told him about herself, her life, and her stupid need to see and experience the world. What was the point of any of those conversations? Did he find it amusing? Had this been his intention all along; to have her eating out of the palm of his hand just so that he could close his fist and withdraw it when she needed him the most?

Justin could think of nothing to say that would make things okay between him and Leah. Things should change, he decided. They should not become any closer, they should not be alone together in the car or in the loft. He should have orchestrated a change even if it were not for the baby. But knowing all of the things that should and should not be was irrelevant. The reality, in all his selfishness, was that he didn't want less. Less would mean a slow, drawn out suffering. Less meant missing her; it meant not being able to make her smile, it meant not touching her skin or smelling her hair when he hugged her.

Justin felt sick. All of the blood in his body rushed to his head and stayed up there. He wanted to chase after Leah, to explain, but he wasn't sure what he would say. *It doesn't change anything.* Ridiculous, it changes everything. *I'm sorry.* Utterly useless and feeble. *I still want us to be close.* Selfish but true. *I will leave Marcella to be with you.* Impossible.

He thought about 'possibility' again. As long as no one ever said no, possibility was still there. When he had made that statement he hadn't taken into account the life-altering news of his unborn child.

Marcella eventually left to do some shopping; Ella and Andy left soon after. Justin closed up and retreated to his office.

It was uncomfortably cold but he didn't light the fire. He lay in the bed, on the sheets he still hadn't changed, and remembered their night together and the tears Leah had finally trusted him with. She would not allow him to comfort her and look after her again. There would be no more letting in. No more trips to Eastbourne. And no more trust.

★

Leah sat down in the evenings to do her homework and found it almost impossible to focus. She stayed up for hours trying to complete what should have been straightforward revision exercises. She slept little and ate almost nothing. Food made her feel sick; when she did try to force some down, it sent a burning sensation up into her throat and made her choke.

She could feel herself coming undone, panicking all the time that she was running late or forgetting something, checking her bags several times over to make sure she had everything she needed for the day, doubling back to the front door several times to make sure she'd locked it. She lost count of how many times she turned into the street and forgot which way she should be walking.

The day at the cinema found its way into her head frequently, and she saw the whole scenario play itself out, over and over again. Each time one detail or another became more horrific, more intensified. The weight of the boys leaning on her limbs became heavier and more painful, slaps and kicks were more violent, and she was suffocating in the small space she was trapped in on the floor between the chairs.

She began to wonder if the boys might find her somehow, or if they might just appear one day in front of her in the street. She might not be so lucky next time. They might be more determined, and this time she would be even weaker and more incapable of defending herself. Justin wouldn't be there to interrupt. Justin was gone. Completely gone.

At school she felt paranoid that everyone hated her for shutting them all out, and she imagined that they somehow all knew that she had fallen for a married man. Fear of exam failure kicked in. Had she done enough? Had she spent more time thinking about Justin than she had on her schoolwork? Had she fucked up her entire education for all those wasted moments alone with a man who was not only married but had a child on the way?

Justin and Marcella and their baby found their way into her thoughts too. It wasn't just jealousy she felt, it was betrayal. Why would he have spent so much time getting close to her while trying for a baby? It didn't make sense. He'd just played with her; entertained himself with her while he waited for something more exciting to happen in his life.

Leah examined her body in the mirror and found that it was pale and thin and, more notably, that all of the marks were gone. Nothing remained from the day at the cinema, not one bit of evidence. She tried to recall where everything was – the carpet burns on her lower back, the bruises on her upper arms and thighs where she had been kneeled on and pinned down. She was repulsive, physically repulsive. And yet not repulsive enough, not suffering enough. She needed the outside of her body to reflect how she felt inside.

She made her way to the kitchen and looked through the drawers and cupboards, one by one, until she found something suitable: a marble pestle. In her bedroom she hit her left arm with it. It hurt, but the pain was not enough and nothing substantial appeared on the surface of her skin. She gritted her teeth to keep back her screams and tried again, and then again, harder each time, until she was satisfied that it would leave the evidence that she needed it to. *That's it*, she thought to herself. *You can do this.* Her adrenalin rose with the success of her efforts. She changed hands and worked on her right arm, then her thighs, until all of the bruises were back where they belonged. And more. Which felt right too. She felt sick, sick to the core, but better. Better enough to be able to continue with her homework. Everything was as it should be. She was as unhappy as Justin had ever wanted her to be. And she deserved it.

Justin, humbled by his hatred for himself, kept a low profile at The Potting Shed. He had to give Leah time to digest the news, but whenever she was ready to lay her wrath on him, he would be ready to take it. He didn't want to be let off the hook, didn't deserve it. He braced himself for a tirade of recrimination every day that she was due to come in and work, and waited for it until her shift ended. He thought he could feel it in the air around her – her anger, her disgust – but every day he was disappointed.

Justin began to notice that the way Leah dressed was different. She was layered in heavy, almost masculine clothing. Spring had arrived but she was wearing more clothes than she had in the winter – long sleeves, thick cardigans, dark jeans. It was as though she was disappearing under protective layers, hiding from him and from the world. Had he done this? Had he made her withdraw into herself? He tried to make eye contact; tried to find things to do beside her so that they could exchange a few words. At one point he touched her arm and she pulled it away quickly, as though he had physically hurt her. He hated that the most, that his touch could make her recoil. She slipped into the shop, did what she was supposed to do and then left. It wasn't that her manner or her tone was brittle, or even cold, just a million miles away from where it had been that night in the loft. He expected nothing else, but it still stung.

'Hey. How are you?' he asked, trying to sound happy to see her but deeply repentant at the same time.

'Hi. Good thanks.'

'How's the studying?'

'Okay. Thank you.'

'Are you winning?'

'Not really.'

And off she walked. A boss and his employee. Work colleagues. Almost strangers. A horrible, hateful reversion.

★

Leah hated Justin's chirpiness and his attempts at small talk. She hated him asking her how her studying was going when he was the one who had distracted her for the better part of the last year; the single, most important year of her academic life. She wanted to shout in his face that she was fucking up her entire education, that she was failing at everything because of him. Her resentment, something that she had never felt towards him before, was a multiplying virus and she had no way to contain it.

She spent her Mondays feeling anxious about having to be alone with Justin. Most of all she didn't want to have a conversation about the obvious need for them to be released from each other and for him to ask her, beg her even, to keep everything that had happened between them a secret. They'd never had such a conversation; they'd never needed to. They'd only ever talked about not having that conversation; about possibility being something that would sustain them, something they could live off and hold on to forever. But he would want to have that conversation now that there was a child that needed to be protected from the lunatic teenaged stalker that had fallen in love with its father. Leah avoided Justin, refused to engage when he tried to initiate a conversation – if they didn't speak then he couldn't turn the tables on her.

Leah thought about making up some excuse and telling Justin that she could no longer do Mondays. It would be less awkward and easier to manage. She would keep the other shifts, so that she could continue to save up. They would always be busy but it wouldn't be just the two of them, struggling to know how to behave around each other.

And then she thought of quitting altogether and just getting a job somewhere else. It would be easier for both of them to just forget whatever it was they did or didn't have and carry on with their lives. Justin would be relieved, as it was now clear that he had made a definite choice to remove her from his life and devote himself to his family. He would even thank her for it one day, and she would thank herself. It sounded clean and sensible and she could just get on with studying for her exams, go to uni far away from London or take a gap year and forget to come home.

She was committed to her plan to leave for all of sixty seconds.

Ultimately, the idea of leaving filled her with an excruciating feeling of loss. She couldn't do it. She didn't know how she could return to the life she'd had before she'd met Justin. She thought about the emptiness of her flat and the hours she'd spent on her own waiting for her mother to come home; only to be told that she was 'so tired', 'quite drunk', 'ready to collapse'. Then there were the endless conversations with her school-friends about things that simply didn't matter to her: parties, drugs, getting pissed, who had shagged who. And the fact that she had slept with Ollie because she felt she should get it over with. She hated herself for losing her virginity for the sake of it, but her treatment of Ollie was unforgivable.

Justin had somehow made it impossible for her to walk away. He had positioned himself in her head, in a space that now only he could occupy. She looked at what her life would be like without him in it – without his warmth, his concern and his encouragement – and she felt utterly alone and flat and weak, and no longer interesting, beautiful or promising. She would no longer be the girl with the world at her feet. She just wouldn't. No one else saw any of these things in her.

★

On Monday, when she saw Justin sitting alone, going through some paperwork in his office, Leah was overcome with guilt. He looked up and smiled at her – the way he always had – but overshadowing the love and warmth, was his remorse. And then he looked away, perhaps because he thought she would want him to, or perhaps because he felt he didn't deserve anything from Leah in return. Justin could hide nothing from Leah. It was all there in his eyes, in his body language, too; the way he held himself, sort of doubled over, without any of his usual energy. He looked fragile, vulnerable – much smaller in stature than she had ever thought of him as being – and sad, just really sad.

Leah immediately felt ashamed and childish for her complete lack of understanding. Her jealousy and anger had made her turn on Justin, made her want to block him out and have him suffer alongside her. She'd somehow managed to cut her heart off from the rest of her body and still function without it. Just like that. It was not a side of herself that she'd even known existed.

But seeing Justin now, with this deep sadness inside of him, she knew that he was completely incapable of all of the manipulative, life-destroying qualities she had assigned him. He was genuine; he did care and he did love her in a unique, otherworldly way. She had felt it in his every word and touch and she wasn't sure how she could possibly have come to doubt it.

Justin hadn't made Leah think of him too much; she had let him in and allowed herself to fill her head with him. He hadn't forced her to come with him to Eastbourne, or meet him at the cinema, that choice had been hers and hers alone. And he certainly hadn't fucked up her education. She was the only person responsible for the amount of time she devoted to her books. Justin had known that he and Marcella were trying for a child, and that Marcella was pregnant for much longer than he had shared with her, but she wondered if the pain of his keeping of this secret from her outweighed everything else they had shared. He had never promised Leah that he would leave Marcella or that he wouldn't have a child with her.

Leah felt desperately that she wanted to hold Justin and convince him that she didn't feel overwhelmed with resentment; that it was perfectly okay for him to want to have a child. Who was she, after all, to take that joy away from him? She wanted to say something, but no words came out of her mouth. The sore parts of her insides, all swollen and blistered, were getting in the way of everything.

The shop and outdoor areas were all clean and perfect. She assumed this was a ploy so that she wouldn't have to do anything. She imagined Justin thought it was the least he could do; pay her to sit around and do nothing. But she couldn't just sit around for the next two hours straightening pots that didn't need straightening, she'd go mad. She looked around the office, the one area she'd never been expected to tidy. It was disgusting: a filthy haven for a man struggling with his guilt.

For some reason, on that Monday, Justin sensed a slight change in Leah's demeanour. He felt it in the air when she entered the office, saw it in her eyes briefly when she caught his gaze. He watched her as she put her bag away and tied her apron on, expecting her to walk away as soon as she was ready to work. But she didn't walk away. She was quiet and she stayed. He continued watching as she began to tidy up the shit-fest that crowded his desk – the mugs, rubbish, plates, old food and junk mail – and his heart melted. He wondered if the crippling indifference that he had been feeling from her might be very slowly dissipating. She gently lifted his left arm to get to a discarded sandwich bag, then placed it back down on the clean desk. He let her, not daring to move or make a joke about her manhandling technique. And then she smiled at him. That was excruciating. She was still so bloody unbearably sweet. He'd lied to her face for weeks, well, technically withheld information; but it was as repulsive as lying. He'd thrown the most life-altering news at her in the most cruel, public and gutless way. And yet there she was being sweet. *Fuck!*

When she was finished in the office, Justin thanked her.

'You're welcome. Did you leave anything for me to do out there?' she asked.

'I didn't water in the greenhouse today.'

'On it.'

'Thank you.'

Hiding in the greenhouse gave Leah time to slow her breathing down and remind herself that she could do this; she could rise above her pain and be the person she so desperately wanted to be for both of them.

Justin came in and joined her.

She had been in the greenhouse with him many times before. They had shared emotions without words; they'd touched in the smallest, most innocent way and felt everything the other had wanted to give. But now Justin was acting like a scolded child who had done something unforgivable and been told not to touch and not to speak unless spoken to. He acted with the politeness of a stranger, stumbled over a few exchanges and didn't know what to do with himself. He seemed terrified of her, which she couldn't tolerate. So Leah did something she was not expecting to do. She walked over to him, put her arms under his and wrapped them around his middle. All of the bruises she had inflicted on herself pressed up against him and she imagined that his warm, radiating body was healing them; taking the pain away. She lay her head against his chest and listened for the rhythm of him.

After a few seconds Justin allowed himself to touch Leah; softly, at first, almost not at all. Then firmly, until he was sure he would crush her with the weight of his want of her. She was thinner, that he could tell. Her shoulders were sharp, her ribs and spine covered only by her skin and clothing. He assumed that was his fault too.

'It's okay,' Leah whispered.

He didn't know for certain what she meant by okay: okay that he had told her the way he did, okay that he had let her down then hurt her again and again, okay that he was going to have a baby with a woman he was now certain he loved much less than Leah?

Justin didn't seek clarification, didn't want it. The fact that she was consoling him and comforting him, though entirely unjustified, was bringing him back to life. Leah could do that. She could alter his heart rate with a look and pull the two split halves together with just a few words. She offered forgiveness when it wasn't deserved, she offered love that he hadn't earned, and she admired him when all he was made up of was deceit and prickery.

'Can you forgive me, for not telling you sooner?'

'There's nothing to forgive. You should be having a baby. It's time. You should enjoy it: the pregnancy, the waiting, the birth, all of it.'

There was so little he could say in response to that. She was right; the child didn't deserve for him to feel anything less than joy. Actually, Marcella didn't either. But it wasn't for Leah to come to these conclusions; it was up to him to think and say these things, because he was the adult and she technically was not.

It occurred to Justin that the announcement of the pregnancy had pushed the incident at the cinema to one side.

'You've been through so much... I can't believe I have added to it. I mean, it wasn't that long ago that... '

'No. I'm okay. I'm feeling a lot stronger about that, too.'

He wasn't sure whether or not to believe her.

Leah pulled herself gently from their hug.

'Will you have some mint tea?' Justin asked.

'Okay. I don't think I want to talk, though. Is that okay?'

'Of course. Absolutely. I understand. I'm not sure I know what to say either. I could say a lot of things, but it would all go around in circles and come out wrong anyway.'

'Then don't.'

They left the greenhouse together. Leah picked the leaves for the tea from the new spring pots and Justin put the kettle on. She brought the leaves over and they danced around each other; each of them being overly considerate to the other as they prepared the little silver tray with sugar and biscuits and Justin's delicately etched Moroccan tea glasses.

It seemed warm enough to sit outside – the days were getting longer – so they sat on Leah's favourite bench, she with her legs drawn up as always. Justin left and came back out with a blanket and she let him cover her with it. They sipped their tea in silence and enjoyed the quiet of not saying any more than had already been said. It could not be undone anyway. A child was growing by the day and all anyone could do now was wait for it to emerge.

Leah finished her tea and sighed.

'I should go.'

'So you always say. But it would be nice if you could stay longer.'

Leah stood up and wrapped the blanket around herself again, sat back down and rested her head on the back of the seat.

There was always going to be a time like this, when she would lose him just that little bit more than she had already. Even still, she hadn't seen it coming.

★

The pregnancy progressed without any further cause for panic. Justin had hoped that at some point Marcella would actually enjoy it: the changes in her body, the wriggles of the baby inside. But she could not. She demanded fortnightly scans and additional check-ups with the midwives, who dutifully measured her stomach each time and made a note of a slight-but-normal-for-pregnancy rise in her blood pressure. If the baby moved too aggressively Marcella worried that it was distressed; if it didn't move every hour, she agonised over whether it was still alive.

As the weeks passed, Marcella's body softened and curved in all the right places. To Justin it was an incredible, beautiful development; nature had taken over and was doing what it was supposed to be doing. Marcella loathed the weight gain, the thickening that occurred at the tops of her arms and her enormous breasts. More than anything she hated that she was unable to do anything about it. Her consultant had advised her to avoid vigorous exercise after the earlier scare. Marcella was not a woman to let go of the reigns – she liked to be in control – and a big part of that was maintaining her figure. Justin could see that it was driving her to distraction and this combined with the influx of hormones, left Marcella in a constant state of irritation. He couldn't say that she wasn't herself, she was, she was just Marcella amplified. When she was upset, she was catastrophically upset. When she was angry, actual steam seemed to rise from her.

A great deal of Marcella's frustration was directed at Justin, for all of his inadequacies as a husband and a human being. There was very little joy, appreciation or positivity, and no lightness. It seemed to Justin that all of the excitement Marcella had felt at the beginning of the pregnancy had just evaporated. He wondered if she was performing these daily rituals of abuse as some kind of subconscious response to his relationship with Leah and that he was actually getting what he deserved. He ignored it most of the time, pandered to it occasionally, and once or twice completely lost his shit and fired back at her. He never regretted anything more.

Justin tried, though. Despite Marcella's moods. Despite his own guilty conscience. Despite being a distracted bastard. He called and checked on her, a thing he had never done before, texted to see if she needed him to pick up anything on the way home from work, did more around the house, came home earlier and turned up to almost all the appointments she made. He wasn't sure of much but he knew that he owed their baby this; the innocent, unknowing child that was nestled inside Marcella and made of half of him.

★

Once she had started, Leah found it difficult not to self-harm on a regular basis. The tenderness, the lumps, the bruises, the moments when someone touched her arm by accident and reignited a painful sensation that had become dormant throughout the course of the day, were all strangely comforting and calming. The act itself and the relief it afforded her somehow helped her to appear normal, even strong. She told her mother that school and work were fine and that she was managing her time well. She told her friends she was okay, just busy and knuckling down to her studies when she wasn't working. And most of all, she was able to look Justin in the eye and tell him that everything with her was unreservedly okay. She declared to herself and to Justin that she was completely over the experience at the cinema. In addition, she was able to tell him that she was genuinely happy for him and Marcella. The self-harm gave her this strength and there were times when she wasn't sure how she had ever managed without it.

Leah tried different ways of producing the bruises she needed. When her mind was disturbed, when it was full of ugliness, failure, loss and loneliness, she thought only about the things she would do to herself later. It helped that she was so frequently alone in the flat, but her mother being in the next room did little to prevent her from doing what she had to; she simply shut the door and turned the music up. The sensation made her sick to her stomach but she repeated the process a number of times until she felt better and worse in perfectly equal measures. The area she concentrated on the most, given how easy it was to cover and how close the bone was to the skin, was the space between the outer edge of her wrists and her elbows; though she was always careful not to get too close to her wrists, in case a sleeve rode up. Afterwards, she would feel calm, perfectly calm, and able to carry on with whatever she needed to get done.

Still, Leah wasn't totally in control. She went through stages; sometimes she harmed every few days, sometimes only once a week. For a short time, when there had been a succession of days that felt marginally less painful, Leah would find that the bruises had almost faded altogether and wondered if that was it; if her sickness had run its course. But there was always another that she hadn't anticipated. Like the day she had a row with Ollie about how cruelly she had treated him. He knew she hadn't promised him anything but really, he asked her, how could anyone treat another person the way she had treated him? He told her that she was almost completely unrecognisable as the girl he had fallen for. Of course he was right; and she had no answer, no fit apology. And then, more recently, the day Marcella had appeared in the shop to show off her bump to everyone. The bump was perfect, Marcella was glowing and Leah had shrunk down into her hooded pullover and retreated to the bathroom to atone for her rage and jealousy.

As spring merged into summer the temperature began to rise with each new week. The need to conceal the bruises certainly outweighed her need to wear shorter sleeves, but high summer would come, and it would become obvious that she was overdressing. Leah thought about stopping; she wondered if she could just decide to stop and that would be that. The idea terrified her.

★

Justin was still perplexed as to why Leah was continuing to wear so many layers of clothing. The sun was well and truly out; the greenhouse must have been forty degrees. He imagined that it was the attack that had changed things; made her cover up so that she didn't draw unwanted attention to herself. It made sense and yet it tore him up. She had arrived in his life just as she was becoming a woman; a free-spirited young girl in a clinging vest and floral skirt. Now she was almost androgynous in her jeans and hoodies. Leah was still in there somewhere, though. She didn't need make-up or pretty clothes; her allure was immutable. He wondered if she still wore the chain he bought her for her birthday, hidden underneath everything, against her skin.

'Why are you looking at me like that?'

'Oh, I'm not. Sorry, I was on another planet.'

She smiled. God he loved her smile.

'Didn't you say your brother was coming in the New Year?' she asked. 'It will be summer soon and he still hasn't materialised.'

'Yep, that's Tris to a tee. Although, weirdly enough, I heard from him last night and he will be here Saturday week. I'd almost forgotten to tell you.'

'That's not far away. You haven't talked about him much. I think I asked if you were close but I can't remember your answer.'

'We've always gotten along. He's a bit younger, so there was never really any rivalry. Not sure when he'll ever settle down; but he seems happy for now, so I guess there's no rush.' Justin paused. 'I might even be a little jealous of his freedom.'

She giggled.

'How old is he?'

'God, how old am I, so I can count back – twenty-six?'

Had she asked his age out of curiosity or was she thinking Tris might be like a younger version of himself?

'A lot younger, then?'

'Ha, yes, thanks for that. He's a remarriage child.'

'And will he be staying in the loft?'

'God, yes. Shit!'

Somehow, in his head, the loft space remained empty. He liked to imagine that Leah would stay again one day, that it would always be a place where they could find each other. He hadn't changed the sheets and didn't want to. He'd slept in them once or twice, to feel closer to Leah, to draw the last of her scent from the pillow. He wasn't sure if he could still really smell her, or if it was just the memory of the scent that remained, but the idea of washing the sheets made him feel unwell. It would be like he was losing another part of her.

'Could you stay a little later on Saturday?'

Leah knew why Justin had asked her to stay back on Saturday – with Tristan on his way it might be the last chance, for a long time, they could be alone together at the shop. There was so much of her that wanted to say no, it would only make things more and more difficult.

'I think so,' she answered.

★

Saturday was long. Leah anticipated the end of the day with a mixture of anxiety and excitement. Ella hung around for far longer than was necessary; said she fancied doing a bit of a spring clean. Justin rolled his eyes at Leah as if to say,

What the fuck? Why now? Why this Saturday? They could only watch in frustration as she removed the buckets of flowers from the shelves and began to dust and clean. When she had finished with the shelves, she emptied all of the buckets and scrubbed them too, before refilling them with flowers and arranging them symmetrically.

'Can I help you, El?' Leah offered.

'No, I got it. You know me, I have my way of doing things and I'd only go around after you.'

'Fair enough.'

It seemed to go on forever; the cleaning and the ridiculous ritual of rearranging things that didn't need to be rearranged. Just when she looked like she might be done, Ella started on the little cupboard under her desk; pulling out all sorts of odd items and remarking on them. It was maddening to watch.

'You staying back, Leah?'

Justin quickly interjected: 'I've bullied her into some extra planting because she has tomorrow off to study.'

Leah followed Justin into the greenhouse; they pulled out the seedling trays, filled them with soil and worked together in silence.

'I don't actually know what we are going to plant!'

She loved it when he fumbled around chaotically just to be near her.

Justin rifled through a store cupboard and found some seeds. Not exactly a two-man job but they made it one. Soon after, Ella came in and said her farewells. Justin followed her out to lock the door and satisfy himself that she was truly gone.

Leah rolled her sleeves up and continued with the seeds. She wasn't sure why she was still there. A big part of her wanted to resist Justin. To hurt him? To test him? To deprive herself of his affection for her? Or him of hers? To have him miss her, the way she missed him? She was deep in thought when he returned.

'Leah…'

The desperation in Justin's voice completely threw her.

'Oh, no, what? Have I made a mistake?' she asked, looking down at the seeds she had just sown.

He was looking at her arms.

'Your arms.'

Leah quickly pulled her sleeves back down, embarrassed.

'Oh, that. It's nothing.' She held Justin's stare and refused to allow herself any more useless tears.

'It's not nothing. Who did this to you?'

He approached her.

'Please, let me see.'

'No. It's nothing.'

She pulled away.

'Leah, you can tell me. I can help you. No one has the right to hurt you.'

'No one has hurt me.'

Of course he would conclude that someone else did it to her. Because what sort of lunatic would deliberately hurt *themselves*? He could never know the truth, but she also couldn't have him thinking that someone else was responsible.

'We did some marines training. There was an obstacle course: ropes, diving into tunnels, crawling along the gravel. I really messed up my arms.'

Leah congratulated herself on her answer and gave him a wry smile to finish it off.

'I'd better go. I have homework.'

'Please, don't go. We can have some tea, just hang out.'

'I know, but Ella was here for too long. I didn't realise it was so late. I'm sorry, I really must go.'

Justin didn't know what to say, or how far he could push. Leah's obstacle-course story was bullshit, that much was clear, but he couldn't bear to say so to her face – she suddenly seemed too fragile to question. She'd chosen to stay back, she'd wanted the time with him, but when he'd seen her arms she had panicked and now she was leaving.

All Justin could do was watch as Leah untied her apron and left the greenhouse. He went after her as she put it away and gathered her things, but he could think of nothing to say that would make her stay. What demands could he make of her? She was not his to make demands of. But he wanted to know. He wanted a person, a name, a location, a place he could drive to and unleash his fury.

Justin imagined someone, maybe someone very close to her, holding Leah's wrists and screaming at her. He wasn't sure how else she would have ended up with bruises in such an odd place. At the same time, he hoped to God that this wasn't the case. Maybe she'd just done something stupid when she was drunk and didn't want to tell him because she was embarrassed. Leah was full of secrets all of a sudden and he had no way of prising them out of her. He had been steadily earning the right to know everything about her, but he had lost it with his own dishonesty.

Now she was leaving and he didn't know when he might be alone with her again. He followed her to the front door.

'You can't follow me further than this, Justin,' she said, turning to face him.

As ever she threw him with her directness, her ability to

eloquently capture the reality of their situation. Indeed, he could not follow her any further than the door. She wasn't smug about it; it was simply a truth. He would not be able to get her to sit down with him and he would not get to hear the truth about the bruises on her arms.

The minute Leah left, Justin locked the door and ran up to the loft. He stripped the bed, removed the sheets and the pillowcases and bundled them up with the towels. He would take it all home; he would put it all in the washing machine and set it off and then they would be clean again. Clean of her. Of her smell and the sugary sweat from her sleep. And once they were clean and he didn't have them to return to, maybe he would miss her less, maybe he wouldn't ache so much.

★

Leah used the rest of the week to study. She also managed to not self-harm. When Justin had seen her arms, it had shocked her; and even though she felt further and further away from him, his reaction still affected her deeply. He didn't text and she wondered if he was beginning to pull away. But she should be doing that too, preparing herself for his departure. The idea of it, though, of how different things would be when he became a father, was something she just couldn't bring herself to contemplate.

Leah decided that she would try harder on Saturday. She would arrive at work wearing a little make-up, a new skirt and cardigan, hair washed and brushed. If she couldn't feel okay at least she could look the part, and maybe the rest would come later.

★

Justin dragged himself through each day, finding very little pleasure in being at The Potting Shed. Without realising it or planning to, Leah had the power to pull everything down with her when she left on bad terms.

After a week apart, after regretting washing the sheets she had slept in, after cooking up all kinds of sordid possibilities to explain the marks he had seen on her arms, after anticipating the imminent loss of them as they had been, and missing, just really missing her, she looked almost unreal when she finally arrived. She walked in gracefully, not hunched under her layers the way she had been in recent weeks, wearing new clothes that fitted her tiny frame. He imagined her in her bedroom; sitting at her dressing table, brushing her hair and looking at herself in the mirror, maybe even thinking of herself as being pretty. She stopped at the counter as the sunlight fell in through the skylight like a spotlight and lit her up, making everything golden.

Justin had an urge to hug her right there in the middle of the shop. He was not ready to let her go; his feelings for her were as strong as they had always been, stronger even. She never ceased to amaze him. She had handled everything that had happened between them, everything that had happened to her, with poise and maturity. He knew then that he needed more time. He had barely scratched the surface of Leah. Marcella was picking up Tris from the airport. All that he could hope for was a delay, a no show, a text to say he'd stopped over in Thailand for a few days – or even weeks. 'More time,' he said to himself. 'I just want more time.'

PART SIX

Despite being surrounded by customers and staff, Leah felt Justin watching her constantly. She wondered if he was waiting for her to slip up and reveal further signs of abuse. She took off her cardigan in front of him so that he could see that her arms were clean. She needed him to know.

In the late afternoon a heavily tanned man with stubble and wavy, honeyed hair pushed his way through the doors with an enormous rucksack and several plastic bags. He wore sandals, loose black trousers and a thin T-shirt with holes in it. A pair of sunglasses rested on the top of his head. Tristan. There was something of Justin in him; and although she never thought of Justin as being groomed, he was compared to Tristan.

Tristan's energy was a force to be reckoned with; it rippled around the garden centre immediately. Ella rushed out first and almost threw herself at him. Leah looked on in awe. How she longed to be away, for months and months; and return a new, evolved, well-travelled person. She wanted that reinvention and all the experiences that came with travel, and, it occurred to her, she also wanted to be missed. Behind Tristan, Marcella appeared; her hair free from its usual tight bob and her skin glowing.

'The place looks different,' Tristan said in a loud voice.

'Not that much has changed, though,' Ella noted.

'It's cleaner,' he mused, 'definitely cleaner.'

'That would be Leah,' Ella remarked.

Leah suddenly felt like the resident cleaning lady – it was a gift of Ella's, to diminutise her. She walked over to the group, smiling and mouthing her hello to Marcella on the way, and held out her hand to shake Tristan's. She was taken by surprise when he hugged her instead, and kissed the side of her face. He smelt of aeroplane and several layers of sweat but it was oddly compelling. Perhaps it was his freedom, his openness that drew everyone towards him. He was clearly someone who dived in, defied normal conventions, did as he pleased and made everyone wish they had the balls to do the same. The antithesis to what Justin had become lately; the weight of the baby and their connection was all over him, all of the time.

'Good to meet you, Princess Leah.'

Her father had called her that when she was small.

'I haven't been called that in a long time.'

'Suits you.'

Tristan's eyes were dark brown, very different to Justin's; but with a similar intensity. Leah blushed.

Justin came up behind them and gave Tristan a manly hug. She'd never seen him so physical. With her, every move he made was so careful.

'Skin and bones!' Justin remarked. 'You've gone all caveman, too!'

'I know, and I absolutely stink. Dying for a shower. But hey, big man, you're looking fit for an oldie.' Tristan patted Justin's stomach, as if to double check.

'Running to work a few times a week, to hold off the inevitable.'

It was strange, hearing Justin talk so frankly with his brother about himself. As the conversations about how his plane ride had been and the brief descriptions of his last year teaching English in Cambodia continued, Leah felt Marcella's eyes on her. Turning around, she caught her gaze square on. Marcella smiled, not embarrassed to have been discovered, then slowly looked away.

Leah spotted a customer at the till and escaped the gathering and Marcella's scrutiny. After a time, Justin picked up Tristan's bag and the two of them set off for the loft. Marcella took a little wander around the shop, realigned a few vases and candleholders, then spent some time in the flower workshop with Ella; chatting about the impending birth. She had only two months to go. Two months and the baby would take over their lives and cement them forever.

Justin came down to speak to Marcella. He told her that he would go for a drink with Tris after work, if he hadn't collapsed on the bed after his shower. She told him she was shattered and heading off. Justin touched the top of her shoulder and kissed the top of her head seamlessly, as though he had done it a million times before.

'I'll just water in the greenhouse before I leave,' Leah announced.

After a few minutes Justin joined her. He had brought in some bay trees.

'What do you make of Tris?'

'Seems very relaxed, energetic, and super friendly.'

'He seems taken with you.' Justin wasn't looking at her

when he spoke; he was picking at a plant and staring into nothingness.

'I doubt that.'

'Can't really blame him. You're just far too beautiful.'

Leah was taken aback; there was a strange heaviness to his tone that she had never heard before. Without looking at her he turned as if to leave.

'I love you. I'm sorry, I just do.'

And then he left, and she couldn't say it back; but it seemed he didn't care if she did or didn't, he just had to be sure she knew that he did.

★

On Sunday Justin seemed a little distant. Leah assumed he was worried that Tristan would intuitively pick up on their connection. The two brothers talked constantly and rearranged an entire section of the garden centre. In doing so they created some more space in the outside storage area, where she had hidden for her lunch break when she'd started the previous September, the little suntrap where Justin kept the bags of potting mix. Leah sat down there to eat her sandwich; to feel the healing power of the sun revive her after winter. She was tempted to lie back but the bags were still wet with morning dew. Tristan joined her with a mug of tea and a banana.

'Is this the staffroom, then? Mind if I join you?'

'Of course not.'

He had a rugged warmth to his face. He put his tea down and paced around her while he ate.

'Are you not tired from your flight? I can't believe Justin has you working within twenty-four hours of being in the country.'

'He'll always be my bossy big brother, making me earn my keep. I don't mind, though. I kind of need to stay on my toes or I go a bit mad.'

He continued to pace.

'Would you like to sit? If it won't drive you mad, I mean.'

'Ha! Sure, love to.'

'Why Cambodia?'

'Amazing country. Beautiful people. It's warm. It's not warm here. Perhaps I feel like I can make more of an impact there… and I feel more valued. The kids struggle to even fit into the classroom but they don't care. I love their energy; it's the best thing about teaching. Actually, it's not just the kids – their parents come in for evening classes in English and IT. Even the monks sneak in. Over there you don't need much; the kids I see every day have nothing, which makes me realise I don't need anything either. Over there I don't need a mortgage, central heating, big heavy jumpers.'

He spoke in short simplified sentences and jumped from one thought to another as though he had been asked the question many times before and was trying to recall the best answers he had come up with.

'How long have you been out there?'

'Cambodia? Three–four years, on and off. And I'll go back – I can't not, I'm not done yet. The cost of living here is just crazy; I'd really struggle to get my shit together in the UK.'

Leah listened.

'I'm intrigued.'

'You should come out. Do some volunteering for a few weeks. It would blow your mind. The kids would never let you leave, and you'd fall in love with them. They'd be all over you.'

Leah thought about it; pictured herself away from The Potting Shed, away from Justin and his new baby, away from self-harming, her family and her peers. She knew so little about Cambodia, about the world, actually. She was too embarrassed to ask if it was near Thailand or Vietnam.

'It's one of those things you do when you don't know what else to do, or just need a break from doing what everyone expects you to do. And sometimes we just need to be reminded of what's actually important in life. I can sense a restlessness in you. Sometimes you have to leave everything that is familiar behind to find yourself.'

It began to feel like Tristan could see straight through her; instinctively knew that something big needed to change in her life.

'You've definitely got me thinking.'

'And by the time I leave London you will have booked your ticket.'

Tristan obviously didn't do small talk. He went straight in. There was a lightness to it, though. He had an easy way about him that made anything seem possible.

'I could set it all up and make sure you were perfectly safe. You really would get so much out of it.'

'Thank you, I'd love to know more. I better get back to it, though.'

He jumped up to join her.

'Yes, me too. The boss will be after me.'

Justin was heading their way when they came out.

'You two look like you've been smoking behind the bike shed.'

'Just talking about other worlds, big man.'

Justin was immediately irritated by Tristan's familiarity with Leah. He had known her for all of five minutes and was already getting into her head. And she looked so relaxed walking out with him, like they'd known each other for years. 'Other worlds' was *their* topic. Other worlds, parallel worlds and travelling, these were *their* conversations – his and Leah's. He wanted to warn her about this older man who would fill her head with romantic, ethereal stories… to impress her – to become closer to her. However, it occurred to him that he might well be talking about himself.

Marcella and Justin both ate out with Tristan after work. Tristan had never fully warmed to Marcella – he found her unnecessarily argumentative and controlling – but he had matured over the years and seemed more tolerant, or perhaps just less bothered, and he had lots of stories to share. He talked about how a baby had been left on his doorstep only a few weeks earlier.

'I'm astonished that there is still an assumption with some people that the Westerner will sort it out. It was tiny. I took it to the nearest hospital and the nurse told me she would call social services and the baby would end up in an orphanage before the end of the day. The mother had to be someone local, someone who knew where I lived. I looked for weeks at the faces of the local women to see which one looked remorseful.'

Marcella shook her head and rubbed her belly as if to reassure her unborn child that she wouldn't be leaving it on any doorsteps.

'That is just heart-breaking,' she said, 'she must have been in such a terrible place to feel she had to do that.'

Justin tuned out. He was tired, frustrated, distracted. He wasn't sure when he would be alone with Leah again and every day that passed was narrowing the time that was left between now and the due date of the baby. He wondered if there was a job he could create for Tris that would mean he was out of The Potting Shed on Monday afternoons. The terrible aching was always there, both when he was with Leah and when he was without her. In the evenings it turned into an unbearable weight that made him want to crawl into bed and stay there and just sleep and sleep.

He recalled the look on Tris and Leah's faces after their chat over lunch. They were smiling, relaxed – comfortable even. He tried to imagine what they had talked about. He knew his brother; knew that he would have easily charmed her. He couldn't be angry with him for befriending her, though. Why wouldn't he? She was beautiful. She was mysterious. She was young and sweet and perfect. It was impossible not to want to know more, not to want to engage her in conversation, not to want to make her laugh, have her bite her lip or blush with embarrassment.

★

Tris had made plans to see friends on Monday so Justin didn't need to find an excuse to send him out. Leah arrived in good spirits and asked after Tristan almost immediately.

'He's off seeing friends. I'm not sure when he'll be back.'
Who cares?
'Just us, then?'
Yes, thank God.
'Yup.'

Leah's wings were opening out a little. There was a shift happening; like the earth's plates moving and readjusting themselves.

'You must have some jobs for me.'

'I don't. I've done everything.'

'You can't pay me not to work, Justin.'

'How many times do we have this disagreement? Okay, no, I have the answer. I will simply pay for your conversation. So you'd better start earning it!'

'Does that make me some sort of escort?'

'I suppose it does! Um, I guess we could carry on sanding the greenhouse. That way we can talk and work and you won't feel like an escort.'

'I'm up for it.'

Justin set them up with sandpaper.

'So what do you make of Tris?' It was the second time he had asked, but he had to know – couldn't resist.

'I don't really know him that well yet, but he's very easy to talk to. Intense, perceptive.'

'Perceptive?'

'I don't know, he just said some things. It was like he knew something about me that I hadn't figured out yet.'

'Like?'

His curiosity was like a loose torpedo in his gut.

'I don't know. Just random things.'

'Did he tell you to travel?'

'Well, he might have mentioned volunteering in Cambodia.'

'God, he's a fast mover. Would you consider it?'

'I would, actually. I quite like the idea of being useful somehow.'

'Useful? You are more than useful.'

'Not really.'

'You're useful to me.'

'Thank you, but you could pay anyone to do what I do here. Probably someone better, stronger, more knowledgeable about the plants. Someone that didn't take days off to study… Not that I mind scrubbing your floors, but it would be good to be useful in another way.'

'You are useful in so many more ways than scrubbing the floors. And yes, I suppose I could replace you; but where's the fun in that?'

'Is it fun?'

'Having you around? Sometimes. Other times it is actually very painful.'

Leah stopped sanding. 'Painful. Why?'

'You know why.'

Of course Leah knew why it was painful for Justin, but she felt her pain was greater, that he had hurt her more than she had hurt him.

'I don't cause you pain. You have everything you want from life.'

He looked at her for a long time.

'Do you actually believe that?'

She shrugged. The sun was coming down on their backs; it should have warmed her but she felt shivery and cold.

She ran her fingers down the wood; she had stayed on the one section for too long and a dent was forming. She sat down.

Justin sat down, too. He looked beaten. She had belittled him and denied him his feelings for her. She didn't want to hurt him but she was losing him and before she lost him altogether she wanted to be reassured that he would suffer as much as she would.

He put his paper down.

'I don't know how to live with it. I know I have so much, I know how vile and selfish I am, but I can't change the way that I feel. It is just there, all the time. Can you not feel anything from me? Not my pain, my endless fucking quest for more time with you, the ridiculous amount of love I have for you.'

It still didn't make sense to Leah, that he could be in love with her, but there he was saying it again, evidently crippled by his feelings. She put her sandpaper down, dusted her hands on her clothes, then crawled over and sat down cross-legged right next to him. His knees were bent and his arms rested gently on them. She lifted her hand and traced her finger across his skin, from his wrist to the tips of his fingers.

'I know. I'm sorry I said that. I can feel your love, of course I can. I don't mean to… I feel weak from loving you, though, not liberated or high or light. Love isn't gentle when it's like this; it doesn't give, it just takes away. And sometimes, all that's left behind is nothingness. One minute we are talking, we are present, we share so much. And then I leave, and there is the nothingness again. And I don't know how that feeling can get any worse, but it will. As time moves on, as you have your baby, as I leave to go off to uni. This, right here, right now, is as close as we get.'

'Leah, all of this time I've wanted so desperately for you to tell me how you feel; but now that you have, I feel awful. I don't want you to feel weak or flat.'

'Don't worry about me. I will be okay. I'm sorry that I'm mean and take a long time to forgive.'

'You have nothing to apologise for. And I don't deserve

your forgiveness. I deserve so much shit from you and you throw nothing at me. It's torture… there's so much I want to say to you.'

Leah ran her hand up Justin's arm, watching as he closed his eyes. In his breathing she could hear something of the slow torture that he was experiencing. She lifted his sleeve and kissed the top of his arm, then rested her head on his skin. It was so warm there, where the sun was falling on them both.

A distant sound of whistling came from inside the shop. Leah moved away, back to her side of the greenhouse and picked up her sandpaper. Justin lifted his head. They both began to sand again.

'There you are. What you up to, guys?'

Tristan was carrying groceries and beer.

'Just finishing off the sanding.'

'Let me put this away and come and help.'

And off he trotted into the office, whistling to himself.

They carried on in silence until Tristan returned with three beers and offered the first to Leah.

'I know, I know, you're underage. I'm corrupting you. It's a Monday. It's not even six. You have homework. Your mum will come and smack me around the ears.'

Leah took the beer, smiling at the idea of her mother coming and smacking anyone around the ears. It occurred to her that her mother had never even been to the garden centre.

'Mate, can you lock the door. Time to close if we're going to sit here and drink beer!'

Tristan returned from locking the door armed with a radio, and found himself an area to work on. The three of them sanded, sang, ate crisps and drank beer. It felt natural and strange all at the same time; for both of them Tristan had become a normalising buffer.

'Have you thought any more about coming to Cambodia? I was thinking that you need to start looking into jabs now if you are keen.'

His persistence made her smile; but there was something in the idea, something that was drawing her in the more he talked about it. The idea of running away, far away, while Justin was enjoying his new baby, might actually be the only way she could manage her emotions.

'Despite Leah obviously being bright, mature, sensible and clearly able to look after herself, don't you think she's a little young to be in Cambodia? It's not entirely lawless, but the poverty…'

'Yes, Dad, I hear you,' Tristan mocked, 'but she would be with me and I would show her around and look after her. There's a spare room for volunteers in the same place I stay. It's part of the school and no one messes with the school; it's like an unspoken pact within the community. She would get to know the Khmer teachers and they'd look out for her too. They'd love her, in fact, and the kids would go nuts for her. She'd have an amazing experience.'

'What would your mum say?'

'I actually have no idea. I don't think she would object, though. She's pretty busy and it would mean that she could go away for a summer break with a friend without me tagging along!'

Justin didn't like it. That was obvious to Leah. She wasn't sure what it was he didn't like about it. That it would mean traveling without him, travelling with Tristan, leaving the UK, or that he actually thought it wasn't safe.

She felt a little giddy – the combination of the sun and the beer and being between the two brothers and their conversation that had somehow ended up about her.

'I should probably get going.'

'Think I'll start on the primer, in case it rains later in the week. The wood will soak it up like a sponge,' Justin cut in.

'That sounds like a big job. I can stay if you need me to.'

'You would be most welcome. But I don't want to exhaust you on a school night.'

'It's okay – I have spares most of tomorrow.'

'Stay, definitely stay,' Tristan said. 'Don't leave me alone with him. He's so much nicer when you're around.'

Leah laughed.

They painted. She accepted another beer but drank it slowly, not wanting to make a fool of herself.

'So, how did you end up spending so much time abroad?' Leah asked Tristan.

'I caught the travelling bug from my big brother. He always went on about how important it had been to him. After taking a gap year and seeing what I could on almost no money, I forced myself through university and a few years of teaching in the arse end of London. After that, I was off, never to return.'

It seemed like a clever way to weave one's way into another culture. Teaching and being in permanent, much-appreciated employment.

It was late when they finally finished. Justin offered to drive Leah home. She declined, not wanting to appear too keen in front of Tristan. Justin insisted. He obviously wanted to finish their conversation.

She relented. She too needed to have a little more time alone with him. Although she had stayed all afternoon, it had only made her want more.

She and Tristan hugged as she was leaving. Even though he was more overtly physical, there was nothing awkward or loaded like it was with Justin. She felt Justin watching them and sensed his discomfort.

Justin pulled the car out quickly – he wanted to get Leah away from The Potting Shed. He couldn't shake the vision of his brother grabbing Leah into his body for a hug. How long had he known her? He wanted the journey home to last forever and prayed in his head for an enormous traffic jam.

'I don't want you to go to Cambodia,' he blurted out, regretting his words the second they had passed his lips. He had sounded possessive, patronising and, above all, like a father.

'I doubt I will, but why?'

'For all the reasons I said.'

'It doesn't sound that unsafe, though. Not really. And I'm not completely stupid; I wouldn't take any risks.'

'And I would miss you.'

'And I would miss you. But I miss you now.'

'Then don't go.'

'You do remember telling me about all the exciting countries you've been to, don't you. You got me all excited. You can't take that away from me now!'

'I was lying. Travelling is shit. The dysentery, the malaria… you'd hate it.'

She laughed at him and he couldn't help but smile.

'Pretty soon I am going to disappear one way or another.

I've applied to uni, remember! You will have a brand new baby. You will be knee deep in poo and sick and you'll be so tired that you'll want to tear your own eyes out. You won't even notice when I leave.'

'That will never happen. Please, don't say that.'

'What, you won't be knee deep in poo? I've got news for you…'

'Very funny. You will never disappear from my thoughts.'

Justin parked up in a random street near her house. He undid his belt and turned to face her.

'Did you forget where I live?' she joked.

'Yes, but we can just camp here for the night and find your flat in the morning.'

'I might get cold.'

'I might keep you warm.'

'Feel my hands, they're already cold.'

She put them around the back of his neck and he grimaced, took them in his and held them.

And then he could wait no longer, or resist no longer, he wasn't sure which but he knew he had absolutely no control over what was about to happen next.

The kiss was light and playful, not friend-like, but not entirely forceful either. And it could be felt for a long time after. Anything more, for any longer, would have been too much; they would have been unable to pull away. He would have kept on kissing her until his tongue was inside her mouth, until he could taste all of her.

They sat in silence for a short time; each recovering from the barely there kiss.

'I did tell my mother I was on my way.'

'I know, yes. I'm sorry.'

'No, I'm sorry.'

Justin shook his head. 'Please, don't be. I am the only one that can say that. I am the only one doing anything wrong here.'

'No, it's me. I hate me for this.'

'Leah, no... don't ever hate yourself.'

But the door closed on his words so that she couldn't hear them.

Justin got out of the car.

'Let me drive you the rest of the way,' he called out over the roof.

'It's okay, I can walk from here.'

But she didn't walk, she ran. And he couldn't bring himself to start the car and drive past her as she did.

Leah ran all the way home and up to her room, disrobed and lay on her bed. She wanted Justin's hands on her skin, she wanted him to hold her face and kiss her properly, for longer. She wanted him to feel inside her, how wet she was, how ready, how much she wanted him. She still had the sharp, sinking feeling in her lower abdomen from the kiss – the light, barely there kiss.

But the euphoria of their moment together in the car didn't last long. Leah was in love with Justin and he wasn't hers to love. By allowing herself to fall in love with him she knew that she was setting the rest of her life up as a series of painful disappointments. She imagined herself as his depressed and pathetic mistress; living in a badly furnished studio flat after forgoing university, working to make enough money to live on her own and be accessible to him at any hour of the day or night. To the outside world, she would remain single, of course, having not met anyone that would live up to her Justin standard. Everyone would think it was weird and wonder why she never met anyone she liked. She would cry herself to sleep, night after night, waiting for her allotted time with him. She would grow bitter in her aloneness and resent herself, Justin and everyone she knew who was happy to be seen in public with their appropriately aged (and previously unmarried) partner. Ten years would turn to twenty and then thirty. He would want to carry on with the affair, out of habit, and Leah would not be able to resist, despite the terrible sadness she would feel each time he fucked her and left. Justin would be content and his life full, with Marcella, his glorious gardening centre (that Leah would no longer be allowed to visit let alone work in) and his adorable children. Justin and Marcella might even take up travelling together again, prolonging the time between his visits. Leah would put on weight, her skin would wrinkle and pale and the visits would be fewer and fewer. The innocence and youth he desired so much would become a receding memory and he would wonder why she was not blossoming into the extraordinary woman he thought she was capable of becoming. Justin would never see that it was their affair that was crushing her. She would grow old and cynical because she had fallen for him but would never be able to call him hers. What she would give up by choosing him she would never know.

Leah received a text message from Vanessa. She made every effort to be friendly and normal in her reply, even promising to hang out soon, said that she was just so tired from work that she could barely move and had lots of exam prep. She asked after Ollie and was informed that she'd broken his heart – he apparently kept telling everyone that he was moving on but went on about her all the time anyway.

Leah wondered why she couldn't find it in herself to just be normal and be with Ollie. He really was such a sweet person, and so right for her in so many ways. Her head was a mess; a swirling, hurricane of madness and confusion. Ollie had taken her virginity, he'd done the deed, and had been completely discreet about it; but the thought of sleeping with him, with anyone, after what had happened at the cinema, was completely terrifying. Would it always feel like this? Would she avoid sex for the rest of her life? She remembered the hands again, on her breasts. Sometimes she still felt them there, just a shadow now; but if she thought about that day too much the shadow grew heavier and heavier until it was no longer a shadow but real, heavy, rough hands. She didn't feel like that around Justin. He had safe, gentle hands. She trusted everything about him. Perhaps he was the only man she would ever trust, and yet she would never be able to be with him in that way, so would just never be with anyone.

Leah thought about hurting herself then. The pain might help her sleep; it had been like a drug for her and she wanted it again. Just one more time, one more replica of the bruises and welts from that day at the cinema to deal with the barely there kiss, then she could say she had chosen the last time.

Leah moved around her room and settled for her desk. She didn't want her mother to hear her so she put some music on. She threw her forearm at the desk; at its sharp wooden edge. Again and again she hit the place where there was just skin and bone and no fat for protection. The best part. The part that she could feel the most. She longed to feel something beyond the numbness that always followed the end of her time with Justin. The intense stabbing sensation felt better. Didn't it? It was better. It was what she deserved.

★

When she woke the following morning and saw herself in the mirror, Leah was embarrassed about the bruises she had created. For the first time she truly regretted what she had done. She had come so close to feeling normal again. She wanted to undo the damage, have the night back. But she couldn't; she would simply have to cover herself up and wait. She recalled the feeling she had been filled with as she had thrown her arm at her desk: she had really felt like she was winning. But now, in the harsh light of morning, she could see that she was right back where she had been when she had arrived home from the cinema; when she had taken off her clothes and looked at her reflection in the mirror and not been able to recognise herself. She was still a mess but couldn't bring herself to talk about it with anyone.

Leah was careful to cover the bruises; though part of her longed for someone to see them so she could fall heavily into their arms and cry until the pain lessened, until the burden was shared, and she was reassured that she would be able to stop, that she would recover, that she was not the only living person to have done anything like this. She thought about telling Vanessa but just couldn't. And her mother would only blame herself and then Leah would feel guilty, on top of everything else she felt guilty about. For a moment she even thought about telling Justin, after all he was the only one that knew what had happened that day at the cinema. But he would never look at her the same again; he would simply pity her even more than he probably did now.

★

The weeks were passing too quickly. Andy had taken the opportunity to have some time off and booked a trip to Turkey with some friends. Ella flirted relentlessly with Tris, much to the amusement of Justin and Leah. Justin encouraged it, despite knowing Ella was not even remotely Tristan's type. He wanted something to take his brother's attention away from Leah. He was too old for Leah, of course – despite being more than a decade younger than Justin, the age gap was still too big – but regardless of that, he was also completely wrong for her. For one thing, he would always leave her. Even if she followed him to Cambodia, he would one day leave her there and find another country to teach in. She would never be happy following him around the world and she would never realise her own potential. Tris never committed to anything or anyone for long.

At home the arguments with Marcella had begun to abate. Justin had perfected a strategy of avoiding them simply by not responding to her provocations. Now he waited for her to calm down before he spoke to her again. He wondered if he would carry on like this forever, for the sake of harmony. It hadn't felt right shouting back at her, but he could feel that he was losing himself. All of the joy Leah had created in him had been redistributed back to wherever it had come from.

Marcella had become tired and cumbersome. She was short of breath and unable to do up her shoes; she napped and went to bed early. Justin was attentive, but it didn't feel genuine. He felt like he was instructing himself on how to be a better husband. Hang out washing: tick. Make dinner: tick. Compliment wife on glowing appearance and have her throw it back in your face: tick.

Preparing for parenthood gave them a direction, at least. Most of their conversations began with 'When the baby arrives...' Together they had prepared a genderless room and purchased furniture and equipment that had immediately reduced the size of their townhouse by at least fifty per cent. However – and he could have predicted this – Marcella's meticulous preparations had resulted in him feeling alienated and inadequate, and the baby wasn't even born yet. He knew that he was about to be left out of this epic journey; only called on when needed and probably for the shittest, most uninvolved jobs.

Marcella had packed a bag; one for herself and one for the baby. Justin felt that there was something symbolic in seeing them lined up together in the hallway; there was no bag for expectant fathers. Marcella would be an exceptional mother who would know exactly how to feed, bathe and comfort; she would simply excel at it. He would be the learner; the clumsy idiot that groped around in the dark making stupid, irritating mistakes. Her strengths would be highlighted, as would his uselessness.

He had flashes of Marcella telling him he was doing it all wrong and taking the baby right out of his arms, tutting him the way she did when he cooked – she frequently took the wooden spoon out of his hand and shooed him away. He often stopped participating, he realised, because of his fear of being chastised and belittled. The only place he felt he was free of it was at work. Even then, Marcella knew the books inside and out and questioned his every purchase, so nothing was entirely his domain. Also, every time she came in she couldn't help but make 'suggestions' as to how things might be more effectively displayed and arranged; always ending her unrequested contribution with 'just a thought'. The comments never failed to piss him off. He let her have her say, said he would take it on board, then left things as they were.

The more he thought about their dynamic the more he became determined that he mustn't fall into the same predictable pattern as a parent. He'd allowed Marcella full reign in the house, let her plan their holidays and social lives; but bringing up a child, that was something quite different.

What sort of a father would he even be? It mattered more than anything else he had ever done and yet he'd barely given it a moment's thought until now. He thought of his own father and how terrifying he had been at times, back when smacking was not considered to be a form of child abuse. He knew he would never hit a child. He also knew that he would not be absent like his own father.

And what sort of a child would he and Marcella have? What obscure combination of the gene pool had beaten all of the other possible combinations? Would their child be a thinker and dreamer like him? Or would it be pragmatic and determined like its mother? It would have elements of both of them, of course, but he wondered what that would mean all mixed together. Chaos? Or harmony? He and Marcella as a couple had been both over the years.

He also tried to imagine a time when he would come

to a place of calm and acceptance about Leah. A time when he would just know that it could never be. But every time he tried to imagine them as friends, working alongside one another in a superficial way, or just keeping in touch via the occasional text or e-mail, the picture wouldn't come into focus. It wasn't something he was ready to imagine or accept. In some small way, since the news of the pregnancy, and after Leah's initial shock and anger, he had thought he could feel a natural, gradual shift; a distance growing between them. But then he went and kissed her and now all he wanted was to kiss her again and again.

And then there was all this talk of Cambodia. Would she actually go? How long would she go for? When he thought of Leah he always imagined her in The Potting Shed, tying her apron on, offering her smile to the customers. She wouldn't always be there, though. Of course she wouldn't. He hoped that she would at least work over most of the summer. Would uni be here in London or somewhere miles away? He couldn't bear the idea that she would move to another part of the country.

Justin imagined that Leah would find a way to move on from their connection quite quickly. She was young, she was resilient, and her life was about to happen. She had everything to look forward to: university, travel, boyfriends, the beginning of her adult life. And when, not if, all of those things, or even one, did take her from him, he would have no choice but to carry on; to make things work with Marcella. He couldn't spend his entire life feeling the way he felt right now, that much he did know.

Justin also knew that Leah needed to be released, to be allowed the freedom to fall in love and one day marry and have a child herself. If she didn't leave of her own accord he would need to release the latch on the door and push her through it. There was no doubt a better man out there who would love and adore Leah and explore the world with her. It was sickening, but true. The heaviness would surely subside after a time and maybe he would eventually return to the person he was before Leah came into the shop that day. But the more Justin tried to remember who that man was, and recall what his life was like, the heavier he felt. He wasn't unhappy then, but he wasn't happy in the way that he was when he was with Leah. He didn't want to return to that half version of himself; he wanted to feel more and do more and know that every day wouldn't be mapped out until he was old and dead. All of a sudden he wanted to travel again; he wanted to re-explore the world with Leah, see her eyes full of wonder. He was sure that he would never be loved again the way that Leah loved him, not by Marcella, not by anyone. And, if he was entirely honest, he wasn't sure he would ever be able to love Marcella in the way that he used to because she was not Leah. How would that ever be fair on Marcella?

*

Leah stayed back with Justin and Tristan on Monday afternoon to finish painting the greenhouse. Justin had to leave for a dinner he'd forgotten about and gave Leah strict instructions not to stay for more than an hour. She was beginning to sense that he was strongly opposed to her being alone with Tristan. She found it amusing that he was being so protective of her, so unprepared to share her.

'Fancy a bite after we're done?' Tristan offered.

'I should probably go home and study.'

'Just a quick one. Food will only improve your ability to concentrate. There's a good Thai place around the corner.'

She could see no reason not to.

They finished up, closed the shop and made their way to the restaurant.

'How are the stress levels?'

'Pre-exam? Pretty high.'

'Do you feel prepared? You seem very studious.'

'I have no life so maybe I am finally getting on top of it, after losing focus for a little while.'

'Uni?'

'I hope so.'

'You don't really want to talk about school, do you?'

'I'm kind of full of it. It would be nice to talk about something else.'

'Then we shall!'

They found a table, ordered a selection of plates to share and a carafe of wine.

They talked about work, about Ella, Andy, even Justin; though Leah quickly changed the subject.

'Can I ask you something?' Tristan was never shy to address the thing that was on his mind. 'But you have to promise not to run.'

Everything in that sentence told Leah to run now, before he even asked. Of course, it was about Justin – he was about to ask her if there was something between them. He took hold of her wrist very gently.

She must have looked petrified.

'Would it be weird for you if I did this?'

He pulled her wrist in closer and kissed the underside of her hand.

Everything in her head was screaming yes, it is weird, so weird, and wrong. Justin would be mortified. But then everything about that thought was utterly ridiculous. There was no her and Justin, not now or in the future. His feelings couldn't come into it. Why should he have his wife and his imaginary girl too? She didn't belong to Justin and he didn't belong to her. She was becoming a spirit between worlds: a spirit that never entered the next life but never partook of this one either.

Leah hadn't spoken. She had let Tristan kiss her hand. She looked around the busy restaurant. Of course, Justin wasn't there but she felt his presence.

'I don't think it's weird,' she smiled.

'Phew.'

They were both coy, not sure where to look or what to say next.

'I should get back, though. I have to…'

'I know, you have to study. Perhaps on Friday you could stay back late and we could just hang out.'

'Maybe.'

'Maybe is good. We could just keep it really light. No pressure. Something tells me that the last thing you need is anything heavy… Sound good?'

'Okay. But whatever happens, can we keep it just between us?'

'Of course. No doubt everyone would think I was much too old for you anyway. Which I am.'

'Even Justin. I mean, he can't know.'

'Absolutely. He'd judge me the harshest of all. And he has a thing for you; a sort of fatherly, protective thing. I think he'd probably take a swing at me!'

The notion horrified her – that people thought of Justin as a fatherly figure in her life – but she decided to eliminate the thought from her mind and just be relieved that Tristan hadn't considered Justin's behaviour around her too deeply.

Tristan drove her home in Justin's work car. It felt very strange to be there with him and not Justin, almost disloyal. She wasn't sure how things had ended up this way. Her life had been so uncomplicated, so predictably dull before she walked into The Potting Shed. She wondered again if perhaps she should leave her job. Justin would go on to have lots of babies and be perfectly content. And he would never need to know that she was stealing this moment with Tristan right now. But, at the same time, she liked that Tristan was attracted to her. It would be hard losing Justin to his new life – the baby was due in only a few weeks' time and Leah knew that she would fall flat and feel completely alone. Wasn't it fair that she had a distraction, just as he did?

Leah directed Tristan into her street. When they pulled up outside the flat she leaned over, held and kissed the side of his face. Tristan covered her hand over with his own; then he kissed both of her cheeks, the top of her nose, her forehead and her lips, just once. Leah couldn't figure out how this was happening; she had known Tristan for such a short period of time and yet it felt completely natural to be intimate with him. It wasn't forbidden; it was free and easy and not full of heavy emotions. It made her think that she might be okay one day, if she could just allow herself to be.

Stepping out of the car, Leah said her goodbyes and made her way up to her front door.

★

The following Friday Leah offered to stay back late after work. Justin wasn't staying back himself so she was sure he could have done with the help; but he insisted she left and got a good night's sleep. She assumed that he didn't want her to be alone with Tristan.

Tristan found her in the greenhouse.

'Why not come back after everyone has gone? I'll ping you a message when the coast is clear.'

'Okay.'

Justin saw Leah making her way to the office to collect her things after work. He followed her in and closed the door behind him.

'Hey, are you off?'

'Yes. Is there something else you would like me to do?'

'No. I just haven't spoken to you in a while. Just wondering how you are?'

'I'm a little stressed. I really can't wait for the exams to be over.'

'You'll do brilliantly... I know how conscientious you are.'

He looked nervously out the window to see if anyone was about.

'I miss you,' he told her.

'I miss you too.'

'Really?' he asked, genuinely needing to hear the answer.

'What makes you think I might not?' she asked.

'I think I'm losing you. Not that you were ever mine.'

He watched as Leah dumped her bag and jacket on the sofa. She came back and stood next to him so that they were both leaning on the door of the office with their hands behind their backs, staring down at the knots in the wooden floor. It would be near impossible for anyone to see them at this angle, with the clumps of wisteria obscuring most of the view. Justin leaned to the side so that he could kiss the top of her head and rest his closed lips there. He breathed her in.

There was still so much about her that he didn't know. He had hoped to make his way beneath the layers as time went on, but looking at her now he felt he knew nothing of what she was really feeling. There seemed to be less and less that she was willing to offer him. He had no idea who she was when she left the shop: the friends she saw, the girl she was at school, the conversations she had with her mother.

It was Tristan, of course. His constant presence had reduced the tiny morsels she fed him to almost nothing. She was no doubt being careful – didn't want Tristan to notice anything between them. She always had been the sensible, controlled one. He'd brushed past her earlier and felt the sleeve of her cardigan, but he wasn't sure if she had even noticed. She hadn't looked at him, didn't acknowledge him. The absence of any meaningful exchange between them made him crave her more, made him even more desperate.

Justin looked at his office, at Tristan's things littered in every corner: a half-read book with a broken spine, dusty old desert boots, an empty box of anti-malaria tablets, dirty mugs and glasses, plastic containers he'd eaten from. The rest of it was upstairs: his clothes, his giant rucksack, his ancient toilet bag. Justin wondered when he would leave. He wondered when he would stop touching Leah so freely and openly, the way he wished he could. He wanted to be annoyed with his brother, but couldn't do that either. He was behaving as Justin wanted to; showering Leah with attention and kindness and filling her head with ideas about the world. And the laughter, her laughter, had finally returned. Wasn't that more important as a thing in itself than the fact that it had been Tristan that had been able to make it happen?

'It's not that way around, you know that,' Leah finally said.

He had forgotten what they were talking about and looked at her blankly.

'I'm losing you, Justin. You're about to have a baby.'

All that he could do was shake his head and whisper: 'No'.

She made to leave, causing goose bumps to ripple up his arms. For a moment he couldn't bear the thought and pulled her back by her shoulders; back into their hiding place behind the closed door of the office. He wrapped her in tight, one arm around her shoulders and the other around her midriff, felt her chest rise and fall until their breath slowed and they were in rhythm with each other. He inhaled the scent of her hair, kissed her neck and her ear. She didn't try to free herself. If anything he felt her press herself back into him further. As the minutes passed their breathing became the thing that was holding them there; it felt to Justin that if one of them pulled away the other might stop breathing altogether. He couldn't let her go. Wouldn't.

The distant sound of someone singing grew louder, and then it was so loud they could also hear footsteps. Justin freed Leah from his embrace, unravelled her and watched her stumble over to the sofa and begin to gather her things. He moved away from the door in time for Andy to turn the handle and enter.

'Hey, guys. I'm off. Just grabbing my bag. See you tomorrow.'

They said goodbye in unison and Andy was gone again. But it was too late to return to the moment they had been locked in before he had come in. Leah left too, quietly and awkwardly. Justin closed the door behind her. Then he stood back in the place that they had occupied together only minutes before and imagined that Leah was still there with him. He could still feel her up against him, still smell her hair.

Justin threw himself on the sofa. He thought about how close he had come to lifting up the side of her dress and finding Leah's thigh, moving his hand towards her underwear. It was impossible to think of anything else. He ran upstairs to the bathroom in the loft to deal with it.

Leah sat in the café and drank several glasses of homemade lemonade. She deliberated over whether she should text Tristan and tell him she couldn't make it back to The Potting Shed. She knew she would feel uncomfortable being there with him after what had just happened with Justin. She got out her books and began to read over her notes; she would just sit and work for a while and decide in an hour.

Leah had lost track of time when Tristan finally texted. She made an excuse about being needed by a friend and told him that she might be able to visit the following evening.

She wasn't working, just studying all day, and could do with something to look forward to at the end of it. Tristan replied that he would look forward to it all day.

★

On Saturday Leah distracted herself by studying. She hit the books and tried not to think too much about what had happened between her and Justin the day before. They had both been clinging on to the very last of something, she told herself, that was all.

In the evening Tristan texted to let her know the coast was clear. Leah arrived at The Potting Shed half an hour later, paranoid and carrying a book. If Justin appeared out of the blue she would use the excuse that she had left the book behind yesterday and needed it to study. She had become so accustomed to secrecy that preparing lies almost didn't feel strange anymore.

Leah knocked on the old Indian wooden doors and heard Tristan fiddling with the lock to let her in. His hair was still wet from his shower and he was wearing a clean shirt, and jeans that didn't actually have holes in them. It was clear that he had gone to some sort of effort. He took her straight into the office, where he had lit some candles and plumped the cushions on the sofa. Beautiful acoustic music was playing on the old record player.

He looked embarrassed.

'Oh, it's too much! I just wanted you to relax…'

'No, it's lovely. I am feeling relaxed already.'

He handed her a glass of white wine. Noticed her book.

'You're not going to sit here and study, are you?'

'God no; it's my excuse for coming here, just in case Justin arrives.'

'Ah, very clever, but he won't. Try not to worry about that. Sushi okay?'

'Absolutely. Lovely.'

They talked about her day at the books and the fact that she would be doing the same tomorrow. Eventually they moved on to Cambodia and he showed her some photos on his phone of smiling children. As he flicked through the pictures Leah noticed a few shots of women; some Cambodian and some young white women she assumed were volunteers or fellow travellers. She wondered how many of them he'd slept with and if there was one in particular he would be returning to. The pang of jealousy she felt at the thought surprised her.

The wine quickly went to her head. When Tristan stood up to change the music she took the opportunity to lie back on the sofa and stretch out.

Tristan crawled over.

'Don't fall asleep on me now,' he whispered, moving her hair from her face.

'I'll try not to.'

He leant over and kissed her forehead, then her cheeks. Leah closed her eyes and he kissed them too; then her mouth, which she opened so that she could kiss him back. He traced her breastbone with his fingers. He was so close to her breasts. Something rose in her; flashbacks to the day in the cinema, heavy, dirty hands all over her chest. She must have tensed because he paused.

'Hey, are you okay? You're shaking. I'm sorry... I didn't mean to move so quickly.'

'No, it's okay, it's not you… I just…'

A tear slipped down the side of her face and wet her hair. She was ruining the moment and wondered if she would ever feel comfortable being touched by a man again.

'Hey it's okay, if you're not ready, or if you just don't want to.'

He hadn't recoiled after her reaction; that was something. He was stroking her hair, smoothing away the tears.

'It's not that.'

'Okay. You don't have to tell me, but you can if you feel like it.'

'Something happened, not that long ago… It was pretty awful. But I want to be able to get over it. I want to move on and not have one bad experience dictate the rest of my life.'

'And that is exactly how you should feel. It's not easy to trust again, or to believe you deserve something better, when you've been treated like shit. But we're not all bastards…'

'You're definitely not a bastard.' She smiled. 'Everything feels okay, with you. That's the surprising thing.'

'There's no rush, Leah. I'm happy to just hang out and talk, listen to music.'

Leah turned on her side so that she could see into Tristan's eyes. She trusted him. And she really wanted to feel okay about being intimate. She leaned over and kissed him. As long as she was in some sort of control, she might just be able to disassemble her anxieties and free herself of them altogether. She picked up Tristan's hand and put it on the side of her hip, on her skin where her top had ridden up. His hand was so warm, and soft, not insistent, not hard, not unclean. She didn't want to pull away but she liked knowing that she could. He was being careful, really overly careful, in a way she was sure he had never had to be with another woman. It made her want him more.

Leah guided Tristan's hands over her body with her own, so that it almost felt like she was touching herself. They both removed her clothes and then Tristan removed his. When she moved his fingers to between her legs she let go of the top of his hand, closed her eyes and thought only of the present. And then she felt something even softer there – his lips, and then his tongue – something Ollie had never done. It was overwhelming, unlike anything else she had experienced, and then she came, and everything that was bad in the world ceased to matter. As she did she pushed his fingers deep inside of her; she had to have him there.

When she finally regained some control, Leah took Tristan in her hand, which he seemed not to be able to get enough of. He stopped to put a condom on, then entered her from where he was kneeling on the rug in front of the sofa. She was at an angle, half lying and half sitting on the sofa, but he made it work. He was very careful and gentle at first, until she wrapped her legs around him and forced him in deeper and faster until he came.

Tristan left to use the bathroom. When he returned he curled up on the sofa behind her, holding her naked body with his free arm.

'You okay, gorgeous girl?'

'Yes, absolutely,' she whispered.

Tristan drove her back home. It was a warm evening and the traffic was quiet for once. Leah felt less heavy and less anxious. She thought of the orgasm Tristan had given her and immediately wanted to come over and over again.

Leah's mother was dozing on the sofa. Leah lied about where she had been, chatted for a short time then closed herself into her bedroom; relieved to be alone.

She climbed into bed. She needed sleep. Exams began in two weeks. She had to focus. She had to not hurt herself anymore. She had to allow herself some time to just be and maybe enjoy whatever short-lived fun she would have with Tristan.

She thought about Ollie, about how she had used him to lose her virginity, someone familiar and inexperienced, and how she had maybe even walked away from him because he was those things. What boy her own age would ever be able to live up to her ideals now? She wanted to talk to Ollie and explain that her head was just too messed up to do the right thing, to allow her to maintain a normal relationship, or to behave in a way that was not self-destructive and selfish. She wanted him to know that it wasn't him, that he was a wonderful person. He just wasn't Justin. And it was still Justin she wanted to be with, in his space, in his office, in the bed in the loft, doing all of the things that she had just done with Tristan.

Tristan was his own person, certainly not young or inexperienced, but he was also a man with no ties to anything or anyone. She told herself that as long as he was using her she couldn't use him. And she was not about to fall in love with him.

Justin could never find out; the importance of that had to be clear. She texted Tristan; made him promise that he wouldn't tell a soul, especially Justin. He replied that she could trust him and that he wanted to see her again as soon as possible.

Monday came around quickly. Tristan had been sent on a supply run and wouldn't be home until late that evening. Leah wondered if Justin suspected something. It was obvious that he had engineered Tristan's absence. After shutting up the shop, Justin prepared mint tea and snacks. They sat out on a wooden bench in the evening sunshine. Leah was exhausted, utterly shattered from the hours she had spent bent over her books. She brought her feet up as she always did and rested her head against the back of the hardwood bench. Leah felt uncomfortable in a way that she never had with Justin. It wasn't just guilt brought on by what had happened with Tristan, it was also because she wanted it to happen again and wasn't even sure why, as she didn't really have any strong feelings for him.

'How are you feeling?'

'I'm just so tired. I'm so over revising. I feel like I have done all I can and now I want to empty my head of all of it and move on, learn something else.'

'I have absolute faith in you.'

'And what about you? How are you feeling pre-baby?' It was a question she felt she should ask, as a sign of her acceptance.

Justin threw his head back and sighed. He was always surprised by Leah's maturity; the baby was the last thing she probably wanted to hear about.

'Actually, I'm quietly shitting myself. What do I know about babies? I know Marcella will have all the right instincts when it comes out kicking and screaming. But it's harder for a man, I think. I don't know if we have the same skills.'

'I think you're going to be an amazing father. You are a very attentive, caring person; and as far as I can tell, that's a pretty good starting point for looking after a baby. The practical skills you can learn as you go.'

Justin smiled, grateful for the encouragement.

'Thank you. I hope you are right.'

They were sitting opposite each other, as they usually did, knees bent and feet up. He stretched his arm out so that he could play with a loose strand of her hair. He twisted it around his fingers then tucked it behind her ear so that her cheek was exposed.

'I hope that when you come here you are able to forget about your exams, even if just a little.'

'I feel very relaxed here, with you. I don't know how you do it, but you make all of the stressing out feel utterly pointless. In the end we only have so much control over things, don't we?'

'We only have control over this moment, right now, when we are alone and the doors are locked.'

He patted the seat in front of him.

She crawled over to him and he opened his legs for her so she could sit between them with her back to him. She leaned into his body as he wrapped her up in his arms. Her loose top exposed most of her neck and shoulders. Justin swept her hair to one side and kissed her neck several times, until it became too much, until he wanted to kiss her everywhere. Always in the back of his mind now was an urgent need to make the most of the time they had alone together. He slipped his hand under her top and felt the smooth skin of her chest. There was nothing in her resisting him and yet he knew how wrong it was. He just had to be close, to feel her skin and the warmth of her body.

'I should go.'

'Just stay a little longer.'

Justin slipped his hand inside Leah's bra, felt her small nipples between his fingers as he kissed her neck. Leah backed into him and her breathing grew heavier and heavier. With his other hand he lifted her skirt. She arched her back, half pressing down on him and half trying to resist, as his hand felt her wetness and her warmth through her underwear.

And then she did resist. She lifted herself up and pulled away in one swift manoeuvre. Turning around, she looked him in the eyes and kissed his face.

'I want to but I can't. And you can't.'

'Why?'

'Because I love you.'

'That doesn't make sense.'

'I don't want to be hurt.'

'I don't want to hurt you.'

'But you will, this will, after. There won't be possibility anymore because it will have happened and you will go back to your wife and baby. And I will just feel like shit.'

'So you will be strong enough for both of us?'

'If I have to be the strong one, I will. Isn't that what it means to love someone? To leave them with the thing that's best for them, even if it isn't what you want for yourself?'

'If I had known that, perhaps I would have held back… because I would be the worst thing for you. In fact, I have been the worst thing for you.'

'Justin you have a wife, and a baby on the way. Everything that you've done in your life has led up to this point. And when the baby comes, you will know that we were never the best thing for each other. What I want or need doesn't matter. I have to go somewhere else, this spot is taken.'

'I am sorry, Leah. I need to stop being so greedy and selfish because, let's face it, that's what I am being; but I can't seem to help myself. Anyone looking in on you and I would point out that I am just a predator. I have done nothing but mess with your head since we've met, and during one of the most stressful times of your life. God, I can see the years of therapy that will follow – the girl who had the world at her feet, but was fucked over by a self-serving pervert. I'm such a cunt.'

'Justin, stop. Don't take all of the responsibility. How can you? I'm not a child, am I? I know what I am doing and feeling and I have always had a choice. I have loved every minute that I have spent with you… In any case, it's not like anything has actually happened. We haven't slept together.'

'It has in my head, it has in me… I'm more gone and more unfaithful than if I had gotten drunk and had a one-night stand with someone. You are in my head every single minute of the day. I am not fully present in my own life because of you. Not that I blame you, of course. I'm sorry. I shouldn't even be saying these things to you.'

'I don't need you to be sorry. We just need to find a way to be, that we can both live with. I had better go.'

'I know. Of course you must. You must go and not be alone with me. That would be a very bad idea.'

Leah didn't know what to say. She would suffer anything to make things okay between them, but she would not pity him and she would not watch him pity himself.

So she left.

She left him sitting on the bench on his own, pouring the last of the mint tea. He poured it from a great height; the way the Moroccans did, he had once told her, although he had forgotten why they did it that way. She watched him throw the little glass back as though it were a shot and he was sending himself into a state of drunken oblivion.

Justin stayed back to drink Tristan's beer. He'd sounded like such a cock, but then it wasn't the first time. Leah had protected herself. She had foreseen the abysmal outcome of an illicit affair and eradicated the possibility. Maybe she had even fallen out of love with him but wasn't ready to wound him with the news just yet. He drank, then drank some more when Tristan returned, but of course couldn't tell him why he felt the need to annihilate himself with alcohol. Finally, he walked home; which took him almost an hour. When he crept in through the front door Marcella was in the living room.

'Where the hell have you been, Justin? I texted you like a hundred times. What if I was in labour?'

'Then I guess you would have phoned work, which is where I was. My phone was flat so I didn't get your texts. I'm very sorry.'

'Not good enough, Justin. Really, you shouldn't let your bloody phone go flat. I mean, how old are you? Twelve?'

'Okay, fair call. I'm a complete dick. Sorry, won't happen again.'

'You're drunk? Are you fucking kidding me?'

'I had a few beers with Tristan. I'm not that drunk.'

'Well, that makes me feel so much better. Did you drive home?'

'No.'

'But you're not too drunk?'

'Too many to drive.'

'Well, just as well I'm not in labour then. Because I would need to take a fucking taxi to the hospital.'

And with that she stormed out of the front room, thundered up the stairs and shook the house with her well-honed door-slamming technique.

Justin slept on the sofa. He'd managed to piss off both of his women in one night with very little effort.

★

The following Friday Leah stayed back at the café around the corner until Tristan gave her the all clear. They drank a little and played some music. Leah perched on the side of Justin's desk. The evening was warm and she was wearing a shirtdress. It had been a long time since she had hurt herself; she liked looking down and seeing the skin pure again. Tristan appeared in front of her while she was lost in thought.

'You're in another place.'

'Sorry.'

'I think I can bring you into the present.'

Tristan put his hands down on either side of her thighs, resting them on the top of the desk. Leah opened her legs so that he could get closer. She felt his hands on her lower back, pulling her in closer until she could feel him pressed up against her. He kissed her, then lay her down on the desk and told her to close her eyes.

One by one she felt him undo the buttons on the front of her dress – and as he did she felt the night air on her chest, her torso, abdomen and hips – until her entire body was exposed as she lay there on the desk.

For a moment she felt self-conscious. She closed her eyes

to help her relax but when she did both Justin and Tristan appeared there. Although it was incredibly confusing she was relieved it wasn't the blurred faces of the boys that had attacked her in the cinema.

Tristan examined the length and breadth of her body with his fingers and played with her through her underwear. He then carefully removed her knickers and used his mouth again. Within minutes she came and all she wanted was for him to be inside of her.

Justin wasn't sure how long he had been standing outside his office, in the dark, obscured by the wisteria. He had made no sound or movement, and doubted he could even if he'd wanted to. It was only fragments that he caught: Tristan's look of rapture, the slight rise of Leah's breasts, her entire torso exposed and, further down, a neat triangle of pubic hair. He watched her writhe when she came; watched her body contort and heard her make a small, erotic sound that made his stomach convulse.

He wanted to do something, anything; he needed to undo this terrible act, this crime against him and against her. But he couldn't. It was as though he had come down with a deadly, tropical disease – sweat poured out of him as he shivered and shook from within – and his hands just hung there uselessly.

There was no way to unsee it, either. The images were always going to be there now. In his head he screamed at himself to leave, to stop looking, but he couldn't. It was not the first time he had cried over Leah, but this felt different. She was his. And Tristan had taken her. And she had let him. At that moment he saw his brother get his cock out and pull on a condom. Leah made a small, pained noise when he entered her. He wouldn't have done it like that; he would have been gentle. He wouldn't have hurt her.

Justin watched Leah glide up and down his desk on her open dress like a ragdoll; all hair and flawless, glowing skin. And Tristan, deep inside her, having her. Tristan came, like a bull breaking through a gate. The sound was revolting, vile. He'd seen enough, too much. He turned around quietly and disappeared back into the night.

★

As the exams started Leah thought more and more about the possibility of disappearing to Cambodia for the summer. She enquired about flights and began a series of jabs. She broached the subject with her mother, who seemed perplexed and concerned and agreed to talk about it some other time – when wasn't so tired. She found herself making regular trips to see Tristan in the evenings. There was never an expectation that she would come, just an open invitation. She studied for hours and the sex was something to look forward to at the end of it all; it was a physical release, and, after a time, it became her fix. She needed to be touched, needed someone inside of her, needed to come. She didn't mind that it was sometimes too hard or too deep; she liked the feel of her hips in Tristan's grip, especially just as he was about to come. Being wanted by Tristan, and having complete control over when she would sneak in, somehow kept her self-loathing at bay. She'd replaced physical pain with physical pleasure. It had been a neat transition that seemed to have no consequences.

Justin had been quiet with her recently and she

wondered if perhaps he was aware that there was something between her and Tristan. They had been discreet and to their knowledge no one had noticed, seen or heard anything, but she couldn't help but think of it.

'Hey, Leah, do you have many exams left to go? Would you mind working all weekend?'

Justin had only ever asked her to work extra hours when he had wanted to see more of her. But this was different. She didn't remember him ever using her name the way he just had. It sounded strange.

'The baby is being induced tomorrow. It's overdue.'

'Oh wow! How exciting. Of course I can.'

'Thank you.'

'I hope everything goes well with the birth… '

'Me too.'

'You'll be a beautiful dad.'

He smiled.

There was still something in Justin's eyes, something that connected her to what was going on in his head, but recently he seemed to be working hard to keep it from her. He had a number of possible reasons to be cool with her: the awkward way things had been left between them the last time they had been alone, the impending birth, to name just two. And she had probably created some distance herself given that her head was full of exams, and Tristan, and the thought that in the very near future she would no longer be a schoolgirl. But it was probably the right thing, for both of them.

Justin had been sitting at his desk as he spoke to Leah. He had for a moment wanted to tell her that he knew about her and Tristan; to just say it out loud and have her know that it had caused him immense pain. Perhaps he also wanted some sort of reassurance that she had thought of how it might hurt him should he find out. Why his brother, of all people? Surely she knew it would destroy him.

He had restrained himself, though. Revealing what he knew to her would have come out all wrong. It wasn't the right time. He imagined telling Leah that she could have anyone in the universe except his own brother. It would only come out as feeble and selfish. What demands could he make of her when she could make absolutely none of him? But God, he wanted it to be anyone but Tristan. Even that kid that had come in the one day, she could have him.

He ran his palm over the surface of his desk. She had been on here, her naked body, opened out like a peony, only to have his brother's cock shoved in the middle of it. He wondered then why Tristan hadn't blurted it out over a beer, as men so often did. Thank God he hadn't; there was no guarantee Justin wouldn't have lamped him. She was far too young for him, far too innocent, and incredibly vulnerable. She'd been through a traumatic attack. Surely casual sex was the last thing she was emotionally ready for. Her mother was absent at best and her father simply didn't feature in her life at all. Leah seemed almost completely alone and unsupported. Had he himself taken advantage of this? Her vulnerability? Her aloneness? Her lack of a strong parent?

★

Saturday was long and busy and Justin's absence was felt. Every time the phone went Leah looked over at whoever had answered, thinking it might be news of the baby. Ella said it would probably be hours, maybe even the next morning, and went on about her sister's forty-eight-hour labour and eventual Caesarean.

At the end of the day there was still no news. Tristan texted Justin who replied that it was going to be a long night – Marcella was not dilating and was now sleeping peacefully under epidural. Leah watched on as he replied: *Good luck, big bro. Text me the minute it pops out.*

Leah and Tristan closed the shop and enjoyed the last of the evening sun outside before ending up back in the office. Tristan sat down at the desk to look at some old photographs he'd found – they were of The Potting Shed in its various stages of development – and tugged her over and sat her on his knee. They looked through them together: the Moroccan tiles being laid; the reclaimed wooden shelves going in; a half-built greenhouse; empty tables and trays where all the plants would one day go; Marcella pretending to work the till with a daft look on her face; the sign going up; Marcella and Justin standing at the big Indian door, each of them holding out an arm to present the shop. The last one was of Justin in a crisp Potting Shed apron, something she'd never seen him wear.

Leah heard Tristan begin to breathe heavily in her ear. He moved his hands underneath her skirt and shifted so that she could feel how hard he was. She arched her back and pressed up against him.

'That's it! I have to have you now.'

Tristan moved her forward so he could put a condom on and take her underwear off. He then lowered her down onto him. He was hard and she had to adjust herself so that it didn't hurt. She let out a small noise that made him come within seconds.

★

In the early hours of the morning, Marcella had still not dilated enough and the baby began to show signs of distress. A decision was made to perform a Caesarean as a matter of urgency. Marcella reluctantly agreed and was immediately wheeled out of the room. Justin scrubbed in and found Marcella in the operating theatre crying almost uncontrollably.

The doctor tried to reassure her that it was the best decision for both her and the baby and would be all over within minutes.

'But what do you mean by distressed?' she sobbed. 'Will there be something wrong with the baby?'

'That's why we are taking the baby out, to avoid just that. There's nothing to worry about for now. I need you to relax, though. It will be best for your baby.'

The doctor had a soothing but slightly detached tone; he had clearly delivered similar news a thousand times. Justin smoothed Marcella's sweaty hair and kissed her forehead.

'This wasn't supposed to happen, Justin. I wanted to give birth naturally. I don't want a Caesarean,' Marcella sniffed, trying to pull herself together.

'I know. It's okay, though. The only thing that matters now is that we get this baby out safely.'

'That's the thing about babies; they make their own minds up about how they want to come out,' the midwife added.

It was like a remarkably choreographed dance – the way the nurses, midwives and doctor worked in harmony – each doing their part without getting in each other's way. Within what felt like seconds; a wet, pink baby was lifted from the melee.

'It's a girl!'

Justin sighed with relief as the child let out a kitten-like squawk and its tiny fists opened up as if to grasp on to something.

After a swift swaddling their daughter was brought over to them. Marcella kissed her and smiled for the first time in twenty-four hours.

★

Justin sat in the large, plastic-covered chair next to his sleeping wife and cradled his daughter. He hadn't moved for at least two hours; couldn't stop looking at her delicate features as she slept. Part of him couldn't begin to understand how he could be trusted to look after something this precious, without any supervision. The other part of him simply didn't want to let her go.

After a time the midwife appeared. Marcella slowly stirred and eventually woke. The midwife checked her stats and dressing and congratulated them both. She also remarked on Justin's natural way with the baby. She hoisted Marcella up a little, making her grimace with pain and ask if her stitches had come undone. Once reassured and given another dose of pain relief, Marcella was ready to hold the baby. Justin handed her over, feeling the loss almost immediately, and watched on as Marcella admired their beautiful creation.

'You need to try to feed the baby,' the midwife bellowed in her deep Jamaican accent.

Justin watched helplessly as Marcella struggled to undo the buttons on her pyjama top to get her breast out. The baby was more interested in sleeping than latching on. She opened her mouth a little then nodded off with her lips slightly pursed. The midwife told Marcella to squeeze some milk out manually so the baby could taste it. Marcella looked at her as though she'd asked her to piss in public, tried a couple of times and then declared that it just wasn't working.

The midwife handed the baby back to Justin.

'The baby needs to drink. We can try some formula if you can't manage to breastfeed.'

Her lack of empathy irritated Justin.

'Sorry. I'm just so tired. I need to sleep. I'll try again soon,' Marcella told her.

'Okay, but don't leave it too long,' the midwife insisted.

'It's okay, I'm here to look after her, you sleep a little longer. I'm not going anywhere,' Justin assured her.

Marcella turned over and closed her eyes. Justin was happy to be left alone with the baby; she gave him an instant inner calm and gratitude for his life that he had never experienced before.

★

On Sunday morning, when Leah arrived for work, the text had come through to Tristan – *Please tell the gang a little girl has arrived safely by Caesarean. She's a cutie.*

Leah's heart seemed to collapse in on itself. A little girl, a beautiful mini Marcella. She was happy for Justin, of course, but she felt the distance immediately. The fact that she had not been texted stung for some reason, but then why would he text her? He was experiencing one of the most beautiful moments of his life, and it didn't have anything to do with her. She pictured the two of them in a hospital, hugging and kissing their adorable bundle, realising that they would be happier now, that this was what they needed to bring them closer together. *It's right*: she told herself, over and over again. *It just is.*

★

When Justin came into work the following weekend Leah hugged him, quite openly, and told him how happy she was for him. He clung to her for a few moments – as if to reassure her that she had not been forgotten – and whispered his thanks in her ear. Leah closed her eyes briefly, taking in his scent that she had missed so much, until the guilt she felt for going behind his back with Tristan – a condition she seemed temporarily unable to cure herself of – overwhelmed her and she pulled away. She remembered the little gift she had bought for the baby – a soft, velvety bunny with pink ears and a pretty floral dress. When she returned with it, Ella had appeared and was asking all the questions that Leah couldn't bring herself to ask. She learned that Marcella was stoic in her recovery. And that the precious, sleep-loving baby finally had a name, Lucia; which had something to do with her being born at daybreak.

Justin only stayed for a short time. He rushed around in his crazed, sleepless state; placing orders, checking the books and delegating a number of tasks that needed urgent attention. Just as he was leaving Leah handed over the gift.

'So sweet of you to buy a gift.'

'I had one just like it when I was little.'

'Thank you.'

And then he was gone again.

★

By mid-June Leah had completed her last exam. She piled all of her notes and textbooks, all evidence of her education, even a broken protractor, into a two large boxes. She sealed the lids with tape and shoved the boxes into the loft space. She was ready for a new era.

PART SEVEN

In the weeks following the birth, Justin turned up to work for a few hours each day. Marcella's mother, Malena, had come over to help out at home while Marcella recovered from the C-section. What that help basically amounted to was her bossing Justin around – she was, after all, taking her orders from Marcella. He allowed her to cook and clean with absolutely no hesitation, though, as while she was busily carrying out these tasks she had no choice but to let Justin care for his daughter.

Justin had learned from the midwives how to bathe Lucia so when, on their first night together, Malena tried to insist that she would do it after dinner, he politely and then rather flatly refused her. She came to the bathroom anyway, to supervise and instruct, but Justin calmly pretended she wasn't there. Marcella tried breastfeeding and found it too difficult so he was able to give Lucia her bottles and wrestled her away from Malena any chance he could. He loved this time the most; when Lucia was nestled in the crook of his arm, sucking back like a happy little drunk.

Justin spent a lot of time in his head during the feeds – especially the long evening ones that he drew out as much as he could – letting Lucia sleep in his arms when he should have put her back in her cot. He let Leah into his head, but a lot of the time Tristan came with her; images from that night in particular, when he had watched them through his office window. He assumed that his memory of that night and the arrival of Lucia might have helped reduce his affection for Leah; but the aching was still there, still raw, still dominant, and his love for her was as strong as it always had been.

Marcella was heroically temperamental. She was up and about but annoyed that she couldn't lift or drive, and even more pissed off that there was nothing she was allowed to do to lose the weight she had put on during the pregnancy. She sulked more than Justin had thought she would and took full advantage of her mother's presence, almost reverting to infancy herself. Justin assumed it was the hormones that had taken control of his previously strong, capable wife and that as soon as Malena left she would find her way and take control back. For now, though, there were two women to harass and chastise him the minute he walked in the door: Had he ordered the other baby monitor, the one that would work better than the shitty one he had chosen? When would he pick up the thank-you cards from the print shop? Had he remembered the baby wipes from the supermarket? And would he, just for once, take his shoes off before he made it halfway down the hallway? The two of them seemed to feed off each other – a force to be reckoned with, or not, as he preferred. He pretended to himself that Lucia was on his side while the two of them went off on one together. Justin, and the one Argentinian female who couldn't shout abuse at him, would just slip away together to find a quiet place to cuddle up.

He gently asked Marcella how long her mother might be staying.

'I need her, Justin. It's not about whether you get along with her or not. It's not like you can be here twenty-four hours a day.'

'Of course. I was simply asking out of curiosity. But I can be here quite a lot. One of the joys of owning my own business.'

'My arse you were. It's pretty obvious you've had enough of her. And pretty disappointing that you can't see the bigger picture.'

'I was actually thinking it would be nice for us to be alone with Lucia once in a while, just the three of us.'

'Well, there will be plenty of time for that when she's gone.'

Marcella had spoken as though she was not looking forward to this prospect at all. It was clear that Malena wasn't going to leave anytime soon and even more apparent that he had absolutely no say in the matter. He was an imposter in his own home, it seemed. The useless male who appeared and disappeared as he pleased and who often forgot items at the supermarket. His salvation in all of it, of course, was Lucia. Sweet, innocent Lucia; who always seemed to stop crying and fall into a dreamy, content slumber within minutes of being in Justin's arms. It was as though she'd been waiting for him all day and was relieved when she finally got what she wanted. He loved it. He loved that even Malena, with all her experience and know-how and 'sleeping tiger' technique, could not pacify Lucia the way he could. It made him smug; quietly, triumphantly, joyfully smug.

★

Tristan announced to Leah that he was taking her away with him to Cornwall for a few days to stay with some friends.

'You've finished your exams. You need it, you deserve it, and I just want you to. Come on, what do you say?'

'What about the shop? We can't leave Justin in the lurch?'

'It will be fine if we go early in the week. Andy needs the money, so he won't mind working seven days. He could even get Ella to help for a few extra days.'

'But we can't say we're going together, and it will look suspicious; us both taking time off at the same time.'

'But we could say we are were going as friends. Surely that would be okay. I mean, he knows we get along…'

'I don't know.'

'Just say yes! Come on, we're about to have a really hot spell and, let's face it, those are rare in this country. The house is amazing, right by the sea.'

'Do you think Justin will believe us, though?'

'You worry way too much! He's not your dad, you know! He'll get it. You're young, you need to have fun. He used to have fun, you know, when he was your age. With friends.'

'Okay, it does sound kind of cool.'

★

Leah had taken extra shifts during the day as she was no longer in school. The following Monday when she saw Justin, Tristan had already mentioned the trip to him and been given the all clear for both of them to take the time off. Leah was suspicious; she didn't think Justin would have let something like a holiday in Cornwall slip through, not without a single question. For the first time in weeks she was alone with him; she knew it would come up in conversation the minute the last customer left.

'So, I hear you're going away with Tris.'

'And a big group of his friends. I'm kind of just tagging along. Probably like an annoying younger sister.'

'I doubt Tris sees you as an annoying younger sister.'

She couldn't look him in the eye.

'So, how are you finding being a dad?'

She could see the warm glow all over his face at the mention of Lucia; the look made her wonder if anyone had actually thought to ask him.

'It's far more amazing than I could ever have imagined. She's the sweetest little thing. So tiny, so vulnerable and yet so strong and determined – she knows exactly what she wants. I can't stop cuddling her.'

'Sounds like love. She's one lucky baby to have you for a dad.'

'Thank you. I hope so. Not nearly as lucky as I am, though. It's early days, of course. We still have terrible twos and teenage strops to come. I guess this is the way nature works. We fall in love with them when they are innocent and adorable and desperately needy so we can forgive them when they develop into little monsters.'

'I hope you will bring her in soon. I'd love to meet her, this girl who has stolen your heart.'

'Yeah, I guess she has stolen my heart. It's kind of mind-blowing.' He paused for a moment. 'And it happened at about the same time someone stole yours.'

The blow hit her from out of nowhere.

Leah stared deep into Justin and knew at once that he was referring to Tristan.

'No one has stolen my heart. How could they? You still have it in your hands; you have since the day I met you all those months ago.'

Justin looked away for a moment, to find the words. He was tired and emotional, but this had to come out now.

'No. You never fully let me have it. And why would you? That would have been foolish and dangerous and you are too clever and too strong, so you've preserved it and kept it at a safe distance from me.'

'You don't know, Justin, or you've chosen to forget because it's easier to think of me as not being attached to you. It makes it easier for you to walk away.'

'I wish I could.'

'You wish you could what?' she asked.

'Find it easy to walk away, to un-attach myself from you. But I can't. Even now. I still think about you when I shouldn't. I wonder what's going on in your head, how you are, if the people around you have been kind enough and if they know just how amazing you are and tell you every day the way they should. And I wonder what you would think of certain things I do or say in the day: if it would make you laugh, if you would be moved, if you would still lock on to my words and try to connect with me the way you used to. But you are young, so young. You can't possibly understand the depth of my love for you and how it has affected me and completely, permanently altered me for the better. I have no idea what I mean to you, what you feel for me, but it obviously isn't strong enough to stop you from sleeping with my brother. Whether you meant to or not, Leah, you have completely broken me. No one has ever caused me such pain, ever.'

Justin had not intended to say any of what had so freely come out of his mouth. It was too much. He had offloaded; filled her head with his baggage and tried to shame her – a single, free young woman – for sleeping with Tristan; a single, free man. He was immediately ashamed. He'd said it to hurt her, that much was clear to both of them. Leah was silent; looking to the ground for support, or solace. He could see that she was holding back tears; that her beautiful, deep brown eyes were filled with regret. Before she could speak he grabbed her, pulled her in almost violently to his body.

'God, Leah, I'm so sorry. I didn't mean to say that. That was cruel.'

He held her close, kissed the top of her head over and over.

'It wasn't cruel. I'm cruel. I'm sorry, so deeply sorry about Tristan. How did you know? He promised he wouldn't tell you. It just happened. I think I was lonely. Really lonely. I haven't made any effort with my friends because I couldn't tell them about you, so I've just avoided them. And I couldn't come to you; couldn't be with you. I think I needed to find a way to be happy again. After what happened I felt so small and so low, and I really hated myself. I can't even explain why. It's just light with Tristan, though. It's not like it is with you. We're certainly not in love. And we won't ever be. I really didn't want to hurt you. It hurts me, every day, it hurts to see that you go home to your wife, especially knowing that's the way it will always be.'

'I know, and I'm sorry. Tris didn't tell me, by the way. I just know. I can't believe how much I have messed with your head. You need your friends. You need to be able to talk to them. I'm sorry that I have impacted on your life so negatively and somehow made you and Tris happen, because I couldn't give myself to you and he could. Because I wasn't there for you.'

'Because you're married. Because you have someone to do all of those things with. You don't owe me anything, not even friendship. I can't expect anything from you. But I do love you, Justin. And it does hurt. You can't possibly imagine how much.'

'I don't want you to feel bad about Tris. You're right, I am married and you deserve every happiness. But don't let him hurt you. Don't expect too much from him. He's not someone who stays in one place for very long.'

'I know that. It isn't what you think. It's just a physical thing.'

He could think only of that night he had caught them fucking on his desk.

'I'm not sure that makes me feel particularly better.'

'I'm sorry. I thought it might.'

'Then you can't know how much I have wanted you in that way.'

'You didn't try hard; only that once, when it was too late.'

'Out of respect for you.'

'And your wife.'

'I should be thinking along those lines; but no, it was out of respect for you and your age and your fragility.'

'I've never wanted you to regret me. I don't want you or anyone else to look at me and think that I was the girl who made you unfaithful to your wife.'

'I am responsible for my own actions. I would never look at you in that way.'

'But you might regret me, maybe you do now. At least technically you haven't done anything you might detest me or yourself for later.'

'At least.'

'And it might not have been as wonderful as you had thought it would be.'

Justin laughed out loud at the ridiculousness of this notion. 'No chance.'

Leah smiled.

'I feel like you want to say more,' he said; wanting everything out on the table. It felt like the time for honesty.

'Okay, I think I've also held back because I know I wouldn't be able to walk away; because it would be wonderful and I would want more and you wouldn't be able to give me more, only when it suited you. And I don't want to be a mistress; a sad, lonely, desperate shag waiting at the Holiday Inn.'

He laughed again. 'I would never take you to the Holiday Inn!'

'It's not funny! And yes, that is how I would end up.'

'I wouldn't let it be like that.'

They sat in silence for a while. Justin composed himself, helped Leah wipe her tears away. The openness had become a welcome relief.

'I'm not going to tell Tris that I know, though. I don't think I want this out in the open. The thought of him kissing you any time he likes, in front of me, does actually make me feel physically sick.'

'Okay, fair enough. I wouldn't want that either.'

'And you must go away and have fun. You really have earned it. Besides, I have my little bundle to keep me busy.'

Instead of asking Leah to choose anyone but Tris, which is what he had wanted to say, Justin had backed down and almost given her his approval. The truth was that he found it difficult to be angry with her. He did actually want her to feel light again. If Tris was where she found happiness again after what she had been through, he would simply have to get used to it and stop being such a selfish cock. But it did sicken him; the thought that Leah's lightness had been ignited by Tris's soppy reassurances and stories from the poor villages of Cambodia, and, most repulsive of all, by the slick way he had managed to get her clothes off. He couldn't stomach the thought that she would lie down next to him in a bikini on a beach in Cornwall; that they would swim together as he had done with her; that they might shower together after; then have sex, curl up on the sofa and watch films while he stroked her hair. And, most of all, wake up in the same bed together each day that they were away.

Tris was spoiled and self-centred and would no doubt take all of it for granted. He'd probably even forget to tell her how beautiful she looked. Justin had fantasised about having time with Leah; time to meticulously discover every molecule that made up her being, but four fucking days in a beach house by the water in the summertime. 'Prick' didn't really cut it.

*

The trip was everything Leah needed and more. She'd declined to attend the end of A-levels party with her friends. Vanessa had popped over and tried to drag her out. Ollie had even texted, after making a point of telling her he wouldn't anymore, and had begged her to come – for her own sanity. She just didn't feel she could; she felt she had alienated herself from her friends and no longer deserved them. She wouldn't know how to even talk to them anymore. She needed to get away from anything to do with school, The Potting Shed, from Justin too, although she knew she would feel a pang of sadness the further out of London she got. But it was good for her to try to detach herself from him; she needed to know that she could.

Leah was quiet around Tristan's friends to begin with. They were all several years older than her, but they made her feel comfortable and inflated her ego endlessly by congratulating Tristan for landing someone so young and beautiful. During the day they walked for miles along the rugged coastline. They swam and bodysurfed; sometimes in wetsuits, sometimes in swimming costumes, and once, on the way back from dinner, they swam in their underwear. They ate pasties by the sea, ice creams in the harbour on the walk home, and had dinner in the local pub. She drank more than she ever had, and found it completely uninhibited her. She danced and even sang, well into the night, then stumbled upstairs to the room she shared with Tristan for drunken sex. When she couldn't see Tristan's face she imagined it was Justin between her legs, or entering her from behind. It wasn't something she did intentionally; she'd simply wanted Justin for so long that he appeared in the only way he could, without anyone having to ever know about it.

On the last night, she took a walk on her own. Tristan had asked her again about Cambodia; he would head off in the coming weeks and wanted nothing more than for her to come with him. He asked her what she felt was holding her back as she was not beholden to anyone or anything until uni started in October. She told him nothing was, not really.

She wanted to say yes, but the thought of leaving Justin for that long felt unbearable. Justin wouldn't want her to go; he'd made that clear – despite having filled her head with exciting recollections of his own travels.

Leah made her way down the steep dirt path that led to the sea. She needed to be alone, to think through her decision.

She sat cross-legged on the shoreline and stared into the black water as if waiting for an answer to spill out of the next breaking wave.

She was still but for her breathing. She was naked but for the thin chain around her neck; pulled down long and low, to a point between her breasts by the metal bird. She held the bird in her hand. If only she could live her life as a bird and be able to take flight whenever danger approached.

She licked her lips to taste the salt from the ocean's spray and closed her eyes for a moment. Just listening. Just breathing. Just being.

Her hair had grown wild, thick and free; it swept over the bumps of her spine and tickled her cheeks. She couldn't remember having it cut over the course of the entire year.

Her jeans, T-shirt and underwear sat in a crumpled heap beside her. A skin shed. She felt lighter without the layers, and closer to the elements.

She needed to swim. She remembered Justin talking about swimming without any clothes and wanted to try it, wanted to feel like she was still connected to him.

It was as if the water was egging her on: to be fearless, reckless even. The wind picked up and a wave rose to form an impressive wall before smashing itself onto the beach. The answer had come with it.

Leah picked herself up and ran into the black water as though she were being chased. What was going to catch her? The night? A change of heart? She laughed and squealed as a mess of seaweed clutched at her ankles, the exhilaration of the bitter cold washing away her pensive mood.

She had painstakingly perfected her dive over the years; she remembered begging her mother to judge her in their villas and hotel swimming pools during their summer holidays abroad. Each time she came up for air she would anticipate her score.

Leah used breaststroke to take her further out. As her legs opened and closed she felt the freeness of the sea being allowed between her legs, without the usual barrier of her bikini bottoms. If it weren't for her skin she could disperse her liquid self into the sea; every cell separated, unable to reunite. It might be easier to be that way, to be in parts, to live some of your life in one stretch of sea and the rest somewhere else.

She rolled onto her back, enjoying the torture of the cold, splayed her arms and circled them to keep herself afloat. Leah spoke out loud so she could hear herself and believe herself as she said it: 'I have to go.' She would book her ticket to Cambodia the minute she returned home.

*

The moment he waved Malena off at the airport, Justin felt slightly less relieved than he thought he would. It occurred to him, quite by surprise, that he and Marcella would now be left alone; to manage alone, to get along, to bring up Lucia and try to rekindle their affection for each other. He had put the silences and new levels of outward hostility between them down to Malena's presence, Marcella's surgery and endless sleepless nights. However, now that they had become fully functioning zombies, the wound was as good as healed and Malena was on a plane home. He began to wonder what they might be left with as a couple. He felt a tightness in his chest and a twisted knot in the pit of his gut; he was actually anxious about going home to Marcella.

Justin didn't have the energy to confront her about it, but his patience for Marcella's mood swings was wearing increasingly thin. He was tired too; he was still trying to run the business, pay the bills, do the shopping and spend time as much time with Lucia as he possibly could. And he had done this while Marcella had rested, while she watched as her mother cooked and ironed and hoovered and folded up the washing.

Justin arrived home to the sound of Lucia crying; she was in her Moses basket. He lifted her up and rested her against his chest; she was warm and smelt of baby shampoo – Malena had insisted on bathing her before she left. 'It's the least I can do,' she had said. He sat on the edge of the bed and rested his hand on Marcella's hip. She was all curled up in a foetal position; he felt her body judder and realised she was crying.

'Hey, what's up?'

'I'm going to miss my mum,' she sobbed.

'I know,' he told her. 'But she'll be back. She mentioned coming in September. That's not that far away.' It felt like he was comforting a child.

'It feels like an eternity. She should be here. Or I should be there. Now that I have a baby.'

'We will manage, you'll see. Now that you're healed you'll be able to do more and more.'

'I'm not talking about changing nappies; I'm talking about emotional support.'

He'd never thought of Malena as being particularly emotionally supportive – brisk and bossy, yes, but warm and empathetic – he had never witnessed those qualities in her. Not once.

'Well, isn't that what I'm here for? I am your husband.'

'It's not the same; women need their mothers when they have children. They just do.'

It was, of course, possible that Marcella wasn't looking forward to their time alone either. Lucia began to squirm and let out an enormous puff of wind, followed by something far more substantial.

'I'll go and change her.'

He didn't want to get into an argument, simply couldn't face it.

*

Leah reappeared at work looking sun-kissed, windswept and relaxed. She had even managed to put on a little weight, not much, just enough to cover her bones, but it suited her, she looked healthier for it. There was a freeness to her that Justin hadn't seen before, too. Perhaps it was the simple fact that girls grew into women at some point and this was that moment. Originally it was her vulnerability and youthfulness that had drawn him to her. Now it was something else; something that was still evolving, still blossoming.

Justin had heard about the trip via Tris; although thankfully no details of their fucking in the sand dunes were revealed. He was still jealous, wounded and resentful and took to denigrating Tris any chance he could. Of course, Leah refused to rise to any of it.

'Did he mention that as kids I once had to rescue him from the sea? He's an appalling swimmer.'

'He didn't actually, but he seemed to keep afloat in Cornwall.'

'He crashed our dad's car once. He'd barely gotten his licence and rolled it. He was caning it on an open road.'

'I think he's a better driver now. We made it there and back alive.'

★

One Sunday afternoon Justin ducked out at lunchtime and returned, much to everyone's delight, with Lucia. He'd tucked her into a body sling and waltzed in behind a customer. Leah did a double take. It was the first time she'd seen him as a father and she almost didn't recognise him. It was beautiful, though, Lucia's plump cheek against his chest as she slept. Ella rushed over, trying unsuccessfully to restrain herself when she saw that Lucia was sound asleep; she reached in and stroked the top of her head before scurrying back to the flower workshop to help a customer.

It was Leah's turn. She bent down to take a closer look. She could see both of them in her even though she was still so tiny; she had Marcella's olive skin and dark hair, but

Justin's features. A chubby little arm hung out the side of the sling; Leah felt herself reach out to hold it.

'She really is special. So perfect in every possible way.'

'Thank you.'

Justin stayed for some time with Lucia tucked up contentedly in her sling; he wandered around with Andy, who took notes on what needed to be done; the plants that needed shifting and the stock that needed re-ordering. When Lucia woke, Leah watched as Justin expertly whipped her out of the sling and took her off to change and feed her. He came back out with Lucia wide awake in his arms. She really was a beautiful baby.

'Would you mind? I really need the loo!' Justin asked, handing her the baby.

'Of course not. I'd love to hold her.'

Leah took the tiny parcel in her arms.

Justin looked at them. 'You're a natural.'

'Hardly.'

Leah took Lucia over to a bench in the shade and sat down with her. She seemed so small and precious; she didn't want to risk stumbling with her. Once Leah was used to how delicate Lucia felt she let herself sit back and within seconds a complete sense of calm came over her. She used her free hand to stroke Lucia's fine dark hair and ran her finger down her miniscule button nose. She couldn't have imagined a more perfect little being. Lucia looked up at her with an expression of curiosity; not quite acceptance but not disapproval either.

Justin returned and sat down with her on the bench.

'Would you like me to take her from you?'

'No rush,' she replied. 'She's lovely and holding her is so calming.'

'I know. I do it for hours. I literally sit with her in my arms and stare at her all night. Lucky she isn't self-conscious; it would be quite disconcerting if adults stared at each other the way we do at babies.'

Leah thought about how much she and Justin had stared at each other; about how she had examined Justin's features in detail and never tired of them. She remembered being in the car with him and staring at him while he drove them back from Eastbourne. He had stared at her in the same way, from the moment she had met him. She had felt naked and exposed but had loved every minute of it. The day he stopped looking at her in that way she would feel bereft.

Tristan came over and asked for Justin's help with something.

'You okay for another minute.'

'Of course.'

Justin left her to it. Lucia grew slightly restless in her arms after a time so Leah stood up and took a little walk around the garden centre. Within a few minutes Lucia's eyelids grew heavy and she closed them, drifting off to somewhere peaceful.

★

The following week Leah broke the news to Justin that she was going to Cambodia with Tristan for the rest of the summer. She watched as his shoulders fell; it was another blow, but he seemed unsurprised by it.

'I guess working here has paid for your ticket…'

'Yes, it has.'

'Whatever you do, don't thank me for that…'

'Okay. I won't. I'm sorry.'

'I'm joking. You've nothing to be sorry for, this is your life; you have to start living it at some point. I knew it was coming; I just hoped it would be slightly further down the track.'

★

Justin frequently returned home to find Marcella lying in bed with Lucia gurgling in the cot next to her. She got up immediately to tell him how glad she was that he was home so that he could take over. She then rushed around cleaning and doing washing, preparing dinner and working out.

'You can do some of these things with Lucia, Cel. You could maybe join one of those mum and baby bootcamps in the park. And you could pop her on the mat on the floor with that thing with all the dangly toys so you can get stuff done around the house; she'll be okay.'

'Very funny, Justin. I am NOT one of those wanky women in the park doing sit-ups with a baby in their arms. Seriously, I can't believe you would even suggest it. And I do put her on the mat; but she doesn't last long and then she wants to be picked up, or fed, or changed.'

'I don't think those women look wanky! I think it would be a good way to make friends with other mums while doing something for yourself; something you enjoy.'

'You do it, then. You'd fit right in. It's so not me.'

'Okay, it was just a suggestion. Do you want to tell me what's really going on? You seem really hostile.'

'I'm not. I'm just tired and you don't seem to understand what it's like to look after her all day.' Marcella looked on the verge of tears.

'I think I do actually – I'm doing the night feeds too, and I've tried to be around a lot, to help. I'm in and out of work like a yo-yo. I know it's hard work, but we are not the first parents to have to go through it.'

'You really have no idea, Justin. You swan about pruning roses all day... No one is making any demands of you, not really.'

'Okay, that's a little unfair.'

'I'm sorry. I can't help it. I'm just not myself. I don't even know who I am anymore. I can't stand to look at myself in the mirror because I'm so fat, the house is a pigsty and all I want to do is sleep.'

He gave her a hug and let her soak his chest with her frustrated, angry tears.

After a time she came up for air. 'I think it would be good for me to go back to work part time,' she declared.

'What? Already? You just said you're exhausted! How's that going to help?'

'Soon, yes. And it will help, because it will break the routine. And I can't just give up work altogether, it will be too difficult to get back into it.'

Justin had never thought of accountancy as the kind of career where at some point you were at your peak and couldn't stop for fear of falling back down the ladder. He had always seen it as a steady career. Number crunching was number crunching, whichever millennia you did it in, wasn't it?

'But you're entitled to paid maternity leave.'

'I've had enough maternity leave already. I'm going mad. You try sitting around the house all day folding clothes and making bottles; you'd be bored out of your mind.'

He wanted to point out that Lucia was barely two months old and that although these were clearly menial tasks, the joy of looking after their daughter surely outweighed them. He didn't, of course. She would have accused him of suggesting she didn't want to be with their baby. She may have even punched him in the face in her current hysterical state.

'I've already contacted work and they'd be happy to have me return part time, just for a few hours in the morning. That way I get the best of both worlds. I would enjoy Lucia even more in the afternoons because I would have had a little break. We could get an au pair to cover the time that I'm at work.'

Justin put his foot down. 'No, we are absolutely not having some non-English speaking teenager – and a complete stranger, I might add – looking after Lucia. If anything, Lucia can come to work with me in the mornings.'

'While she is small that might be possible, but you can't take her into work once she starts sleeping less and moving around. And that's a pretty snappy assumption; that all au pairs are young and stupid.'

'Let's worry about what happens when she's more mobile when the time comes. I'm not prepared to leave her in the care of a stranger, not yet. No way.'

In all of the chaos of Lucia's arrival, and the excitement and exhaustion that came with it, it had not occurred to him for even a single moment that Marcella might want to go back to work so soon. He could see that she loved Lucia; she cared for her with great affection and was forever taking pictures of her on her phone to share with friends on Instagram. They'd had a steady stream of visitors and Marcella had shown Lucia off with enormous pride. But her moods were erratic; they changed with the hour and he never quite knew which version of Marcella he was coming home to. Sometimes tears, frequently some form of verbal abuse, and often a deep melancholia that he put down to tiredness. He knew that he was more than obligated to love her now, now that things were challenging, now that they had brought another person into the world. He wanted to support her emotionally, to sit down and comfort her in some way. But he had come to find her repellent. The shifts in mood were becoming more and more intolerable, especially since he was in an equally exhausted state. He simply had no energy for it, and almost no will to try.

It hadn't escaped his thoughts that by spending so much energy on Leah, Justin had put his wife's needs to one side and allowed their marriage to quietly come undone. He couldn't remember the last time he and Marcella had been out for dinner together, just the two of them, even before Lucia, when they actually did have all the time in the world but had taken it for granted. Aside from practical support he hadn't done anything remotely spontaneous or romantic and they hadn't been intimate for months. Marcella had done nothing for him either, of course. She'd made no attempt to remind him that she loved or appreciated him. He wasn't even sure what he meant to her. Was he just there to run errands? Act as a punching bag? Cover the bills?

★

On her last day at work, Leah made sure she found a moment to be alone with Justin. She found him in the greenhouse. He hadn't been cool with her, but seemed guarded. It made sense, and she wouldn't ask him to be any other way; she too had prepared herself for their time apart and had even worked through what the time away would most likely do to them. Her feelings for him would always remain, but the intensity of her love for him couldn't continue to be the thing that defined her. She had been foolish to allow herself to run with the fantasy in the first place; it had been beautifully painful to be in love with Justin.

What she needed now was to be released from his hold on her. He would let her go, of course, he hadn't given her wings only to clip them, and he was now quite firmly settled into his life as a family man. Still, she needed a shove; a word, approval of some kind. She wasn't entirely sure she could make the leap of her own free will; even with the ticket already purchased and her case half packed.

'Can I talk to you for a minute? Everyone else is gone.'

He smiled.

'I just wanted to say thank you...'

'Thank you? What for?'

'For being the person that you are: for talking, for listening, for being patient and generous. And for trusting me. I've known you for almost a year now. Can you believe that? I feel so changed for it... inspired, valued... and cared for. And I've never met anyone I admire more. Or that I wanted to spend more of my time thinking about, however wrong that may be. And although it has broken me at times, I think it has made me too.'

She wanted to get it out – all of the things she'd planned on saying the night before as she lay awake, restlessly turning it over and over – but it was hard, even harder than she thought it was going to be.

Justin listened intently as Leah struggled to get the words out without breaking down. She paused and bit her lip, looked down, took a deep breath. He remembered how few words she had spoken in the beginning and how he had to gently encourage her to come out of herself more. He had longed to know every thought in her head. It was usually he that broke down and made himself vulnerable. He didn't think he deserved to be thanked, though, and she was throwing far too many accolades at him, considering he never should have allowed their connection to ripen as it had.

'You have nothing to thank me for. I adore every minute I spend with you. No one has ever made me feel completely alive the way you do. I should be thanking you. I don't think you will ever fully understand what you mean to me or what you've changed in me, and I do mean that in a positive way. I know I've been telling you how much I don't want you to go, but I do really. I am actually proud of you for doing this. Pride is not the right word, of course. Excited for you, a little jealous and full of admiration. You must go and have your adventures and swim in other waters…'

There was so much more he wanted to say but he restrained himself. It no longer felt appropriate to talk about possibility and the future; it would only confuse both of them. She deserved her freedom and his blessing.

'I'm not sure who I am without you now. But I know

that one day I will be a better me because of knowing you, because of the talks we've had,' she half sobbed.

He had to pull her in and comfort her.

'It's okay. It isn't goodbye forever,' he reassured her, and himself, as he kissed the top of her head.

'I know it's not forever, not in the literal sense. But everything is shifting. I miss you already. I miss what we were and what we weren't.'

'I know. Me too. But we both know we need something to change; it is too much for both of us at times. But I'm still here. I'm still me. I'm not going anywhere.'

Leah cried into Justin's chest; inhaled his scent with deep, almost panicked breaths. She clung to his body, missing him before she had even taken a step away from him. For a moment she wondered if she should go at all, if she should perhaps cancel the trip and just stay and work until uni started. But there was another voice in her head; a voice telling her that things must continue to evolve into something more acceptable and more tolerable, and going to Cambodia was right – it really was. This was the road to recovery. She would grow so much as a person and she would come to accept that things had happened in the way they had for a reason.

So why was letting go of Justin, turning and leaving, the hardest thing she had ever done?

'Wait, I have something for you,' Justin blurted out.

'What is it?'

'It's just a little gift. It might seem a bit strange, so, when I give it to you, you must promise not to open it until you are away. Far away. Promise?'

'Okay, I promise.'

She followed Justin back to his office and took the small packet he produced from him. It felt like a thin book.

'Thank you.'

She went through her satchel until she found his gift. She'd forgotten to wrap it: *The Collector*.

He smiled and kissed her forehead one more time.

'Perfect.'

'Bye,' she said as cheerily as she could.

'Bye, my girl,' he said, trying to match her tone.

The terrible emptiness that followed her departure would stay with Justin until Leah returned. Justin knew this the moment she left The Potting Shed and the familiar aching that had started when he first met Leah, once again worked its way around his body.

It was worse for him, to be the one that remained. Leah wouldn't have the familiar corners of The Potting Shed to maintain her agony the way he did: his office, the greenhouse, the benches outside, all the places she should be, all the places they had sat or stood in together. She would be somewhere new and exciting, with her lover, with no trace of him apart from whatever was left in her head. He hoped it was enough for her to remember him fondly by and that she would come back to see him the minute she returned. It was possible, of course, that she might look at him very differently after her time away; like a man she once knew but no longer loved. He would have to brace himself for that possibility.

Justin could see no way of atoning for what had happened between them. He was just weak, without morals or loyalty. There was no cure for his addiction to Leah, he knew that already: not her absence, not a baby, his wife's unhappiness, remorse, guilt, regret, cruelty or even shame. There was nowhere to hide from her, no way of blocking her out or cleansing himself of her. Leah was still everywhere and yet she was nowhere. It was almost as if she had died and he was left to grieve while she got on with her wonderful afterlife.

PART EIGHT

Despite the long flight, Tristan came to life the minute they landed in Phnom Penh and Leah felt at once that this was home to him. He called over a tuk-tuk and they climbed in with their bags. He told Leah to keep an eye on everything as he secured the bigger bags. It took only a few minutes in the damp heat before her clothing was drenched with sweat.

The drive through the city was mind-blowing. The chaos of the traffic and the way everyone negotiated their way through the melee with horns and gestures, despite an alarming lack of traffic lights, was nothing short of a miracle. Leah was shocked to see entire families piled on to a single motorbike, barely a helmet in sight, food and bags balanced precariously between children.

The architecture was an extraordinary miss-match of old and new – a combination of French colonial, functional and extravagance – the result of historical conflict and recovery and the stark distinction between wealth and struggle. The traditional Cambodian curved peaking roofs and the intricate details of the monks' pagodas, with their gilt-coloured spires and their giant Buddha's and shrines, were simply breath-taking.

It felt nothing short of magical to be in Phnom Penh – a city so unlike anywhere Leah had ever been. She caught a quick glimpse of the Mekong River as the sun set; several boats were lined up on its shores and she could make out the shapes of their captains snoozing on deck.

A few miles out of the centre of the city and everything seemed to quite suddenly deteriorate. It was as though they were in a completely different world.

'This is where the poverty has been moved to,' Tristan told her. 'They want PP to look clean and modern, but you don't have to go far to find this.'

The stench hit her then. The smell of exposed, makeshift sewage systems. The smell of too many people living in cramped spaces; all sweating and cooking and finding a way of surviving.

They paid the driver and pulled their luggage out into the dusty, rubbish-filled street. The housing here was cobbled together from sheets of tin and wood and plastic sheeting. Families sat on wooden tables – the only furniture everyone seemed to possess – next to sleeping babies, restless toddlers and resting elderly. She felt their eyes on her, all of them, as she trundled past; trying not to look anxious with her bag full of stuff, her unstained clothing and new footwear. She was the alien in an alien place. They seemed friendly, though, and were more than happy to see Tristan return.

Tristan clapped his hands together as if in prayer and lowered his chin to his chest. Their welcome party all did the same while keeping their hands together. He spoke in a combination of English and Khmer and introduced Leah to a number of people whose names she couldn't pronounce let alone remember.

They finally approached the schoolhouse; a functional concrete structure with bars and shutters on the windows but no glass.

'This is it!' Tristan called out, looking back to see what Leah made of it.

Leah peered in the windows; it was empty of children, but full of wooden tables and chairs that had been painted pink and yellow. Posters covered the walls with letters and numbers – all in English – and pictures of transport and animals. A young Cambodian woman appeared and sang out to Tristan, greeting him warmly as she put her hands together in welcome.

'I cleaned all your sheets and room for you, Mr Tris.'

Her English was excellent. Tristan introduced her as Srey Pov, the finest maths teacher in Cambodia. She blushed and shook her head, then opened the door to their room and said she would see them both in the morning. She didn't seem surprised that Tristan had appeared with Leah and didn't ask whether they would be sharing.

The room was a decent size with a kitchenette in one corner, a small wooden table with two chairs, a large wooden bed with mosquito netting and fresh linen. A door at the back led to a small bathroom and little courtyard with a water tank.

Leah suddenly felt exhausted. Sweat dripped from her hairline and her clothes were soaked through.

'So, what do you think?'

'I'm absolutely overwhelmed! But really excited and happy. Everyone seems so lovely. I'm just shattered.'

'Me too. You will love it, though. And there's so much to see: the temples, boat rides, the provinces, silk island…'

'I can't wait. Really. Thank you for inviting me.'

'No, thank you. And the best is yet to come; the kids are going to adore you. You take the first shower and I'll grab us some food. We'll be straight into it tomorrow, at the crack of dawn. There'll be kids banging down the door, wanting their first lesson, just you wait!'

Tristan disappeared and Leah was left to compose herself. She suddenly felt a million miles away from anything familiar and comforting, quite alone and completely daunted at the prospect of having to teach. Did she know Tristan well enough to be here with him? What if they fell out? What if he turned out to be a bastard? As she washed the dirt and sweat away in the shower, she couldn't help but cry. She'd done this to get over Justin, to spread her wings and become the woman he thought her capable of becoming. She'd talked herself into it, knowing she would always regret not taking Tristan up on this opportunity of a lifetime. But she wept: like a child, like an idiot, like a spoilt, pampered first world princess, like someone who was afraid of everything. She tried to put it down to jetlag and tiredness. A little fear was natural, wasn't it?

After her shower Leah dug out her phone and texted her mother to tell her she had arrived, and that it was simply amazing. She had no idea what the time was in the UK but her mother replied within minutes, told her to be careful and just enjoy every minute of it. She hadn't expected her to be so positive; it was encouraging. She took out the gift from Justin she had tucked underneath her clothes and opened it. *The Velveteen Rabbit* by Margery Williams. She remembered it from her childhood, remembered the sentiment behind it. She couldn't read it now, couldn't bring herself to, but she liked knowing it was there, liked knowing that Justin had chosen it for her. She had a little piece of him with her. She found her way under the netting and between the cool sheets and fell into a restless, tearful sleep.

★

Justin found solace in the one thing that was capable of giving him pure, uncomplicated joy: Lucia. Not even The Potting Shed gave him the slightest bit of pleasure anymore, not without Leah. Lucia was always happy to see him. He took her into work each morning and returned her to Marcella after lunch. He carried her around in a sling until she grew restless, then popped her on a mat on the floor of his office where she could stretch out. She took naps in her buggy, which he wheeled to the different areas of the shop where he was working. She grew more expressive, animated and demanding each day. Ella took hold of her a few times but Lucia wasn't fond of her. Andy, with his casual charm and confidence, always managed to get her to stop crying by pulling daft faces.

The kid Justin had hired in Leah's place was pleasant enough, but Justin almost resented his existence – simply because of who he wasn't.

Marcella seemed more content when he dropped Lucia off, but by the time he returned in the early evening she was tired and fractious and usually took to bed the minute they had eaten. He'd attempted to take some time off when he could; suggested they go out for lunch or dinner, or to the cinema. Marcella always had a reason not to go; she was too tired or disapproved of the time, the day, the place. They were becoming strangers who lived completely separate, parallel lives; passing a baby to each other in the hallway with little acknowledgement of each other. Justin needed to say something; he felt he owed it to Lucia to at least try to regain something of what her parents had once been, and what they should be, for her.

'Cel, we really need to talk.'

'Not now, I am absolutely exhausted.'

'Yes, now. It has to be now. You will still be exhausted tomorrow, as will I, and next week and the days and weeks and months after that and by then you and I might not even know each other anymore.'

'I don't even know what you're talking about.'

He was perplexed that she could possibly think they had nothing to talk about.

'I think I need to know if you still love me.'

She guffawed at him, as though he'd said it as a joke.

'Marcella, please, I need you to tell me.'

'Um, let me think. We are married. We've been together since university. We have a child together. I'm pretty sure that constitutes love.'

'No, that is our situation, it is not the same as loving someone.'

'Okay, then. Yes, I still love you. I can't believe you feel you have to ask me that.'

'Okay, you say that. But you don't have a kind word to say to me, you don't want to go out anywhere with me, you don't think of me in the day unless you need something from the supermarket. You don't even touch me anymore. So, yes, I am questioning whether you still love me.'

'I could ask you the same question. You're not exactly giving me much either, Justin. I don't see you appreciating anything I do or showing any affection towards me.'

Justin hadn't tried to be intimate with Marcella for several months before Lucia was born. Marcella hadn't mentioned it and she didn't seem bothered about re-establishing their connection.

'Maybe I haven't. Perhaps it's because every time I try to make time for us, you refuse me. And you practically recoil when I touch you. I'm asking if you still love me because there is nothing about us at the moment that proves we are in love. I know you can feel it too. You just don't seem to want to address it. At all.'

She began to cry, as she so frequently did. Her face didn't soften, though. She just looked more hostile, and nothing about her made him want to comfort her.

'Please, talk to me, Cel. Something is not working. We have the most beautiful little girl in there, we have our own home and great friends, what more could we possibly want? And yet we are both completely miserable, stumbling around not knowing what to say to each other anymore. How do two people who have known each other as long as we have forget how to be nice to one another? You seem utterly depressed and I need to know if it's because of me.'

'I don't know,' she sobbed.

'You don't know if it's because of me, or you don't know if you love me anymore?'

'No, I don't know why I am so unhappy. I don't know why none of this is making me happy. I can't feel anything anymore. I feel like someone who has woken up in hospital after an accident and the doctor is standing there touching my leg, asking me if I can feel it. He touches again and again in different places, and each time I tell him desperately that I can't feel anything at all. Nothing. I'm just numb.'

'Is it me? Do you not feel anything from me, or do you not feel anything for me?'

'Sometimes... Yes... I don't know.'

'Which? Both?'

'Both. Yes, both... I think... I told you, I'm just numb.'

She was almost incomprehensible. Justin couldn't believe that she was unable to pinpoint the origin of her misery; Marcella had always been able to articulate her feelings, loud and clear. If he was as depressed as she obviously was he would know the cause. He may not want to verbalise it, but he would know. As it was, he knew perfectly well the cause of all of his unhappiness.

'What can I do differently? To make this work? We have a baby together. I'm not ready to throw the towel in on this. Are you?' he asked.

'No, of course not. I don't want to lose you. I love you. I love our little family. I just don't know who I am anymore.'

'Do you think maybe you could try a little more? Maybe go out somewhere with me? Try to not bottle things up? Stop shutting me out?'

She shrugged and sniffed.

'Maybe it's just that you've had a baby and that, in itself, is taking some getting used to?'

'How can you say that? What do you even mean? Other women seem to manage. Do you think I wish we hadn't had Lucia?'

'God no, but is it possible that you could be suffering from some sort of post-natal depression?'

'That is a repulsive thing to say! You're practically telling me that Lucia has made me depressed, that I don't love our child!'

She was hysterical again. It was like diffusing an unexploded bomb; one dodgy move and the whole thing was blowing up in his face.

'There are millions of mothers out there who struggle emotionally after giving birth. It does not mean that they don't love their babies; the transition just hits some women harder than others.'

'Oh really, Justin, is that right? You are such an amazing amateur psychiatrist. Transition. For fuck's sake. Where did you learn that one? Why don't you just say it? I'm a complete and utter failure; chronically depressed and unable to look after our child. That's it, isn't it? I can't even look after our baby. It's no wonder that you've fallen out of love with me. Christ, there are women out there with full-time jobs and four children and I can't even look after one. That's what you think of me, isn't it?'

'That isn't what I think of you. Stop telling me what I think. You're an amazing mother.'

'I'm not. I'm so not, Justin.'

Marcella began to weep.

'This is just not me.'

'I know. I know it's not. We will get through this. You could see someone.'

'No! I don't need a therapist. I'm not fucking crazy. And I'm not suffering from post-natal depression. I wanted this baby more than anything in the world.'

He wasn't sure why, but any mention of a possible solution seemed to completely set her off.

'Okay, okay, of course you're not. I know you wanted Lucia, we both did. But if this is going to work, and if we are going to work as a family, you are going to have to try. Will you?'

She nodded and let him hold her for a moment.

'Sure.'

Although he wasn't sure if she'd said it because she believed it or because she needed to end the conversation. She left the room to blow her nose and Justin heard her draw a bath. Marcella either needed to accept help or just decide to enjoy life again; it was as simple as that in Justin's mind. He knew Marcella well enough to know that he could not persuade her to see a therapist if she refused one, and he could see that she could quite easily go even further downhill. He also knew that the fact that it was out there now, the possibility that she was depressed, might just be enough to trigger a recovery. What he wasn't certain of was what there would be left of them at the end of it.

Justin went to the bedroom where Lucia was sleeping soundly; oblivious to how badly her parents were screwing themselves and each other up. He lay down on the bed next to her and listened for the little noises she made. Leah came to him then, in her ethereal form, with her gentle, unspoken admiration for him; something Marcella had lost or perhaps never had. He could almost feel her fingers on his arm and the back of his neck. The way she and Marcella loved him were so completely different; he shouldn't compare, it was pointless and unfair, but it was when he needed Leah's gentleness that he couldn't help but notice that Marcella had none. He texted Leah a brief message; asking if she was okay and telling her that she was missed.

★

Leah woke to an unfamiliar room, drenched in sweat, surrounded by netting and mosquitos. She disentangled herself from Tristan's naked body, his heavy, wet limbs, and wrestled with the netting. She was so dehydrated from the flight and the heat that she almost blacked out as she crossed the room to find some water. The shower gave her some relief as she once again rinsed off her sticky skin. She could hear banging on the door and window as she made her way back into the bedroom, followed by lots of giggling.

'Mr Tris! Mr Tris!' tiny voices sang out, as heads bobbed up and down to see into their window.

Tristan jumped out of bed and surprised them; the children screamed and jumped for joy. 'I'll see you soon. Too early, too early!' Tris told them as they scurried off.

Class began at half seven and the school day finished at two. Leah was amazed by how many children fitted themselves into the classroom – each and every age, from four to twelve – all squashed in and listening with interest. There were varying degrees of preparation: some with their own pencil and meticulously cared for notebooks, others arrived empty handed and used loose sheets of paper from the store cupboard. All wore the uniform – a royal blue skirt or shorts and a white shirt – but hardly any of the clothes fitted well, being either too small or oversized.

Each of the children introduced themselves to Leah in English, one after the other, and offered their age and favourite food. They all chose meat – preferably fried (chicken, pork, beef, fish heads or prawns) – served with lots of rice. Tristan told her later that meat was a luxury, something they all dreamed about. Together they then stood and sang the English songs that they had been taught by various volunteers from Australia, Europe, America and the UK. They sang every song with equal gusto; their high voices filling the classroom. At the end they awaited applause and further instruction from Tristan.

'Tomorrow we can show her the Khmer dancing you've been learning.'

The girls became shy and shook their heads.

'Not ready!'

'Not good yet!'

'Soon, soon you will be ready. We can teach Leah the dances too!'

They all cheered and laughed.

★

As Leah settled into her new routine, she began to come out of herself. There really was no need to be self-conscious or embarrassed about her abilities as an English teacher; she could do no wrong here. The children didn't know she had no idea how to plan a lesson. They just wanted to learn. They asked her endless questions about herself: her home, her family, London, if she had pets, drove a car, owned a television, if she was going to marry Tristan. They plaited her hair and admired her clothes and shoes and bracelets. They told her she was very healthy and strong. Compared to them she felt like a fat, white giant. When they saw her in the street they would shout out and run up to say hello and show off. And there was always a tiny hand slotted into hers as she walked around the small school.

The children really were the best tonic, the best distraction she could have hoped for. They had so little in life but whatever they did have – some biscuits or sweets she and Tristan brought in, an old toy someone had found in the dump, a game of football at lunchtime or five minutes playing a game on her phone – they were happy. It was difficult not to compare them to the overindulged children in the UK, who never seemed to stop wanting more stuff. Tristan reminded her that it was easy to become self-righteous and rant about the unjust balance of the world, but in the end everything was relative. All they could do was make their contribution, however small.

Leah napped briefly most afternoons, after class, when the humidity had really wiped her out. She and Tristan would shower and set off for food, frequently meeting up with Tristan's various friends and acquaintances. Despite the heat they had sex every day, almost without fail, even when they were exhausted and covered in sweat. To begin with Leah insisted on showering first, but after a while she gave in and let him enter her as she was. They'd barely be back in the room before he'd start unwrapping her as though she was his reward for making it to the end of the day. Most nights they struggled to sleep at all in the heat with the click-clicking of the fan hanging on its loose cord above them. Tristan would pull her into his body and tease her with his fingers until she was unable to resist.

They spent a weekend in Sihanoukville, another in Siem Reap and several evenings on boats on the river with Tristan's friends. They also visited Tuol Sleng, the school that had served as a torture and execution compound when the country had been ruled by the Khmer Rouge, and the evocative mass graves of the Killing Fields. In the afternoons they visited orphanages, a hospital and a number of initiatives in the slum areas. Extreme poverty and poor education had been passed down like unlucky genes through the generations. And both invariably led to many other problems: bad hygiene and poor health, HIV transmission, drinking and domestic violence. Learning English opened a potential route to employment in the tourist industry and was therefore one of the best chances the children in the slum areas had.

Being so close to such desperate poverty produced emotions in Leah that she had never experienced before. Some visits fired her up to somehow make a positive impact; the volunteers she met at the NGOs they visited, the spirit of the Cambodians themselves – to choose life, to work hard, to help their fellow people – inspired her. But other visits made her cry quietly to herself in the tuk-tuk home; some problems would take years to resolve, some children would always go without, and some cycles would take decades to break.

There was always a quiet moment in the day when Leah was on her own and she allowed herself to think of Justin. She missed their emotional connection; there were so many times she wanted nothing more than to reflect on everything with him, talk it out, and feel the comfort of his arms around her.

Tristan was there, of course, but she found him to be quite detached, which possibly came from years of living in similarly impoverished areas. He just seemed to fit in; didn't see what she saw or perhaps just didn't see it in the same way. He didn't find it desperate or uncomfortable, and he didn't feel like a voyeur. Nor did he seem to notice how much all of it affected Leah. It was probably a good thing – she hadn't come to Cambodia to feel sorry for herself because she had to witness other people's suffering – she had come here to find strength, to learn, to give and to engage.

She and Justin texted every other day, but it was difficult to gauge how he was getting on without her in his life. She couldn't be sure that he missed and needed her as much as she missed and needed him. Without being in his presence, without actual words spoken out loud, she couldn't be certain. It was possible, of course, that he had let her gently slip away from his every day consciousness, or even made a concerted effort to banish her from his thoughts, and was simply responding to her texts out of common courtesy or fear that by not responding she might retaliate somehow. She hoped the thought would never cross his mind but it was impossible to be sure; he had so much more to lose than she did.

They exchanged messages about work, Lucia, the volunteering programme, other projects and people she had met, and how busy and shattered they both were. It sufficed, it was something, and she had no right to ask for more.

Leah and Tristan were around each other day and night. Considering how little they really knew each other, and how unused to sharing space with someone they both were, it could have been a recipe for disaster; but everything pretty much revolved around sex. They had sex when they drank too much, or when they were too hot and couldn't sleep, they had it when they ran out of things to talk about, or couldn't be bothered to talk at all. Sex just seemed to be the most effective way to resolve everything; no heavy feelings were delved into, no deep conversations begun. Leah wondered, though, if she had somehow become addicted to it in the way that people became addicted to drugs or smoking or alcohol. She had used it to replace the self-harm and regain control of her body and was now using it to keep her time with Tristan on an even keel.

*

After a few weeks, Tristan arranged for Leah to spend a couple of weeks in an orphanage out in the provinces. It came up one night when they were out and she had jumped on it immediately. She wasn't sure if it was because she subconsciously wanted some time out from being with Tristan or just needed to experience something on her own. Before she knew it she would be on the plane home again; she had to make the most of her time and really push herself. Leah wasn't sure what she felt for Tristan. It wasn't love; he was just always there, always taking her clothes off any chance he could. They hadn't talked about what would happen when she went back to the UK and she felt no need to bring it up.

*

Justin tried to keep himself from contacting Leah too much, but as the days turned into weeks he became increasingly frustrated. He knew he should just allow her to get on with her life and let her be, but he wanted her to know he was still there if she wanted him to be; without proper contact he couldn't be sure she didn't need him in some way. The text messages were perfunctory; they provided a temporary, tenuous link, but were in no way comforting or reassuring. He needed to see her and hear her voice. He wondered if he should try to arrange a chat over Skype or Facetime. Just a phone call would have placated him.

Things were not improving with Marcella, despite the distance Leah had put between them, despite their shared love of Lucia and the conversations they'd had about trying to make it work. Justin wondered what he had left to give; anything that might have been good or positive was overshadowed by their exhaustion and precarious mental states. He wondered how he had managed to let Lucia down, right from the beginning of her life. He tried to make up for it by spending all of his remaining energy on her; smothering her in love.

As a final attempt he recruited Marcella's closest friend, Anna, to come and look after Lucia one evening.

'I can't believe you would go and organise something like this behind my back. I am so embarrassed.'

'Embarrassed about what?'

'That Anna has come all the way over here to babysit!'

'Are you kidding? Anna was over the moon. She said she was desperate to be asked. I would have asked my mum but she's away.'

'Justin, Anna would have felt obliged to say yes. That's not the same as wanting to.'

'She didn't. Stop looking for the negative in everything. She just really wanted to come and spend the evening with Lucia. You would do the same for her, wouldn't you? And you wouldn't do it out of some misguided sense of obligation, you would do it because you wanted to. Anyway it's done now, so just go get ready.'

'You should have asked me first.'

'You would have said no.'

'I would have had a choice; a say in the matter. We could have waited until your mother came back from wherever she is.'

'Us actually spending some time alone together can't wait. Please, Cel, stop arguing with me about it. I don't want it to ruin our first night out together in months.'

'We are only going around the corner, right?'

'Yes, of course. Anna will call us if she is worried about anything and we can be home in minutes.'

'I have nothing to wear! I'm so fucking fat!' Marcella screeched as she stomped down the hallway on the backs of her heels.

It felt like a first date with a complete stranger; the forced small talk about the general ambience and the weather, the perusing of the menu and, of course, the discussion about whether to order red or white. It was like they were meeting each other for the first time. He knew she would have the fish; she knew he would have some sort of red meat, probably lamb, but they asked each other just the same. Justin wondered, as he sat across the table from Marcella, if he would have pursued her if he had just met her and this had been their first date. It seemed harsh, but the simple truth was that he doubted it. She was attractive, of course, but her lack of affection for him made it difficult to return any and he was beginning to resent her. She'd managed to slowly diminish him as a person and he was no longer certain that it was entirely his fault. She sat across the table from him and looked absently around the room. He tried to get the negative thoughts out of his head, tried to be in the moment and focus on the things he still loved about her.

As the evening progressed Marcella loosened up a little, and there were glimpses of the woman he had once known: the way she laughed with her nose screwed up and rolled her eyes at him when he made a terrible joke, the way she stretched back in her chair then used her fingers to loosen her hair. Her pashmina slipped from its place around her shoulders; he had always loved her olive skin.

'You look beautiful right now, just like that, all relaxed.'

'Slightly drunk, you mean. The wine's gone straight to my head.'

'My plan has worked, then.'

She laughed.

'Ha! I'm not fair game at the moment.'

'In any case I've missed you, in that way.'

'Well, we did have a baby.'

Marcella smiled, took another sip of wine and looked away from him.

Justin called for the bill and they walked home together in silence, both slightly giddy, both looking down at the pavement. And there, somewhere on the cement, was the overwhelmingly obvious need for them to try to be intimate; to actually make that first step. He thought of how he might initiate it, how he might be immediately rejected and then what he would do if she did reject him, how it might deter him from ever trying again. He wondered if they would end up as one of those couples that just never had sex, who just shut that side of themselves off completely but stayed together out of habit 'for the sake of the child'. He also wondered if it would be different somehow, since the birth, if she would be more self-conscious and inhibited, if he would look at her differently now that she was a mother. For the sake of their entire relationship, for the sake of the child they had created, he had to try. He put his arm around her shoulder as they turned into their street, pulled her in closer and kissed the top of her head.

They sat and chatted to Anna while she finished the tea she had just made. After they said their goodbyes, Justin poured some more wine, which Marcella said she didn't want, but drank anyway. His intuition told him she wanted to try too, but that it was proving difficult; the thick nothing that had built up between them was hard to break through, really hard. They had experienced shitty periods before, like any couple, and had somehow found the holes and mended them as they went along. This felt different, though.

Marcella lay back on the bed with her hand covering her Caesarean scar and let Justin kiss her all over. She was nervous, almost shaking; he could feel the tension in her body, the tightness of her legs as they almost clamped together, resisting him. He remembered everything that she had liked before, the way he had used his mouth and fingers. She imitated the noises she used to make, but there was something holding her back, something false in it, and it annoyed him that she thought he couldn't distinguish the difference. She didn't pretend to come, at least, she told him that she was too drunk so he should just get a condom. He entered her. He was gentle at first, thinking he might ease her in and help her to relax. She pretended to enjoy it, pushing him in deeper and telling him to go harder and faster. He knew her too well, though. This is what she did when she wanted him to come quickly so that he would be done.

★

Tristan drove down to Kompong Speu with Leah. He wanted to introduce her to the orphanage director, Heng, who he knew well. Heng had started teaching kids maths and Khmer history years earlier, under a tree in an area where there wasn't a school for miles. Each day more and more children would appear. At the time he was living in a small hut. In the morning he would wake to find some of the children he had taught during the day sleeping on his veranda; they had stayed all night because they had nowhere else to go.

One by one he learned their stories, of being kicked out, of being abused, of going hungry, of family members dying of illnesses they couldn't put names to because they were too young to remember or understand. Relatives and neighbours heard about the kind man teaching orphaned kids and started to send other children with similar stories to him; he would take care of them, they said. At one point he had as many as fifteen kids sleeping in his tiny hut and on the veranda. Heng was barely able to feed himself on the small income he made from his crops of salad and vegetables, let alone all of the children.

Over the years he gained support from various NGOs – some promising continuing support, others offering one-off donations – it was always just enough to get by on. Eventually they moved him to another location where two buildings were paid for and erected; one for the girls, one for the boys. Later came the schoolhouse and a small, separate hut for him. Over time another building was donated; containing a proper kitchen and dining area and a small bedroom for the cook. Another year, a guestroom was added to the schoolhouse in the hope that volunteers would come and stay for long periods of time. It had been empty for a while, though, and the kids were forgetting all the English they had been taught, so Heng welcomed Leah with open arms.

The youngest children were apprehensive at first. They huddled back in a group behind a small, smiley woman with deep lines who was introduced to Leah as Srey Nat, the head nanny. She spoke a limited amount of English but Heng spoke exceptionally well. Some slightly older children, who attended a high school in the next village, appeared and, after much encouragement, tried their English out on Leah and Tristan.

Leah was taken on a tour: the hacienda-style orphanage surrounded a small courtyard garden decorated with beautiful paper mobiles and wind chimes.

'All this made by the children with Srey Nat. Very clever lady,' Heng bragged on Srey Nat's behalf. Srey Nat shooed away his compliment with her hand.

There were also several beds of salad and vegetables and some young fruit trees, which Heng proudly showed off. In the kitchen she met Nita, the cook. She had no English so she just smiled and waved and carried on with her work.

In the girls' dorm, sparse but for several wooden beds all lined up next to each other and a few cabinets, were three sleeping babies: one in a sling, another in a cot, the third on a bed. Leah walked over to the one on the bed. She was dressed only in a cotton vest, with a half-drunk bottle abandoned by her side; she let out a tiny sigh, as though the dream she was in had worked out well after all. Leah gently stroked her face and thought of little Lucia, of her innocence and the complete trust she too had that everyone around her would look after her and give her everything she needed.

'You going to be okay?' Tristan asked her.

'I think so. It's kind of overwhelming, isn't it, but this place has such a nice feeling about it.'

'Yeah, it's one of the good ones. There are a few I wouldn't take you to.'

'I feel a little bit like a fraud, though, like a voyeur or something. Do you know what I mean?'

'Don't. Just get that out of your head. You're not here as a tourist. They need the extra pair of hands and the kids need something, anything. They have nothing. You coming here makes them feel important. And it gives them hope that more people like you will come after.'

'I don't suppose my internal conflict and general disillusionment with the world means anything to them?'

'It means jack shit. They just want to have fun and learn; they want someone to give them the time of day.'

'I can give them that.'

'The town is only a short walk away if you need anything, but don't go anywhere alone at night. Or in the day if you can help it. And text me lots. I want to know how you're getting on. I'm going to miss you!'

'I'll miss you too, but don't worry about me. I'll see you soon.'

By the evening most of the children had warmed to Leah and

fought to sit next to her for their meal of greens in a garlicky broth, with some pulled-chicken and rice. One desperately shy little girl, Sopheak, who looked to be around nine or ten, huddled up close and watched Leah's every move, but was reluctant to engage in conversation.

Leah washed herself using a bucket of water that Srey Nat had brought her and used some of her bottled water to brush her teeth. She pulled out her copy of *The Velveteen Rabbit* and sat it on the bedside table as she settled into her little, airless room. Not being around Tristan made her instantly feel closer to Justin again.

★

The message from Leah took Justin by surprise. She had asked if she could call. Said she was helping out at an orphanage in a rural area, not with Tristan, and made some excuse about it being a work-related conversation; he assumed in case Marcella read the message. They figured out a time, given the time difference, her need to be near a decent signal and his need to be alone; and there he was, pacing the shop again on a Monday morning, waiting for her, thinking of her, feeling nervous and overexcited.

'Hey, stranger.'

'Hey, beautiful.' It was forward of him to call her that. He had not planned to say it but it had come out anyway. 'How are you?'

'I'm okay. I'm tired and sweaty and covered in mosquito bites but really loving it. The children are amazing.'

'I can only imagine. Sounds like you're having the time of your life.'

'It's been pretty emotional.'

'In a good way?'

'Sometimes. I feel a bit useless, though.'

'It's only natural. I bet the kids don't think you're useless.'

'No, I guess not. Thank God they can't see how inexperienced I am. There's such an element of trust – it's bizarre. What do I know about looking after babies or teaching English! They think very highly of me for some reason.'

'I know how they feel.'

Leah was silent.

'Do you miss home yet? Just a little?'

'Not home so much, not yet. But I miss you. I think I did the moment I arrived. Like an idiot.'

'I missed you the minute you walked out the front door. Like an idiot.'

'I thought you might heal. I hoped you would.'

'It's not the kind of thing that feels better with time. It doesn't close over.'

'Stitches perhaps? A skin graft?' Leah suggested with a giggle.

The time apart had changed things. Justin was being pushed forward by all the things that he had mulled over and longed to say to her while she had been away.

'When will you come back? This place is not the same without you.'

'Soon. I have a moveable return date. Depends on… I haven't called my mum to ask her to open my results.'

'You are strange. I would be desperate to know! Will you let me know?'

'Of course. How's that cute baby of yours?'

'Getting so big! And demanding!'

'Send me a photo.'

'I will.'

'How's my brother?'

'You don't really want to ask that.'

'True. I'm sure he's fine. As long as he's being nice to you.'

'He is. Or was. It's nice to get a little space, though. I'd better go. Can we do this again?'

'I would love to.'

'Lots of love.'

'Yes, lots.'

And that was it. She was no longer on the other end of his mobile phone but he held it to his ear anyway, as if her voice might linger somehow.

Leah texted her mother and asked her to open her results letter. That evening she opened the text reply she was hoping for and dreading in equal measure: *A*AA, you got into Bristol!*

She felt strange, light-headed. The feeling began in her stomach and rose slowly up her body until she thought she might pass out. Bristol had been her first choice. She had deliberated for months about which course to go for and in the end went for English. Now it was happening.

She walked outside, into the courtyard where the temperature was a few degrees cooler. She could hear the children chattering in their bedrooms. Srey Nat was away so the girls were up late and being particularly noisy. She thought about going in and encouraging them to get to bed.

'Miss Leah, a baby has been left,' Heng said, rushing over with a wicker basket. 'Very small. I heard the crying but I thought it was a kitten. Then the crying keep going so I look and find him.'

Leah looked into the basket and sure enough there was an unbelievably tiny baby, she assumed a boy, with his mouth open as if he was trying to make a sound. Leah immediately assumed that he must be dehydrated.

'He needs to drink, Heng. Let's take him to the kitchen. Wake up Nita and have her make up a bottle. But she must sterilise. This baby is very small; we can't let him get sick.'

Leah sat down at the table in the kitchen holding the premature infant in her hands. He felt too small to cradle the way she would a normal-sized baby. She thought she would harm him just by touching him – there was not even a slight amount of fat under his loose skin. He was covered in a fine layer of dark hair and his tiny mouth was almost white his lips were so dry. Leah kept him wrapped in the blanket and tried holding him to her chest to keep him warm and comfort him.

Nita brought over the bottle and tested it for temperature. The teat looked enormous. Nita spoke no English so Leah asked Heng to find out from her if there was a smaller one. Nita shook her head and raised her arms up in the air. It would have to do. Leah tipped the tiny baby back into a feeding position and tried to encourage the teat into his mouth. He seemed to want to try but it was just too big, too foreign and too exhausting for him. Leah asked for a syringe. When Nita brought it over, again Leah told her to sterilise it. She held him in her arms while she waited; stroked his tiny, soft head.

Leah drew some liquid up into the syringe, gently prised the baby's mouth open and released a small drop inside. He half choked, half welcomed the milk and tried desperately to swallow it. Heng and Nita hovered around looking anxious and watched her closely. She had no idea what she was doing but they seemed more confident in her ability than their own.

'This is going to take some time. But we need to take him to hospital. He's too small to drink properly.'

'Tomorrow, you can try to take, too late now, but I think they send him back here,' Heng said, shaking his head.

'Send him back here? But he needs to be in hospital; he's too small.'

'I know how this work. We get small baby from hospital before. Lot of times.'

Leah believed him but she still thought she would try. He was premature; they were not qualified or equipped to look after him.

'I'll keep him in my room tonight and try to get him to drink.'

'Thank you, thank you. I am not so good with small baby,' Heng joked nervously.

'It's okay, I will do my best.'

Leah spent at least an hour trying to feed the baby. They would get so far and then he would fall asleep and the little pool of milk she had managed to get into his mouth would just dribble out again. She found some muslin squares and fashioned him a little nappy, wrapped him up in her cotton pashmina and nestled him on to her bed. She stroked his little head and the soft downy hair on his face; she'd never seen anything quite so small and desperately needy in her life. He fell asleep within minutes. Leah didn't, though. She was worried she would roll over and crush him in the night. She kept as far away as she could without falling off the bed and placed rolled up clothes all around him to create a barrier that she hoped would prevent anything happening if she did manage to fall asleep.

In the morning Leah woke to the sound of kitten-like squeaks. He'd come undone and his little hands were flailing about in search of something safe. She picked him up, re-swaddled him so that he felt a bit more secure and carefully carried him outside and into the kitchen. The children were all up and eating their breakfast; they rushed over to see what she was holding. Even they said he was a very small baby. Leah was worried about them all being too close and passing on their germs so she told them the baby was not well. They backed away with concerned faces.

'You'd better get ready for school,' she told them.

After Nita had prepared some more milk and the syringe, Leah tried again to feed him. She wasn't sure that any was actually going in but she reassured herself that if even a few drops managed to slip down through his splutters, it might be enough to hydrate him until they made it to the hospital. As Srey Nat was not around, Heng had to stay back with the children while Leah made the trip to Phnom Penh on her own. She decided to pay for a driver; the bus would be far too busy and full of dust and germs.

Before she left Leah gave him a wash in a basin. He didn't like being naked, out of his swaddling, but once he was in the water he fell asleep; she imagined it felt like being in the womb, all warm and familiar. She found some more cloth for a nappy and took the smallest baby clothes she could from the orphanage's limited selection.

Leah had never felt such purpose; sitting back in the car, carefully cradling the baby. She found it difficult to imagine how anyone could abandon their own child. However, her time in Cambodia was teaching her that these decisions were made by mothers under desperate circumstances and perhaps even with the view that they were offering their child something better than what they could provide themselves. Abandonment, suffering and loss were all a part of life out here, not altogether shocking, just something so many had to go through. Having enough to eat every day, having the opportunity to grow and receive an education and get a job and even survive were not a given. These things had to be fought for.

★

Justin had managed to turn up to work one Thursday morning without Lucia's changing bag; it didn't occur to him until it was too late. He popped her back into the car, hoping the contents of her nappy wouldn't squish out, and drove home.

He was surprised to find Marcella at home, lying on the sofa in the living room watching television, curled up with a blanket over her. She was even more surprised to see him.

'Are you ill?'

She got up to a sitting position, began to cry and shook her head. 'I'm not working anymore. The company is merging and all the part timers went first.'

'But why didn't you tell me? How long have you been home?'

'I don't know why. Just this week.'

'Marcella, this doesn't make any sense.'

'I've been looking for another job.'

'That doesn't answer my question. Why didn't you tell me?'

'I don't know! I've never been made redundant before. I feel like a complete waste of space. This wouldn't have happened if I was full time.'

'Anyone can lose their job. It's not about you.'

'Not anyone, Justin. Only the people that matter the least.'

'Well, you have never mattered the least to your company; so just get that out of your head. Anyway, it's happened. You can look for something else. You'll be snapped up in no time. Still doesn't explain why you didn't tell me.'

She sort of laughed and looked down at the ground, unable to meet his gaze.

He tried to soften his voice.

'You still don't seem okay. I'm worried about you.'

'Oh, that again. You think I'm crazy because I'm crying! I lost my job. This is normal! It's normal to cry when you feel shit about yourself.'

'You're just not yourself, though, are you? You're angry, you're down on yourself and you've kept this from me. How long were you planning on keeping it a secret? I mean, that's not you, that's not what we are. We don't lie to each other. We're married!'

'It's not that big of a deal.'

'It really is. Can't you just say sorry, I should have told you?'

She looked up at him, clearly hating herself but wanting to blame him for her senseless behaviour.

'I'm sorry. But it has only been this week.'

'Here I am taking Lucia into work every morning, trying to accommodate your wish to work, oblivious to the fact that you are currently unemployed.'

'I needed the time to look for a job.'

'And how's that going for you?' he said, looking at the sofa and blanket and then at the television. He couldn't help himself – he wasn't sure if she was looking for jobs or not but he was sick and tired of her excuses for everything.

'Cheap shot, Justin. I had a headache so I lay down for half an hour. I've applied for three jobs this morning.'

'Good for you, maybe tell me about that sometime. Right now I have to get back to work.'

'You can leave Lucia with me.'

'No, it's fine, you have a headache.'

Justin stomped upstairs with Lucia, changed her and brought the bag back down.

Before he left he returned to the sitting room.

'Here's what's going to happen,' he began, 'I'm going to continue to take Lucia in to work in the mornings, for now, while she is still small enough. Why don't you use the time to go back to bootcamp, get your energy back, look for work, see friends for coffee, whatever. I don't really care. But you need to find a way to be happy again. I don't think I can do that for you.'

And then he left her to it; to her tears and her depression. It felt harsh but entirely justified.

★

Leah carried the baby into the hospital and spoke to three

different nurses before being sent to the back of an enormous queue. She got up again after an hour and explained that it was an emergency – that the baby was too small, dehydrated and not well – anything she could think of to have him seen quickly. She had never used such a tone before in her life. The baby had no voice; she felt someone had to stand up for him and fight for his right to survive.

'Okay, I try for you, madam,' was the reply. It was better than being told to join the queue again.

Leah paced the waiting area and tried to feed the baby again. He took tiny sips but she had no idea what she was doing and it just didn't seem enough. Every half hour she went back up to the desk to ask how long it would be.

'Doctor very busy, madam.'

'Baby very sick,' Leah replied, sounding patronising and growing more and more agitated by the minute.

'Please sit down and wait, madam.'

'Okay, this is not my baby, so I leave him here with you and you will have to take care of him.'

She held him out to the nurse.

'No, no, madam,' she replied, flailing her arms about in protest. 'Just stay. I will try one more time.'

Leah had her now. If she left the baby the nurse would have no choice but to deal with it. If it meant him being seen sooner, she was prepared to do it.

Twenty minutes later, Leah was called over and followed the nurse down a corridor. She led her into a curtained booth where she was made to wait for another twenty minutes. When the doctor arrived she placed the baby on the bed and told him she was working in an orphanage and the baby had been left there. She said she thought he was dehydrated and looked premature.

The doctor examined the baby, listened to his heart and did some reflex tests.

'Yes, he is most likely premature and definitely dehydrated. We can put him on a drip.'

'Thank God.'

Arrangements were made with a nurse and within minutes he was attached to a bag of fluid. Leah stayed with him and helped him to fall asleep. She too closed her eyes and nodded off in the seat beside him.

When she woke, a nurse was unhooking him from his drip.

'You can take him now,' the nurse told her.

'Take him where?'

'Back to orphanage.'

'Doesn't he need to be in a humidity crib? Doesn't he need to be monitored?'

'That's for babies that are just born.'

'But he is just born.'

'He is not the newest baby we have here. You can take him back to the orphanage.'

'I think he needs to stay here in hospital. I want to leave him in your care. He's not even feeding properly.'

'He cannot stay here. We will send him to another orphanage; they will come today or tomorrow, depending who can take him.'

Leah thought then about what Tristan had said, about the orphanages that he wouldn't have taken her to; the not so good ones. Whatever he'd meant by that, it wasn't going to be good enough for this baby.

'I need to see the doctor.'

'He will say the same thing.'

'Please. I need to see him.'

Leah had the same conversation with the doctor. She told him how the baby wasn't feeding well, that he'd refused the bottle and needed the syringe but that she wasn't sure the milk was even going down. The doctor said she should just keep trying until his sucking got better. Leah was infuriated. She phoned Heng who told her it was what he expected and to just bring the baby back.

She left the hospital with the baby; he did look a little better for being hydrated at least, and maybe it would get his appetite up and give him a little strength. She asked the driver to go to a supermarket or chemist selling baby things. She bought some disposable nappies, a smaller teat and two of the smallest baby grows she could find. Exhausted, she collapsed back into the car and fell asleep with him in her arms on the journey home.

*

Justin's blow-up with Marcella seemed to spur her into action. She got up each morning and jogged down to the park to begin to get her fitness back. She began to communicate with him about the jobs she was applying for. She seemed fine when he came home at lunchtime and handed Lucia to her. He could see that she wanted to be forgiven and he felt no need to make her feel any worse about herself than she clearly already did. He hoped that it was real; that she really was determined to get back to her old self. If not for the sake of their marriage then for Lucia, who needed her mother to be herself again.

The pressure of looking after Lucia and the business, and worrying about Marcella, was beginning to take its toll on Justin. He was struggling, both emotionally and physically, and felt incredibly isolated. He didn't feel he could talk about any of it with friends: not that he had time to see any of them anyway. Depression was such a grey area, if that was what it even was. Marcella had never been depressed before, so it was clear to him that it had everything to do with giving birth and having to adapt to the massive changes Lucia had brought about in her life.

He missed Leah and yearned for the relief of her presence. Leah had always known when he needed some sort of reassurance. Sometimes it was just a tracing of her fingers across his back or arm, other times it was a hug; but it always worked, always lifted him out of his heaviness.

He sat down at his desk one afternoon after dropping Lucia off and was about to text Leah when a photo came through from her. It was of a tiny baby wearing a little cotton hat, sleeping on a pillow. *Look who I'm looking after at the moment.*

It alarmed him a little; the fact that she was taking care of such a tiny baby. She was going to become so attached to the orphanage that it would be almost impossible for her to leave. He wanted to protect her, as he always did, but she was so far away.

Justin asked her how old the baby was, noted that he looked incredibly small.

He's brand new, premature, apparently not the responsibility of a hospital.

She was so young herself; too young to be getting involved with premature babies in orphanages.

The texting could go on forever. He desperately wanted to hear her voice. He called her.

'This is a lovely treat.'

The signal wasn't great so he waited while she moved around. He could hear the sound of children playing in the background.

'I'm worried about you.'

'Oh no, don't worry about me!'

'They're asking a lot of you. You're supposed to be teaching English not looking after tiny babies!'

'Srey Nat, the nanny, is away. I had to help out. I think she'll be back by the end of the week. But I'm okay, really. It's a challenge, but a good one. He's such a sweet thing. So tiny, though. Not like Lucia with those lovely big cheeks!'

'I can only imagine you are handling everything beautifully, but just be careful with yourself. It's easy to get too attached.'

'It's too late. I'm attached to all of the kids here, not just this little guy. This one girl, Sopheak, won't leave my side.'

He wasn't sure how to express himself without sounding patronising.

'And I am sure they are attached to you. They won't want you to go.'

'Now I feel bad!'

'Sorry. I don't want you to feel bad. You're doing what you can in a difficult situation.'

'It means so much to me that you are worried. But really, I am okay.'

'I know, I know that you're strong. What's his name?'

'The baby? Heng gave him a Khmer name: Ravi. I'm

not sure that he looks like a Ravi but what do I know about Khmer names!'

'Sounds like a really lovely thing you are doing.'

'He's just so adorable. I feel so privileged. I would never be given such a fragile new life to look after back in the UK; I wouldn't be qualified. Here there seems to be an assumption that I know what I'm doing. But it's so hard to get him to drink; it literally takes an hour to get a few drops in. At least I'm learning patience, if nothing else.'

'You're amazing, you know that.'

'I'm not! I had no choice. Anyone would do the same. I'm not amazing, really.'

'I think you are.'

Justin felt so much pride, as though he had nurtured her and was now seeing her become someone extraordinary. He was concerned too, though. He could hear in her voice how attached she was already to a baby she would only look after for a short period of time, but concern wasn't what she needed from him at that moment. She needed him to approve: to tell her she was doing something good.

'Thank you,' she whispered.

'Text me tomorrow?' he asked her.

He needed to hear from her; not just because he missed her, and his own life was a complete mess, but because he needed to know that she was handling the situation. He wouldn't tell her about Marcella, though he wished he could. Leah would be sincere; she'd listen and be mature and probably tell him how he could be a better husband. But he wouldn't tell the girl he adored that his wife was not coping; that would be more disloyal to Marcella than anything.

'Okay, I will.'

'Oh wait, you didn't tell me about uni…'
'I got into English at Bristol.'
He felt like he was about to collapse.
'Wow! I knew you would do it. I'm so happy for you.'
'Thank you.'

★

Leah was in no hurry to get back to Tristan and the school, or back to the UK. Uni wouldn't start until October so she could stay a little longer than she'd planned. She wasn't ready to hand over Ravi just yet anyway. She felt he needed her and that was the most wonderful feeling in the world, no one else had become as close to this baby as she had.

She texted Tristan to tell him about the baby; that she was needed at the orphanage more than she was at the school, so it made sense to stay. He understood, said he admired her decision but that he missed her and he would come up soon. She told him she missed him too, but the truth was she was so busy with the baby that she hadn't thought about him at all. In Tristan's absence, she had, without even thinking about it, immediately rekindled her connection with Justin. Justin didn't have to say much, just the sound of his voice gave her all the comfort and encouragement she needed. Even if he was being a little too overprotective, she loved that he cared.

She carried Ravi around the orphanage in a sling fashioned for her by Nita. She didn't want to leave him out of her sight in case one of the kids tried to pick him up. They were pretty unpredictable at times, and many had come from big families where they were expected to help look after their younger siblings. Ravi was still fragile and, she was sure, not drinking enough. She began to weigh him on the kitchen scales and found that he had barely put on a few grams.

Leah still slept with him on her bed, surrounded by barriers so she wouldn't crush him in the night; but she found that she instinctively curled herself away from him and woke in the same position each morning. It was as though she knew subconsciously that he was there. When she couldn't sleep, which was often, she just watched his little heart working overtime: willing him to sleep well, eat more and get stronger.

Srey Nat finally returned. Leah thought she might take over Ravi's care but she didn't seem confident around such a small baby. She watched as Leah fed him and tried to help, but actually had less luck and less patience.

'He like you, Miss Leah! I'm too strange for him!'

Leah laughed. 'You mean, you are a stranger to him. Not strange. You're not weird!'

Srey Nat laughed out loud, showing all her rotten teeth.

'I don't know which one more trouble. Big one keep us too busy and make too much noise and mess, or this one, no eat enough.'

Leah nodded in agreement. 'This one is more worrying, that's for sure.'

'I get kids ready for bed, you stay here, you very tired now you have baby in your bed.'

Leah sat out in the courtyard, which was so much cooler than her room, and tried to coax Ravi to take a little more milk. She draped a mosquito net over some trees to create a little tent for the two of them, which the children all found hilarious as they skipped across the courtyard after their evening ablutions.

'You look funny!' they all chanted.

'Yes, but no bites!'

'Can I sit with you?' Sopheak asked.

'Of course, come and keep me company.'

Sopheak crawled under the net and sat cross-legged by Leah's side.

Leah managed to get Ravi to take more milk than the day before, which felt like something of a milestone. She propped him up against her chest and tried gently patting his back in case he had any wind. He made the sweetest little grunting noises and then drifted off to sleep. She stayed like that for a while; stroking his soft hair that smelled of baby shampoo from his bath that morning. Sopheak stayed with her and held his tiny hand.

★

Marcella had mentioned the interviews she had been on and was interested in one company in particular. When she was offered the position, the fact that it was full time was finally brought to Justin's attention.

'There were so few part-time opportunities. I thought if I at least got my foot in the door I could then negotiate.'

'Marcella, please, be honest with me, what indication did you get that they might offer this job to you part time?'

He realised he sounded like a condescending prick, but if she would insist on behaving like a petulant child and keeping secrets from him, he felt he had no choice.

'Okay, so there really are very few good part-time

opportunities. I am not making this up. And I don't want to take a career plunge for the sake of working part time. I don't want to be a bloody bookkeeper. Nor do I want to travel to the other side of London for a part-time job; that would be ridiculous and I would never see Lucia. I would prefer part time, of course, but, if I can't, then I need to accept a full-time position. It's not like the money will go to waste!'

'I understand your points, now that you have made them. My confusion is over why you didn't find it necessary to make them to me in a conversation before you went for it? I feel like I don't really feature in your decision-making process at all.'

'You would have told me not to. As it is, all I feel is hostility and disappointment from you.'

'I wonder why that is? How do you know I would have told you not to go for it? If I don't know what it is that you really want, then should I just guess? I'm not your father, Marcella. I'm not here to make you do anything. I'm your husband. I'm here to support your choices. But this decision doesn't just affect you and I, it affects Lucia, so I think it is only fair that we should make it together. She's already becoming too animated to just sling on my back or leave in a buggy to sleep.'

'Well, I'm coming to you now and I haven't accepted it yet. But, Justin, I didn't ask you to give up your job when we had Lucia; so why do I have to be the one to give up my career? I bring in more money than you, anyway.'

'Okay, for a start, I don't have a job, I have a business. You can't take time out from a business; it doesn't run itself.'

'Okay, true. But to me the principle still applies. You haven't had to make any sacrifices.'

'Well, right now, I actually feel like I have lost my wife. I mean, is this really about money? About who makes more? What about all those conversations we had years ago about what makes us tick. I care more about enjoying what I do than making shedloads of money; that's what's important to me. And I've worked bloody hard to get the business to a point where it is does actually make enough.'

'I didn't mean it the way it came out. I'm sorry. I was just trying to make you understand.'

'And I didn't ask you to give up your career. I assumed, wrongly it seems, that you would want to take maternity leave for the first six months or so. I shouldn't have assumed that.'

'I don't think anyone can really know what they want until they are in the situation. I don't think being a full-time mum is for me. There, I've said it. Call me a bad parent, a bad person; call me cold and un-maternal, whatever, it just isn't for me. I love Lucia, with all my heart, but I don't want to be in the house all day with the washing and the vitamizer; nor do I want to take endless walks in the park with the buggy. I just don't. And I don't mix with the kind of mothers that do like those things.'

'It's not for everyone, Cel. I get it. I do know that you love Lucia, despite not wanting to be at home with her full time. I'm not completely callous. We will have to adapt, that's all.'

He was trying not to lose it with her. He wanted to shout in her face: *Why did you want to have a baby in the first place?* He really didn't get it. Didn't she envisage herself in the park with the buggy? Isn't that what women who desperately wanted kids did? Did her visions involve pushing a baby out and packing her briefcase for work the next morning? But he refrained, not sure how close it would send her to the edge.

He knew he lacked empathy, but it was quite simply because none of this was how he'd thought it would be and she kept everything from him until the very last moment. He felt heavy, alone and resentful. This was hard for her and he was supposed to be seeing that and supporting her. But who was supporting him? Who was left holding everything together because Marcella wanted to do what Marcella wanted to do? Part of him wanted her to go back to work full time as then she'd be even more absent and exhausted, and they wouldn't have to bother going through the motions of trying to be a happy couple again.

'I think I just need the balance. I feel so anxious when I'm in the house all day. I start looking at the clock and wondering when her next nap will be, and when you will come home again.'

Finally, an attempt at giving him insight.

'I have tried, but nothing feels natural; it all feels like a struggle. Knowing when and how, and how much is too much, and what is not enough. When I look at other mothers, they're almost crying with pride – talking for hours about first words, first teeth and the smell and consistency of their baby's shit – and I just feel worse. I feel completely inadequate and alienated.'

That was perfectly clear.

'What I do love is the first smile she gives me in the morning when I pick her up out of the cot. I love that the silliest things make her laugh. I love that she is made of us and that all our best bits are in her somewhere waiting to come out as she gets older.'

Justin softened.

'Look, you don't need to be one of those mothers you

see in the park or in the street. You just need to be you. Lucia isn't holding meetings with other babies and comparing notes. If she feels happy and safe and loved then you're not getting it wrong. The problem is measuring yourself against others, because it isn't healthy and it isn't you. You've always been strong and confident with who you are. And the other thing we need to get to the bottom of is why you're at a point where something you love this much is making you depressed and angry all the time.'

'I don't feel like that confident person anymore. I feel like if I go back to work I might regain something, and maybe that will help me be a better mother and a better wife. Maybe you will even love me again.'

'I haven't stopped loving you,' he reassured her.

Marcella shrugged. It was clear that the jury was out on that one for her. As it was for him. Even though he had said it he had no idea on what level his love for Marcella actually still existed.

*

The sun was at its peak when Leah woke; the room starkly illuminated. She felt hotter than normal and the bedding was soaked with her sweat. The children were all outside getting into their tuk-tuk for school. Leah had slept through the night, the whole night, without being woken. She hadn't done that since Ravi had arrived. She immediately had a sinking feeling, like she'd forgotten something really important. Ravi had not woken her for milk. She rolled over quickly to find that he was still sound asleep. He looked so peaceful; possibly more content than she'd ever seen him.

But she couldn't see the rise and fall of his chest as he breathed.

He was still, very still.

And when she reached out and touched him, he was not just still, he was no longer warm.

Leah cupped her mouth and flew out of bed backwards, across the room, towards the door, slamming her body against its hardness. She turned around to face the door and pressed her forehead up against it; she couldn't look at the bed with the dead baby in it. Her body began to convulse and shake as she screamed and heaved and struggled to breathe; thumping her fists weakly against the rough, splintery wood. Her legs gave way and she folded to the floor, her forehead pressed to the ground.

When the door finally opened she fell through the opening and crawled out in an awkward, tilted hurry.

Srey Nat crouched down to get hold of her, to try and ascertain what was wrong. From somewhere deep inside a howling noise came. It was disturbing, hysterical, loud.

'Please, Miss Leah, I want to help. What happen to you?'

'Ravi! I want him back. I want him back,' she repeated, clinging onto Srey Nat. 'Please! Please!' she begged. 'Give him back to me! I won't let him die. I will do better next time. Please, just bring him back.'

Heng arrived at that moment, but she couldn't look him in the eye. He stepped over the two women, entered Leah's room, and walked over to the bed.

'Oh, Miss Leah, I am sorry, so sorry,' she heard him tell her gently, over her sobbing.

'It's my fault!' Leah cried. 'I should have made the hospital take him!'

'No, no, Miss Leah, not your fault. You cared very well for Ravi. This hospital fault. You tried, they did not take him. This happen before. Too small. He born too soon. Not your fault.'

Srey Nat hugged her tighter; stroking her hair. Leah's body remained stiff; she was too afraid to move, afraid to see, so they stayed where they were on the floor.

'Not you, Miss Leah,' Srey Nat whispered. 'You good girl.'

'I will take him away,' she heard Heng say.

Leah wanted to plead with him. It was all happening too fast. Ravi was going and she still didn't know how he had died.

She looked up and saw Heng tucking Ravi into her pashmina, as though he were still alive and needed to be kept warm. She forced herself to keep looking, to see it all, as Heng came to the door.

'I want to say goodbye.' Leah held up her arms.

Heng looked a little reluctant, as did Srey Nat, but she nodded to them that she needed to.

He didn't weigh anything in her arms. A little doll he was now, a doll with its eyes permanently closed and its limbs all fixed in one position. All of his features were so perfectly formed; it didn't make sense that a person, a whole person, could just not *be* anymore. All of her tears were falling onto him and disappearing into her pashmina; her soft shawl that smelled of her and that helped him to fall asleep at night. She looked up at Heng and raised the baby. She needed to pass him back. If he wasn't going to move, if he wasn't going to open his eyes, then she needed to hand him back.

Heng bent down to carefully take Ravi and turned to

leave. Leah watched him walk away: his tufty black hair streaked with grey, the back of his crumpled cream shirt, his long and faded green shorts, the worn leather of the back of his sandals, the corner of her pashmina that hung down by his side. Heng must have some kind of super-human strength, Leah decided, to be able to carry Ravi away and do whatever needed to be done with the body.

Srey Nat tried to steady Leah so she could stand, but it was a struggle to find her feet again.

'Thank you,' Leah managed. 'I'm okay. I think I will wash.'

Srey Nat went over to the bed and started to remove the sheets.

'No, not yet, I can do it later.'

'I change sheets for you, is good idea.'

'I can do it later, it's okay, really. Can you please take these, though?'

She handed Srey Nat the milk bottles, the syringe and the nappies; she couldn't look at them anymore.

'It's okay. I will come out later,' she reassured Srey Nat, who looked incredibly worried.

'Okay, okay. I can bring you breakfast.'

'No. Not today.'

★

It was two weeks until Marcella would start her new job. Time for her to look for a nanny who could take care of Lucia for three days a week. Justin's mother would do the other two. It was a compromise Marcella had to make; she had never bonded with Catherine, but it was irrelevant, this was about what was best for Lucia.

The contact with Leah had for some reason ceased all of a sudden. As far as Justin knew she was still on her own in the orphanage without Tristan, so it wasn't anything to do with his brother. Their last conversation had been natural and open and he had finished by thinking to himself how much he loved and admired her.

Justin didn't want to trouble Leah but he was a little concerned about her welfare. He casually texted Tristan; talking first about himself, as though it were an out of the blue catch-up, and then asking how Leah was getting on.

Tristan replied after the longest time and told him that she had taken on the care of an abandoned premature baby but that he had died. He said she must be devastated but hadn't heard from her himself, only the orphanage director. Said he was going up on the weekend, most likely to bring her back to the school with him – he would have gone straight away but took Leah's lack of response to his texts to mean that she really needed some space.

It all took Justin's breath away; this was probably the most horrific thing that could have possibly happened. There he was worrying about what she would be like when she had to leave Ravi behind at the orphanage, but for him to die… Leah would be beside herself, she would feel responsible, she would be grieving heavily and on her own. He knew her too well; knew she would be in utter turmoil. It hurt, to think of her in that state without anyone around her to comfort her in the way she needed. Tristan wouldn't be able to understand or help her through this. He wanted to bolt out of the shop, drive to Heathrow and buy the first ticket out. Of course, he couldn't. He would never be able to give her what she needed when she needed it; his frustration was turning to blind anger and yet there was no one to blame for the impossibility of the situation.

Justin tried to call Leah but there was no answer. Of course she wouldn't pick up, she was in pain, and this was when she needed him the most; when she pretended she didn't. He had been down this path with her before and when she had finally let him in the release had been immense. He began to compose a message. She would read it at some point, he knew she would, and maybe she would be able to draw some comfort from it. It was the only thing that he could do to reach her.

★

Leah stayed in her room for three days. She had ignored Justin's call despite wanting nothing more than to speak to him and tell him what happened. She couldn't bring herself to; he had been so proud of her, he had called her amazing for taking care of Ravi. She wasn't amazing, though. She was none of the things he had built her up to be. The battle went on all the time that she was awake, to answer or not to answer. She had never needed him more.

Srey Nat brought her food and water, but she only took the water. She had not changed the sheets; she lay down next to the small space Ravi had occupied, just as she had done when he was alive, the shape of him still formed in the folds of the linen. There was a very faint smell of him, she thought, although it could have been just a memory that came to her.

And then, once again, she found solace in the brutality of physical punishment. She bruised her arms, the insides of them; she went for the nook in her arm that Ravi's tiny head had rested in, the part that should have been holding and protecting him from harm. It was the only thing that kept her in the now and offered her some sort of atonement for being unable to keep him alive.

Leah drifted out into the courtyard when she thought everyone was asleep. Heng was sitting in the old wicker chair.

'Heng, I need to know how he died.'

Heng looked thoughtful for a moment.

'I think you should not worry about that. He just die and that what happen sometimes.'

'But I am, I am worried. I will always want to know.'

Leah realised she sounded like a demanding child wanting answers to impossible questions, but she couldn't hold back.

'Heng, please, I need to know, I need to be told something, some detail that will help me to move on. I am in so much pain because I miss him, but also because I don't know if I did something wrong, or didn't do enough.'

More tears. She had cried for days, but still they came, her endless supply of sadness.

'I took Ravi to the volunteer hospital and met an Australian doctor. I tell him Ravi die in his sleep. He said it was most likely organ failure – because he was premature, or, he call it Sudden Infant Death Syndrome – which means they don't know. He said he was just too small and he did not have a good chance. But you did everything right, everything good by him. You must believe that. You cannot be sad your whole life thinking about this.'

'Thank you, Heng. Thank you for telling me. I will try to accept what you are saying, but I wish they would have done an autopsy. I know that sounds awful, to have them open him up, but just to know…'

'They would not, not for very small baby that belong to no one. Who will pay? Who will have the time? And what different it make? It happen and there is nothing that could stop it. You did very good job, Leah. You look after him better than anyone, better than hospital.'

'Did you leave him with them?'

'Yes. The Australian doctor said he will take care of cremation for me. Ravi was going to receive blessings from the monks, with other child who die in hospital.'

'Thank you. I am so glad. That makes me feel a bit better.'

Leah wanted to hug him but wasn't sure if it would make him uncomfortable. She stood up to return to her room, perhaps too quickly; everything went black and quiet and she could feel herself go, just go. It felt calm and peaceful, though, a wonderful journey away from the torture of being.

★

Justin pressed send on his lengthy text message:

Leah, I know about little Ravi and I am heartbroken for you. Please try to remember that without your love he would have had nothing to take with him to the other side. You gave him something his real mother could not: your time, your care, your devotion. Death is a part of life and mostly we have no control over when it comes; sometimes it comes at the beginning, when we are small and vulnerable, sometimes in the middle, when we are loving every minute and at the peak of everything. I will always remember how extraordinary you were to have done this; to be where you are now, to have taken risks, to have known that with love also often comes great pain, and still gone for it anyway. For this I love you more, if that is at all possible. Yours, always. J xxx

★

The fever came in waves. More liquid left Leah's body – via every orifice that was able to expel it and every pore in her skin – more than she could physically put back in. She hallucinated as she fell in and out of restless sleep. She had visions of everyone she knew, just staring at her as she lay on the floor, naked, all skin and bones, violently convulsing and vomiting until all that was left to vomit were her intestines; which were stuck, of course, still attached to her dying organs. She had visions of dry retching her intestines up to her throat and then pulling them out with her hands until there were metres and metres of them on the floor beside her curled-up body. Her stomach would be empty then. It would have been easier not to be alive, she would have welcomed death because when it came, the pain, the sickness, the longing, and all of her grief would not be felt anymore.

Heng and Srey Nat said it was most likely Dengue Fever or some bacterial infection in her gut; or perhaps a combination of both. The cramping and expelling was relentless. *I'm going to die here*, she thought calmly to herself as she lay on the bathroom floor, with everything spinning and buzzing and the blackness coming and going. *I'm going to die here.* She didn't want to die in Cambodia, she wanted to die in England; a little old lady who had travelled the world and married and made babies.

Srey Nat appeared with more water, fruit, bread, soup and plain rice, in the hope that Leah might take some. She tried a little, but it was such a challenge, she had no appetite and was terrified it would all come out again.

After what seemed like days, Leah had lost count, Heng appeared with some sort of antibiotics. He said they were the good ones, the ones that worked; he was sorry not to have been able to get them sooner, but the local pharmacy had run out and the delivery was late. Leah took two straight away and thanked him. She apologised for being a useless volunteer and promised she would be well again soon, play with the kids and hold some more English classes. Heng told her there was no hurry, the kids could wait, that all that mattered was that she got well again.

Leah switched on her phone, ignored messages from her friends and her mother, which she didn't have the energy for, and read Justin's text. He knew about Ravi; it hadn't occurred to her that Tristan might pass the news on to him. She was grateful that she didn't have to tell him and he had also reassured her of his continued devotion, without her having to ask for it. She wasn't sure why she had ever doubted him; his love for her had never wavered.

She could barely focus on the tiny keys, but she had to write back.

I can't thank you enough for your warm words. Especially when I am perhaps at my lowest. I miss Ravi every day but I know I need to find some strength so that I can be here for the kids. I've come down with some nasty bug and haven't the energy to leave my bed. Feeling utterly useless and kind of fading away. When Srey Nat isn't around to marshal them away, the kids knock on my door and ask if I am better yet. Yesterday some of them were singing songs outside my window. Ultimately, it will be the thing that will help me to recover; those sweet, high-pitched serenades. I miss you. Always. L xxx

Justin was momentarily placated by Leah's message – the fact that she had written at all was a good sign – but the illness, whatever it was, that was worrying. He tried to get hold of Tris, to see what the fuck he planned to do about it. Again, he waited and waited for a reply. His brother had no concept of responsibility.

*

Justin saw Marcella come alive with the impossible task of choosing a childminder for Lucia. It became a small project she could throw herself into, and it was clearly something she wanted to do well, which he was more than relieved about. She called everyone she knew for recommendations and suggestions, then narrowed it down, researched all of the references in person, leaving only one possibility; a twenty-six-year-old Polish woman named Margaret. For the first time in as long as he could remember, Justin appreciated Marcella's meticulous attention to detail.

They met Margaret as a couple. Justin sat there with Lucia on his lap as Marcella fired questions at her. He wondered how he would be able to bring himself to hand his child over to a complete stranger. However, he liked Margaret almost instantly and could see that she would only bring more love and fun to Lucia's life. She had a vibrant personality, a permanent, genuine smile, exceptional English and indisputably glowing references; not to mention her qualification as a Montessori teacher. To top it all off Lucia was smiling at her within minutes and held her arms out for Margaret to pick her up. Despite how difficult it had become to manage, and even with the knowledge that Lucia would be well cared for, Justin was going to desperately miss his mornings with her.

★

On his first Monday morning without Lucia, Justin looked around the empty shop; it was dirty, unloved and lifeless and he felt nothing but emptiness and apathy for it. It occurred to him that since Leah had gone, and since having Lucia, he had lost a great deal of his love and energy for The Potting Shed. It had been his baby once: his sanctuary, his treasure-trove of plants and ornaments and statues. It now felt like a dank waiting room; a place to sit and brood until Leah returned.

The business had made a decent and consistent income, but could probably make more. He thought about rearranging everything, redecorating and getting in some new stock; he needed to find some inspiration again, keep himself busy or he would go mad. But just looking at the space, it dawned on him: it needed an area for customers to sit down, to drink tea and eat cake, something to keep people for longer. The longer people stayed, the more they bought. There was definitely room for a counter and a few tables and chairs. There were things that could be shifted outside to make more space inside the shop and till area, so that people could sit and eat and drink whilst looking over the flower workshop. There could be outdoor tables too, for the summer and spring, strategically placed next to the most popular plants like lavender and herbs. He could even place little pots for sale on the tables themselves. He wasn't sure how long it would be before Leah would return; perhaps a matter of weeks. They would sit down together at one of the tables when it was all finished and drink mint tea and talk for hours and hours and not notice or care what time it was. She would look at him the way she always did, with admiration and affection, and he would reach over and stroke her hand and it would make her shudder simply because it was him. And it would be him, always him – that she would come back to – in some shape or form. Justin found a notepad and started sketching and writing lists.

*

Leah could tell by the look on Tristan's face that she did not appear at all well. She had made it out into the courtyard and was curled up in the old cane chair.

'I think I need to take you to a hospital.'

Tristan stroked his stubble and stood back a little, as though she had leprosy.

'Oh, God no, that would be a complete waste of time. I'm actually a lot better, despite appearances!'

'There's nothing of you. You've literally disappeared!'

'I managed some fruit this morning and some soup at

lunch. I am well on the road to recovery. The antibiotics have definitely kicked in.'

'I don't know. Looks like you need to eat a lot more than soup.'

'I'm not contagious; you can actually give me a hug!'

'I'm sorry. I'm just in shock.' He moved closer, bent down to where she was sitting and hugged her.

'I can literally feel every bone in your back!'

'Don't worry, now that my appetite has returned I will fatten up in no time. Tell me how you've been, how the kids are…'

Tristan sat down in a plastic chair next to her.

'The kids are brilliant. They ask about you constantly, of course. They say you are the prettiest teacher they ever had. They're wearing me out, but you know me, I'd rather be kept busy. Actually we took them to the fun park for a day out, paid for by an ex volunteer. They went crazy! We might be getting another volunteer in a few weeks, probably just after you go back to the UK. Will you stay here until then, or come back with me? Might be better to come back. We can get you checked out by a doctor. And you need more rest. You don't really get a break from the kids here; it's twenty-four hours a day.'

Something had happened in the time that she had been away from Tristan and seeing him sitting there now, in front of her, looking at her so pitifully, she knew what it was. She hadn't really missed him; she had barely even thought of him. Their relationship, if that's what it was, was based entirely on sex. And once she'd removed herself from it, and occupied herself with looking after the children, she no longer needed it to make herself feel alive and wanted. She needed something more, something she couldn't get from Tristan.

'You are sweet to worry, but I don't think I need to see a doctor. I think I am more needed here. This last week has been such a write off that I feel I owe them a little more time. I talked to Heng before you came. He said he understood if I wanted to go, especially after Ravi, but that he would be most happy if I stayed.'

'I'm so sorry about what happened – it must have been awful. Do you want to talk about it?'

He was sincere, of course, but there was nothing in his tone or in how she felt about him that made her want to open up. It wasn't what they did, it was what they didn't do: the layers, the depth, the delving. All they did was have sex.

'Thank you. I'm okay. I don't think I can talk about it just yet; it still feels too raw.'

She didn't want to cry with Tristan. She wanted to cry with Justin, share the experience with him, no one else would really do, no one else would heal her the way he could.

'It's okay if you want to stay, of course. This is your trip and you have to do what you have to do, get out of it what you need to. I get that. I miss you, though. I kind of got used to having you around.'

She wondered if he realised that he didn't really miss her, just the sex.

'I miss you too. I can get a bus or car back to PP. My flight is the twentieth of September; to give me a bit of time before uni starts.'

'Where are you going? You didn't tell me!'

'Bristol. I still can't believe I got in.'

'Amazing! Well done you!'

★

Ella and Andy thought the café was a brilliant idea and Ella was keen to help out with it as much as she could as the flower shop wasn't often that demanding.

Justin set everything in motion immediately, keen to have the bulk of it completed before Leah returned. The cakes would have to be ordered in and stored, so he replaced the small bar fridge in his office with a new, larger one. He purchased a butler sink and an eclectic mix of tables and chairs that he found in a number of second-hand furniture shops. A friend measured up the counter, which would be made from recycled timber and two large offcuts of marble. His mother found the fabric for the seat cushions and whipped them up at home: natural linen with inky blue stripes. Local charity shops were perfect for vintage side plates, tea cups and milk jugs. Justin also picked up some small vases that he could put on the tables with whatever was left over from the flower workshop. There were already lots of Moroccan tea glasses from his trips to Marrakesh, but he ordered a few more, and some more teapots, trays and sugar bowls. He would have loved to have done this with Leah, but the idea of surprising her when she returned excited him more.

In the afternoons, when it was quiet, Justin took time out to call Leah. She didn't answer the phone, but he left her a few answer messages. She had once told him that she loved the sound of his voice, that it didn't matter what he was talking about she would always want to listen to him.

He asked Tris again about the illness and how Leah's recovery was going. Tris replied that he had been to visit but that Leah hadn't returned with him. She had wanted to stay at the orphanage for the rest of her time in Cambodia. Justin was quietly pleased that she had prioritised doing what she wanted over being with Tris and hoped their relationship was perhaps coming to its natural end.

Tris added that Leah refused to go and see a doctor, despite looking awful. This worried Justin enormously. He found it hard to imagine finding her in a state and not doing something, anything, about it. He was disappointed in Tris. Not only had Leah suffered a traumatic loss, she was now trying to get over a terrible illness, all on the other side of the world, away from her mother and anyone or anything that was remotely familiar or comforting. Justin would have insisted she see a doctor. He would have picked her up in his arms, flagged down the first moving vehicle and taken her to hospital. Simple as that.

He enquired to Leah herself but she skimmed over the details and, when he pressed, said Tristan was exaggerating as she was now almost fully recovered. Justin asked her to send him a photo so that he could be sure. She refused, of course, said she looked like a sweaty pig. She did however send him a lengthy message, quite out of the blue:

> *I keep forgetting to tell you that I love The Velveteen Rabbit. I remember it from my childhood but I don't think I fully appreciated it then. I've read it so many times now I think I know it off by heart. Actually, I read it to Sopheak just the other night. She listened intently for a long time, despite not really knowing what I was talking about because the English is too advanced, but she seemed to find comfort in the tone of my voice. As*

I began to cry she stretched her arm around my body, as far as she could reach, and told me that she loved me. She knew that I needed her to tell me that, or that I just needed someone to tell me that. Little angel. I read on and by the time I got to the end Sopheak's eyes were closed and she was sound asleep, but her little arm stayed tucked around me. I moved her to her bed and she said again that she loved me. There are so many layers to that book: so many hidden, deeper meanings. It is so beautifully written and exquisitely conceived. I wanted to meet the author and hug her, tell her I understood everything she was trying to convey. Of course she is long gone, but it is a shame that I will never meet her, and that I may never meet anyone with a mind like that. People make us real by loving us, and the real love comes when we are old and worn and not pretty anymore. It's just there, unconditionally. Could there be a greater affirmation of the meaning of life than that? Am I strange for feeling this way about a children's book? This book means so much more to me now; now that you have given it to me. Xx

*

Leah's strength slowly began to return. She spent all of her available energy on the children. Heng insisted that she only teach a couple of English lessons a week to begin with, to ease her back in. During the midday heat Leah adopted the same exhausted pose as Srey Nat and Nita; she plonked herself down in the shade, against a cool white cement wall, and played with the babies and toddlers one by one as they climbed on her legs and reached for her hands. She helped Nita with the meals and spent some time hanging out with the older girls after supper; sitting up on their beds as they plaited her hair and talked about boys, make-up, clothes, career aspirations and dreams for the future. She hoped they would all go on to qualify as the teachers and doctors they imagined themselves becoming.

Leah stumbled into bed early each night after holding sleep off for as long as she could. Her mind wanted to move on and do more, but her body was still relatively weak. When she was back in her room, where her sheets and every corner of the room had now been cleaned by Srey Nat, Leah was able to reflect on how ill she had actually been. She remembered in some detail what was going through her head at the peak of her fever; her own death mainly, and the inexplicable feeling that it was imminent.

Now, as she was slowly coming back to life, her acceptance that her death might have been imminent seemed nothing short of ridiculous but the combination of the illness, her grief at what had happened with Ravi and being so far from home, had really tested her. She looked at her arms. She had only hurt herself the once, when Ravi had died. She hadn't the strength to do it after that and, now, she couldn't imagine reviving the bruises. If anything the idea of doing it made her feel ashamed. The children here suffered, really suffered. What she had done to herself was indulgent, selfish and a waste of energy.

As she lay there in the stifling room, for the first time since she had lost Ravi, Leah flicked through her phone and found the pictures she had taken of him. He looked even smaller than she remembered.

Leah heard one of the children singing as he ran across the courtyard to the toilet block. She remembered then the singing outside her window and how calming it had felt that life was going on without her. It was that sound of the children that had coaxed her back to life, children she had only known for a few weeks. She was wanted still, despite feeling that she had failed in her role of carer. The other children needed her to get well and re-engage with them. They had moved on from parents and siblings and other families they had lost or left behind and they needed her to move on from Ravi.

She had missed calls from Justin. He was concerned about her health and requested a photograph, something she declined. She had caught sight of herself in the mirror and felt that she looked gaunt, older. Her hair hung limply and none of her clothes fitted any more. She might send him one in a few weeks when she looked alive again.

★

Justin finally received a call from Leah at work on a Monday. Of course it would be a Monday, Monday was their day.

'I can't tell you how wonderful it is to hear your voice. How are you? Are you feeling better?'

'Yes, really, so much better. I'm up and about, hanging out with the kids.'

'You sound okay. God, I was worried about you. I almost jumped on a plane to come and see if you were okay for myself.'

'Ha! I sound like a spectacle!'

'No, but definitely an attraction!'

'A fatal attraction!'

He laughed. 'Don't say that! No doubt people do die from Dengue Fever or whatever it was you had. You really should have seen a doctor.'

Leah was quiet for a time and he realised then that he actually missed their silences as much as he missed their conversations.

'Maybe, but it doesn't matter, I'm all good now,' she finally said. 'I also got through *The Unbearable Lightness of Being*.'

'Like it?'

'Loved it. Bit of a shock, though. I know I should just savour the book but I think I'd like to see the film so that I can spend more time with the characters.'

'Yes, I remember a very young Juliette Binoche... I read *The Collector*. It was incredibly sad towards the end.'

'I felt like Miranda in my room here, drifting off on my memories of the people I loved and might never see again, wondering if death was tapping on my door!'

'God, that sounds awful. Don't ever die.'

Silence.

'Justin... I miss you.'

Those words, from her, were all he needed to hear; they were enough to sustain him.

'I miss you too. When are you coming home?'

'I arrive back Thursday week.'

'Alone?'

'Of course. You know Tristan – he won't leave, there's nothing for him in England. Not that I would ask him to. I've barely seen him for weeks. We were never serious. We were never in love.'

Justin refrained from telling Leah how delighted he was at hearing this; despite the clear confirmation that they had been together purely for the sex, which still sickened him. No doubt Tris was actually in love with Leah, in his limited capacity; but possibly couldn't recognise it because he was so accustomed to travelling along his own, self-serving trajectory.

'As long as you're okay.'

'I promise you I am, and so happy for hearing your voice. For some reason I just felt too tender to pick up the phone. I thought it would set me off and you would think I was falling apart and, actually, I thought maybe I would fall apart. But I think it's probably okay to feel as sad as I do, isn't it? Even though I retreated a little, you really are the only person I want to talk to about anything that actually matters. Your voice is the only voice in my head, still, after being here and trying so hard to move on from you in that way.'

'Of course. It's normal for you to feel sad. It doesn't mean you're falling apart, it means you are human. Don't move on too much, from me, I mean; I need you close still. In whatever form you come, I will take it. I miss everything about you, every single day.'

Saying goodbye to Justin on the phone, Leah felt her heart plummet. She loved him too much, it was as simple as that. She was heading back to the torture of his kindness and the agony of being in love with him, of stealing moments with him, of sharing him, admiring him from a distance, foolishly fantasising about being intimate with him and then, in reality, saying goodbye to him at the end of the day – knowing he was going home to Marcella.

She was right back to where she was before Cambodia; before she became involved with Tristan. The longing she had for Justin only seemed more manageable because she had bullied herself into believing she could recover. Yes, it helped that Justin was not in her immediate orbit, but on a subconscious level she had always known she would return to the UK. She had never dealt with the idea of losing him permanently.

It was at that moment, when she realised that she was still pointlessly infatuated with Justin, that she knew she couldn't go home yet. She looked around her room, at all of her belongings spread out across the cabinet and the floor and hanging off the hooks, then looked out of the door at the parentless children in the courtyard. This was where she needed to be for now.

Leah was in no hurry to start uni. She would defer. She would get over Justin and allow him to get on with his life too. She would stay in Cambodia until spring and take up her course next year. By then Justin would have had the time to fully realise that their relationship was not something that he needed or should ever have encouraged. The time and the absence, the lack of an imminent return date, would help her heal and move on – and become stronger.

She gave herself the rest of the day to be sure, but the following morning her mind was as clear as it had been the day before. She approached Heng with the idea of staying for longer, much longer. 'Really, do you mean it, Leah?' he asked her. 'This would be the best thing I could hope for.'

This cemented the idea in her head and Leah set about putting her plans into motion. She called her mother first. She seemed shocked but listened carefully to Leah's reasoning and, in the end, said she wished she had done something similar when she was her age, and that actually now was the best time. She said she would contact the admissions officer and arrange the deferment and insisted on sending over some money. Everything was actually falling into place; almost as though it was decided before she had even thought of it.

And then Justin texted.

I am counting down the days until you return. I have a wonderful surprise for you. You are going to love it.

After his text had sent, Leah called him straight back.

'Hello beautiful,' he answered.

'I've decided to stay here until next year, probably around April,' she blurted out.

'That's wonderful, for you, and the children. I'm sorry, I have a customer, I'd better go.'

He knew immediately that not only had he been unable to conceal his disappointment but he had once again behaved like a child who had never been told 'no' before. He walked over to the front door of the shop and locked it to the outside world, entered his office and made his way upstairs where he curled up on the bed and cried. Nothing could have shocked or upset him more; he was completely unprepared for this development. He wondered what possessed her to think that it would be a good idea for her to stay away for that long. Hadn't she decided she was not in love with Tristan? Hadn't she been ill and suffered a terrible loss? Hadn't it been too long already? Hadn't she missed him as he had her? Didn't she need him the way he needed her, to physically be in his life? He had completed the café in a ridiculously short period of time. He had stayed in until midnight five nights in a row to finish off the counter, install the sink and connect the power. He had cleared the shop of excess stock and moved almost everything it had held into new positions. He had scrubbed it inside and out, paying particular attention to the floor tiles, just as Leah had, until he was dead on his feet. He had arranged and rearranged the positioning of the new chairs and tables in the shop and outside. He had even handpicked flowers from Ella's workshop, much to her amusement, and arranged them himself in the little vases he had chosen from charity shops. He couldn't be more ready; The Potting Shed had never looked so inviting. The official launch was planned for the day after Leah's arrival, when he knew she would be coming in to say hello. He knew it, so how could he be wrong about it all of a sudden? How could he un-know her return date and unimagine her reappearance and shift it to some unknown date next spring? He had so vividly pictured her sitting down at the table with a cake fork in her hand, lips slightly open in anticipation of her first bite, wearing that strappy floral dress that he liked so much on her. He had done all of this for her and now she wasn't coming back to see it and be a part of it.

Leah had hurt Justin before. She had slept with his brother, and he had found out about it, and she remembered the sting in his voice when he told her what it had done to him. She had felt awful; as awful as she felt the moment she told him she was staying in Cambodia. He had responded by telling her that he had to go. She knew, of course, it was a lie.

The only consolation was that one day he would thank her for allowing them the distance to disentangle themselves from each other. When he and Marcella had produced a people carrier full of kids and they were as content as two people who did not have a third person in their marriage ever would be, he would thank her.

Even still, there was a moment when she thought: *I can't do this, I have to go back.* It was then she realised why she had set the wheels in motion before revealing her plans to Justin – because he would always have the ability to make her change her mind and return to him, even without actually asking her to.

Leah called Tristan. He was equally surprised, but told her that she would never regret her decision; that her time would be valued by so many that it would be impossible to ever think it had been the wrong thing to do. He said she should come back to Phnom Penh and stay with him for little breaks, though, as it was tough to stay out in the provinces for long periods. She promised she would but wasn't sure she wanted to.

And then there was nothing more to be done. She was officially not going home. She texted Vanessa and shared the news. Vanessa told her she missed her and that she too was taking a gap year but hadn't decided what she would do or where she would travel. Ollie was going straight into his course at Nottingham. Leah allowed herself to miss him. Why wasn't she able to just be with him and be content with that? But she had made her choices and, as always, she had chosen the path of most resistance.

PART NINE

The time passed slowly for Justin in the beginning. He moped a great deal. For several weeks in fact. Every time he looked at another person sitting down in the new café area of the shop, he pictured Leah there and felt annoyed at whoever it was for not being her. The café was a success, and the revenue it generated was great for the business, but there were moments when he wanted to tear it down in the name of his disappointment and frustration.

Justin and Marcella continued along their separate paths; sharing only their enjoyment of caring for Lucia – a truly loved and content little girl with olive skin, honey brown hair and Justin's turquoise eyes. He and Marcella rarely fought, but they didn't try and make love again either. It seemed that they had lost interest in both. It didn't seem to matter that they felt so little for each other, as long as Lucia was happy and thriving.

Justin spent most of the week falling asleep on the sofa, and on the few occasions that he did make it upstairs he crept in quietly and lay on his side of their king-sized bed with his back turned to Marcella.

Eventually, Justin moved into the spare room and Marcella made almost no remark on it. Justin was not sure how long he, or Marcella, would be able to carry on living in this way; it seemed incredibly unhealthy on the one hand and entirely sensible and convenient on the other. It was a pattern he never thought he would allow himself to fall into, but he hadn't the energy to change it one way or another.

Justin continued to communicate with Leah once he had calmed down. He considered allowing her the proper, uninterrupted space she seemed determined to get. But she was as warm and sunny and happy to hear from him as she always had been, and he was as persistent as ever in his pursuit to know how she was.

When Leah worked in the shop and they'd had limited time together, it had never felt like long enough. Now that they were living on opposite sides of the world, they made time. And she had so many stories and thoughts to share. They became even closer; to the point where he was sure he knew everything there was to know about her, every thought that came into her head. In return he shared his life with her: funny and peculiar things that happened in the day, Lucia's milestones, stories of interesting people he met, reflections on his past. He also made a point, every once in a while, of reminding Leah of his unfaltering devotion to her. He spoke little of Marcella and their problems. It seemed unfair to burden her; to moan about his wife to the girl who actually loved him just the way he was.

Justin loved Leah now – not just because of her vulnerability, her warm and gentle way – he loved her now because she was astute, funny and strong. She had the most positive outlook and sensitive perception of the world around her and her place in it. She was doing and being and becoming in the most remarkable, wonderful ways. On her own. He didn't just love her for that, he truly admired her too. Although it was overwhelming, to love her so completely, it was no longer crippling or disturbing; he liked that he was capable of loving someone in that way.

And Leah seemed to love him too. He could be unintentionally arrogant at times, given the years of life experience he had on her, but she let him know when he was out of line, and she questioned him, pulled the truth out of him when she knew he was concealing it, and mocked him a little. Justin needed it all. He didn't want to be on a pedestal; he wanted them to be equals.

Justin loved knowing that there was this other human being, an extraordinary one at that, living many miles away, who thought of him every day, who cared enough to ask him about himself, who missed him and reminded him constantly that he would always feature in her life. He felt her love all the time, despite not believing he deserved it. It helped him to maintain some sort of inner calm in her absence.

★

Once Leah learned to accept how raw Cambodia seemed in those early weeks, all that she could see thereafter was its beauty. When Ravi died, she felt such contempt; she didn't understand how his country could have let him go that way. In time though, it was clear that her judgement belonged in some other place.

When the Vietnam War spilled over into Cambodia, it left unexploded landmines that would cause countless deaths and maimings in the following years; after which the Cambodian genocide destroyed whatever had been left intact. People became torturers and killers to avoid being tortured and killed themselves. Generations of educated people were simply obliterated. Human strength was the only available tool for survival. When peace finally came, the country and the good people that remained had emerged survivors; they had lost everything and had to start again, and they had to do it with the gaping wounds of the past all around them. The effects of any and all of this can never be fully quantified. Ravi was not strong and there were not enough resources to make him strong, so he died. He wasn't the first and he wouldn't be the last.

Leah made a pact with herself to focus on the children and the small difference she could make while she was there. The children had not only endured the unendurable, they had managed to come out of their situations full of ambition and innate joy. They were always looking for ways to amuse themselves, they ran to school eager to learn in their clean white shirts, even though they had empty bellies and last year's exercise books that were already full. They piled into her English classes, rammed up against each other in the crippling heat, to learn a language that might just get them a better job when they were older. She wanted to bottle some of their spirit and determination and take it with her through the rest of her life.

She didn't sleep with Tristan again. The first trip back to Phnom Penh was slightly awkward. They went out for some food, had a few drinks and, back in his room, he kissed her. She told him she just couldn't do it anymore, that she didn't want to become too attached because she would leave and he would stay and there was nothing that would change that. He seemed disappointed and tried to simplify the situation until all she could hear was: 'Yes, but we might as well just have sex.' She couldn't tell if it was the sex that night he was disappointed about or the fact that their intimacy had come to a definite end. He made it clear that they must stay close and he would always be there should she change her mind. The comment, despite being said in jest, cemented it for her; Leah did not want to be one of his shags: not in England, not in Cambodia or anywhere else for that matter. She wanted more for herself; she wanted to be in love with the next person she made love to.

Leah had wanted to let Justin go. She had wanted to be able to breathe without the memory of him somewhere in the space around her, filling her lungs with desperation and want. But it is a difficult thing to do – lie to oneself – the truth will always come out in the end. And the truth was that she simply didn't want to live without Justin somewhere in her life. She loved him, she needed his love; it was as uncomplicated and necessary as that. Justin alluded to the fact that things were challenging at home but he never went into depth and she never asked or delved; it was the one topic they never really discussed. It was up to her, as Justin's friend, to hope that if Justin wanted things to work with Marcella they would; especially for the sake of Lucia.

Leah's communication with Justin was the key to her being able to stay in Cambodia. His opinion, his devotion, his interest and his concern for her never waned. There were always more stories to tell, things she had witnessed and helped with and taken the lead on; and each time Justin told her how brilliant or amazing she was, her confidence grew just that little bit more. And on the days when she felt lonely, useless, low, or just fed up with rice and mosquitos and impossible bureaucracy; the sound of his voice soothed her, lifted her, made her laugh and pushed her forward.

She realised that she kept Justin up somewhere high and grand and began to refer to it in her own mind as her 'Justin standard'. She met a fellow Brit at the Foreign Correspondent Club in Phnom Penh, on one of her two trips in. She noticed that he wore a rubber wristband on his arm with the letters WWJD stamped on it. She asked him what it stood for and he told her that there were certain times in his life that he had to question the choices he was making and he would simply look down and be reminded to think: *What Would Jesus Do?* He asked her if she felt she was missing out by not having a faith. She shrugged it off at the time, made her excuses and re-joined the table with Tristan. Later she thought about an answer; she did have faith, not in his god or any other god, but in Justin, and those same letters on the wristband stood for: *What Would Justin Do?* It made her laugh out loud when she thought of it, but it was true: his voice, his way, his perception of the world, was always in her head. She wondered not only what he would do in any given situation, she wondered if he would think more or less of her for her choices and actions. It mattered as it always had.

By March, Leah still had ample funds left in her account and she wanted to do some travelling before returning home and settling into her degree. An idea sprung from a conversation she'd had with Justin a long time ago. She called to tell him her news.

'I'm going to Nepal!'
'What?!'

'I have some money left. I just want to have another adventure before starting uni.'

'You know it's not going to be hot like Cambodia, don't you?'

She laughed out loud.

'I've had enough heat to last me a lifetime!'

'Have you looked up where you might go? Will you go trekking? Are you going alone or with a group?'

'I have some ideas. I've spent the last four hours in an Internet café and made some enquiries. I want to try a fairly easy trek; I'm not that fit…'

'I'm coming.'

'What?'

'I'm coming with you. I'll meet you there.'

'You can't…what? The shop… Lucia…'

'I can. The shop and Lucia will still be here and they will be fine without me for a couple of weeks.'

'And Marcella.'

'Marcella won't even notice that I'm gone. We don't even sleep in the same room anymore.'

'I'm sorry.'

'Thank you, but you don't need to be. All I need to know is; would you want me to come?'

'Oh, my God, are you kidding? I just can't believe it. And I don't think I will until I actually see you there.'

Justin announced his plans to Marcella that night. She had just come downstairs from putting Lucia down.

'What on earth are you talking about?' she replied.

'I just need to disappear for a couple of weeks. If I'd been thinking about it for some time I would have told you, but the idea just came to me and once it did I have felt nothing but determined to do it.'

'Well, does it matter what I think? I haven't been on a holiday since God knows when. I was thinking about going away with a girlfriend.'

'Of course it matters what you think. And you can. When I'm back.'

'So this is us now? We take separate holidays?'

'Well, we have separate rooms. I don't know what we are anymore; we are all over the place and yet we are nowhere. But this isn't about me deciding what we are, this is me saying that I need to get away; that I really need to do something that is just about me. I have worked my arse off for everything we have in our life but it's beginning to feel like an uphill battle. It feels like I only work in order to buy stuff and pay bills. It's not enough for me. I need to feel like the adventures aren't over yet. I need to feel like life is not just one big series of repetitious events in the same two places: work and home, home and work.'

'Okay, I get it, you need space, you need a break; but isn't Lucia a big adventure? You always go on about me making big decisions without asking you what you think and here you are making a massive one.'

'Well, that depends on what you call a massive decision. I'm not going away forever. I'm not going to throw myself off a cliff or run away to a monastery. I just want to feel alive again, because what has happened to us and to me as a person over the years has sort of flattened me. Of course, having Lucia is an incredible adventure, but, like I said, I am not abandoning that adventure: I am taking two weeks off.'

Justin could feel himself getting agitated; he had to calculate every word he said before opening his mouth or she would pounce on it and use it against him. He took a deep breath.

'So, I am asking you now, if it would be okay with you if I had some time out. Please.'

She looked at him, into his eyes, something they had both avoided doing for months, and he could see that she was trying to figure out what this meant. There had always been this element of non-movement, of not actually addressing the fact that they were fundamentally unhappy as a couple and that something, at some point, had to change.

'Do what you need to do. I'm not going to hold you back, Justin.'

'Thank you.'

*

Leah told the children that she would have to go soon and that it would be a while before she would see them again.

'It makes me feel very sad, because I love being here with you, but I have to go back to school so that I can have a good job one day.'

The children reacted immediately: 'No, you cannot go, Miss Leah! We will miss you!' All except Sopheak. She didn't cry, or shout, or jump up and try to grab on to Leah as the other children did. Instead she sat in complete silence, her devastation forced somewhere below the surface so that she would appear strong and unaffected. Then she got up and walked out of the room.

Leah watched Sopheak as she made her way through

the courtyard and into the dorm; she was old enough to fully appreciate what Leah's imminent departure meant, that nothing was forever, that she was effectively being abandoned – again.

Leah came out later to try to talk to Sopheak but she was in bed already, still fully dressed, pretending to be asleep.

'Sopheak, are you okay?'

She didn't answer at first so Leah gently gripped her shoulder and asked her again.

'I'm not well. I think I need to go to sleep,' she told Leah and turned over.

The following morning Leah tried to take Sopheak to one side and talk to her but she made excuses and ran off.

On the hottest day in April, Leah was finally due to leave. She hugged and shared tears with everyone as the children bombarded her with drawings, cards, letters and demands that she come back soon. Sopheak was nowhere to be seen. Leah searched the compound but couldn't find her; she knew that if she didn't want to be found then she wouldn't be, and she was running out of time. So she left, and began sobbing in the back seat of the car to the sound of the children singing.

'Come back soon!' they shouted as their song came to an end.

'I will,' she mouthed.

As the car bumped its way over the bridge outside the orphanage, Leah spotted Sopheak standing on the other side of the road. She was hiding, not very well, behind a tree. She asked the driver to stop and got out. Sopheak bolted in the opposite direction, back towards the orphanage. Leah chased her, almost losing her footing on the uneven bridge;

the child was like a whippet but Leah's strides covered more ground. Just as she was about to grab her, Sopheak spun around and threw her tear-stained face into Leah's chest.

'I want you to stay,' she cried, locking her arms around Leah's neck. 'Please, don't go.'

Leah knelt down and wiped her tears away.

'I promise you I will come back. I promise.'

Sopheak nodded and tried to stop herself from crying so hard.

'I'm going to write to you, and send photos, and then I will be back; before you even have a chance to miss me.'

Sopheak nodded again, composing herself.

'Wait here, I need to give you something.'

Leah returned from the car with her copy of *The Velveteen Rabbit*.

'I'm giving you this to look after. It's very special to me. I want you to learn how to read it all by yourself and when I come back you are going to read it to me.'

Sopheak took the book, clutching it into her chest.

'I will miss you.'

'I will miss you more.'

Leah waved at Sopheak through the back window of the car; wishing at that moment that she had never come to Cambodia, never made the decision to stay at the orphanage. How could she do this to a child? How could she give so much and somehow end up taking more away? Was it worth it? It seemed brutal and wrong all of a sudden. But what she had done to Sopheak was done now; all that she could do was keep her promise to return.

PART TEN

Justin arrived before Leah. He had arranged it this way so that if she encountered any problems upon arrival, he would be there for her. She had refused to be met at the airport, though. She told him that she wanted to make her own way to Langtang and meet at their chosen guesthouse as equals, as fellow travellers, and start their journey together there.

He spent his first day, his alone day, wandering around the local village in a sort of daze. Jetlagged, blown away by the idea of actually being there; so far away from the familiarity of his life, and overwhelmed at the prospect of seeing Leah again after so many months apart. It was fairly clement but it would grow colder the further into the mountains they trekked. He didn't feel the cold, if anything it invigorated him. Leah would, though, especially after her time in Cambodia. She had told him that she would have to buy some kit locally as there was nothing in PP that would keep her warm enough. He kept his eye out for a good shop for them to get what she needed.

Justin wondered if she would look as he remembered. An image of her came to mind, all windswept and sea-sprayed as she climbed back into the car after their swim at Eastbourne. Would she look the same now or would she seem older, even more beautiful and composed? Would it take time for them to feel comfortable in each other's presence again? He had waited months and yet this last twenty-four hours was impossible, intolerable. He had to be in a room with her again and be held by her gaze. He had to smell her skin again, hear her voice.

Perhaps this could be their other universe: a place where they could exist miles and miles from disapproval. In this imaginary existence he could travel between worlds freely and easily, from Lucia to Leah and back again, for the rest of his life. He imagined Leah in traditional Nepalese dress; her long caramel hair braided and wound into an exotic headdress and her perfect, delicate body covered in vibrant quilted layers and elaborate bangles and beads. He smiled to himself, at whichever twist of fate had brought him here, anticipating this moment that right now he felt he had waited for his entire life.

Back at the guesthouse he sat at a table by the fire with a warm broth of noodles and vegetables, crusty bread and a strong local brew that hit him hard. He had a good view of the door, which was also alarmed with a set of cowbells. Every time it opened he looked up; desperate for it to be Leah and nervous too that it would be her, that the moment had finally arrived. He closed his eyes, just for a moment, just to rest them.

★

Leah stood outside the door to the guesthouse and paused for a moment, her body alive with adrenalin and her hands visibly shaking as she reached for the door handle. What would he make of her? She was different, she felt it in her and knew she looked it, but what would Justin see?

She stumbled in with her enormous rucksack she'd picked up in the local market for twenty US dollars. The bells had alerted the staff to her presence and she was greeted by a small Nepalese woman wearing an exquisite, colourful ensemble and heavy jewellery. Leah offered her name and the woman gestured towards the fireplace: 'This man waiting for you, Madam.'

And there Justin sat, or rather slumped – his head resting on the back of an oversized, plaid woollen armchair – his arms folded and his eyes closed in peaceful slumber. He had been sitting by the door to spot her the minute she arrived and had fallen asleep; of course that's where he would be, waiting for her. She thanked the woman and slowly walked over. She wanted to take in his appearance before he opened his eyes and adjust to being around him again.

He had a little stubble, a few more greys. She recognised his navy pullover and desert boots. There was such an inner calm to his face, serenity even; she had to touch him, just to be sure he was real. That heat was back. It had started as she approached the chair; the temperature had risen and risen until she felt like she was almost in flames. She hadn't expected to kiss his lips but an impulse moved her.

Justin woke, seemingly not even remotely startled by the fact that he was being kissed. He just smiled; perhaps it was simply that his dream and real life had seamlessly morphed together.

'Hi.'

'Hi.'

Justin kissed her back; this time taking her face in his hands to keep her there, so that he could continue to kiss her, and kiss her, and kiss her.

★

There was so much to talk about and yet so little needed to be said. Back in their room they bathed and changed separately then lay down on the bed together. Leah nestled into Justin's side, under his open arm, with her arm over the breadth of his body. They listened to the unfamiliar sounds of the street outside; inhabitants of another world going about their lives, not knowing who these two foreigners were and that they should not be there in that room together – alone.

It was in this position that they fell asleep and in the same that they woke a few hours later; to a darker, cooler room and almost no sound outside at all. Justin stretched over for the lamp, then turned over on his side to find Leah's eyes. He kissed her again and she moved in closer to him. Her small, cool hand lifted his top so that she could feel his skin; she ran it over his stomach and his lower back, giving him goose bumps. She had lost some of her reserve, but her touch was as he had remembered it and the effect just as powerful.

Justin found his way inside of her clothing; her body felt small in his hands. She had not put on a bra after her bath so his hands glided easily over her small breasts and hard nipples, across her back and down into her loose drawstring trousers. Her body writhed with every touch and her breath came heavy and strong. They paused to take everything off, to look, to touch, to kiss and taste. He stayed between her legs until she came. And then she had him in her mouth; but he couldn't handle it for long, it was just too much and he wanted to last. He brought her up until they were sitting opposite each other, her legs on top of his, her perfect body stretched out in front of him. He pulled her in close by her hips until she was on top of him.

'I can't tell you how long I've wanted you like this…'

His emotions took over at that moment; his love, his pain and more than anything a desperate need to be deep inside her when he came.

On the morning of the 25th of April 2015, Justin and Leah ate and bathed together and made love again. They stayed in bed, tangled up in each other's limbs and the crisp white linen of their guest bed. Nothing could have moved them from that place.

As the deep rumbling of the earth began to shake the room and all of the furniture inside of it, and as the shrill sound of panic echoed through the valley, their uninhabitable planet cracked and shifted from within; causing an avalanche to descend from the mountains above them and flatten everything in its path.

ACKNOWLEDGEMENTS

To my partner & best friend, I couldn't be more grateful for your persistent encouragement and firm belief that I was not wasting my time writing this book (or actually putting it out there!). I lost count of all the wobbles you somehow stabilised me through.

And to my fabulous daughters, your own creativity is a constant source of inspiration to me. I will always seek your pride in me and live off your love. Oh, and for all the times you tried to ask me a question when I was mid-sentence and I looked at you blankly… I am sorry!

James Woodhouse – thank you for falling for my characters, for 'getting me', for your brain, your time, experience and passion for literature. I will never forget you telling me that the emotion in this book is like water and we somehow need to contain it! You were right of course.

Last, but not at all the least, thank you Judith, for picking up on my many little errors.

Matador

For exclusive discounts on Matador titles,
sign up to our occasional newsletter at
troubador.co.uk/bookshop